Copyright

Love Me Like That

Copyright © 2016 Marie James

Editing by Mr. Marie James & Hale's Harem Betas ;)

Cover design by Kari Ayasha of Cover to Cover Designs

Dedication

To my grandmother, the most amazing woman I'll ever know.

TAP FOR ACCESS

Love Me Like That Playlist: Love Me Like That

Cover Design: Kari Ayasha of Cover to Cover Design

Cover Model: Justin James Cadwell

Photographer: Shauna Kruse

Wait for You: Elliot Yamin
I Can't Love You Back: Easton Corbin
Over You: Daughtry
The Best Of Me: Brantley Gilbert
Dear Agony: Breaking Benjamin
Don't Close Your Eyes: Keith Whitley
How Far: Martina McBride
Best Days Of Your Life: Kellie Pickler
Almost Doesn't Count: Mark Wills
What We Ain't Got: Jake Owen
Another Try: Josh Turner
Sorry: Justin Bieber
Use Somebody: Kings of Leon
Hello: Adele
She's more: Andy Griggs
She Don't Love You: Eric Paslay
Drunk on Your Love: Brett Eldredge
Break Down Here: Julie Roberts
Love You Like That: Canaan Smith
Like I'm Gonna Lose You: Meghan Trainor
Withdrawals: Tyler Farr
I'm Coming Over: Chris Young
Lonely Tonight: Blake Shelton featuring Ashley Monroe
What Do You Want: Jerrod Neimann
Broken: Seether
Still Holding On To You: SHeDAISY
Goodbye Time: Blake Shelton
Make You Miss Me: Sam Hunt
Hurt: Christina Aguilera

"You good?" Trent asks with a knowing smirk as he backs away from me in the shower.

I grin at him and nod my head. "One of these days I'm going to demand more than just a shower quickie in the morning."

He chuckles and leans in, kissing my lips softly and running a loving finger down my cheek. "I know I've been super busy, Kitten." He kisses my neck, nipping at the skin, even under the stream of hot water the action shoots chills up my spine. "Until we get fully staffed, I need to be at the bar. Believe me; I'd rather be here in the morning with you than there taking beer deliveries."

His fingers skate delicately over my nipple, and I groan when he pulls his hand away and stands to his full height. Even with as long as we've been together a delicate touch still makes me want to beg for the next caress.

He steps out of the shower and grabs a towel from the rack. "What time should I expect you?" He asks as he scrubs the drops of water from his almost scalp length, ice-blond hair.

I work at the bar with him most evenings. I've been an employee of his for the last three months. He, along with my best friend Keira, convinced me my 'day job' as they called it, was interfering with their time with me. I'd already been working part time there on the weekends so that I could see them more.

I shrug. "My shift starts at four, but I'll probably be in a little early," I tell him as I stand up from the tiled bench on shaky, post-orgasmic legs.

I swipe the steam from the inside of the shower stall and watch him, completely in love with every inch of his body as he towel dries his lanky frame. He's not a cut, ripped hunk; he's more like a gangly beanpole with long, lean muscles. He's incredibly tall, but his build isn't imposing, one of the things that played a huge part in our relationship in the beginning. He eats like a horse and never works out, so I don't know how he stays so thin. I joke with him all the time that the fast food he consumes at an alarming rate is going to catch up with him, but he's thirty-two now and he's just as skinny as he was when we started dating six years ago.

I turn the water off and step out of the shower, reaching for a thick, fluffy towel. I hold it to my nose and inhale the clean smell of our laundry detergent.

"Not washing your hair today?" He asks with a joking look of disgust on his face.

I pull the towel from my face and narrow my eyes sarcastically. "I'm hitting the gym first. I'll wash it when I'm done." I inform him.

Unlike him, I *have* to work out…often. I run at least five times a week but no matter the number of miles, the speed, or how often I hit the track my ass never shrinks. At least my chest is proportional. *I'm fit and healthy*. It's the mantra I force myself to repeat when any of my body issue conceptions begin to rear their ugly heads.

"Tomorrow is Sunday, Kitten. I promise you more than a quick fuck in the shower." He kisses the top of my head, leaving the bathroom so he can get dressed and head to work.

"I'm holding you to that!" I shout after him, the smile never leaving my face.

By the time I make it out of the bedroom fully dressed, Trent is gone. He's been working from around ten in the morning until the bar shuts down at two in the morning, and then he oversees the cleanup. He's only averaging about five to six hours of sleep each night; then it's the same thing the next day.

I know it's not healthy for him to live this way. More than once I've tried to talk with him about enlisting a staffing company to find qualified people to help manage the bar. He's waved me off more than once, saying that this bar is our future, and he's not comfortable having another company do something he's capable of doing himself.

He opens *Holder's* later on Sunday and Monday, but every day he's there to unlock the door at opening and relock the door at closing. At least, he has for the last six months.

Staffing has been rough for the better part of a year. Bar staff is excellent but finding, and keeping, proper management has been a huge burden. I think he's given up, having grown tired of people getting trained then leaving to work at the bars in the bigger cities, now with a better resume.

He's working himself into an early grave, but he won't listen to reason. He's asked more than once if I'd start progressing to a management position, but that defeats the purpose of me quitting my office job to spend more time with him, as I'd be working most of my shifts opposite of his. Both he and

Keira have pushed the idea more than once; every time I've told them to leave it alone. I have no desire to run the bar.

He purchased the bar from the original owner when Tom Holder decided it was time for retirement. He was running this bar for Tom when we met but bought it about a year or so after we started dating.

Making my way into the kitchen to grab a bottle of water from the fridge I notice Trent's coffee mug sitting on the counter. He accidentally leaves his coffee more than once a week. I pour it out and add it to my list of things to take him when I get done with my workout.

We aren't rich by any means, but Trent's house is paid for; it was left to him after his mother passed away ten years ago. The bar does very well and because of that we live extremely comfortable. I wouldn't consider myself a kept woman, but the truth is, other than paying for groceries I have no other financial obligations; my cell phone is even covered on his account. The only reason I buy the groceries is because Trent is perfectly okay with eating out for every meal and I'd have to live at the gym if I ate like him.

He assures me this is the way it's supposed to be. A man takes care of every one of his woman's needs. So because of that, I just stick most of my money into savings. I did; however, recently use a chunk of it to buy my car.

My biggest pride and joy is my bright red Mini Cooper Countryman. We don't have kids and have absolutely no time for an animal, so my car is my baby, and I treat it as such. It's the first car that I've ever bought outright with my own money, and I take extreme pride in it.

I jump behind the wheel and wait for my phone to connect with the Bluetooth in the car. On my way to the gym, I call Keira to see if she wants to grab lunch before our shifts start later this afternoon. It's Saturday which means all hands on deck since it's our busiest night of the week. She doesn't answer me, which is not surprising. More than likely she's still passed out with whatever guy she deemed *Mr. Right Now* last night before leaving the bar. She's always used her waitressing job at the bar as her personal dating service. She's been lucky so far that it hasn't caused problems, but she seems pretty up front about her intentions with the guys she hooks up with.

I tilt my head at the emptiness of the parking lot at the gym as I pull up. Saturday morning is usually pretty busy, but this place is deserted, eerie even. Walking up the steps, I see the bright green sign on the door informing me that the gym is closed due to a water pipe break inside. It goes on to say that they hope to be open by Monday at the latest.

I sigh and turn back around. It's winter in Montana, so there's no way I'm running outside. Frostbite and toe amputations are not on my list of things to do this week. I hate when my plans are derailed, and there's nothing worse than not getting my workout in. More times than not it leads to poor eating decisions the rest of the day.

I get back in the car and head to the Starbuck's drive thru to grab a coffee for Trent and myself, suddenly regretting not washing my hair this morning since I won't be working out. I'll wash it after having a cup of coffee with my love; I still have plenty of time before my shift starts.

The emptiness of the parking lot except for Trent's truck is not surprising. The bar doesn't open until two in the afternoon, so besides a delivery truck I wouldn't expect any different.

I make my way to the front door of the bar, knowing it will be open for anyone who may be delivering. I also know chances are good Trent will be in the back office going over the week's paperwork. He's very organized, and I'm certain this quirk of his contributes to how well his business has been doing, aside from the staffing issues.

I'm amazed at how different the bar is during the daytime. It's quiet and weird without music blaring and the sound of glasses clinking; the absence of customers talking and the sound of the balls hitting on the pool tables.

I left early last night with a horrendous headache, and I can tell from the not quite pristine condition of the tables and floors that I was missed. I feel mild satisfaction that things didn't get done last night properly until I remember Trent telling me he had to stay even later last night to make sure everything was taken care of in my absence.

I know it wasn't intentional, but he hurt my feelings when he came home and complained about having too much on his plate to have staff leaving early when he was already limited on employees. I let it roll off my back because I know he has so much going on, but it didn't lessen the sting any. It's not often that we fight or grow frustrated with each other, so it tends to hurt a little more when we do.

I roll my shoulders in an attempt to let the anger wash over me and disappear as I make my way to the back of the bar where the office is. Still holding both cups of coffee I use my hip to push open the door that separates the customer area from the back storage area where we keep all the supplies.

I stop in my tracks when I hear a slap and a giggle coming from the hallway where Trent's office is. My blood runs cold. I take a single step and stop. I listen again, praying that I misheard, knowing the sound was unmistakable.

Crushed, I make my way down the back hallway and stand in the shadow as I see my boyfriend of six years pounding into my best friend. The same person who made friends with me on the playground when she first came to town in the second grade. The woman who has been, before Trent, the only constant in my life. She's bent over the edge of his desk, and he has her hair tangled around his fist, arching her back so he can kiss her shoulder.

"Fuck, Kitten. This pussy gets tighter every time I fuck it," Trent says to her on a moan.

Kitten? Every time?

A shiver races up my spine when he uses not only the same pet name I'd once loved but a phrase he's praised me with for years. Nothing has been sacred. It also informs me that this is far from the first time they've done this.

I'm in utter shock. Later I'll ask myself why I stood there as long as I did. More so I'll wonder how I backed out of the hallway, calmly placed the still hot coffee on the bar, and walked out of there and never looked back.

They'll find the coffee. They'll know I was there because my name is written on both cups courtesy of the barista at Starbucks. Any other conclusions they draw is on them. As for me? I'm done. The only people I have in my life that I love have betrayed me. I have nothing left.

In a form less than myself I make my way home and pray I have enough time to pack and leave before they discover the coffee on the bar.

I sneer at the thought that since Trent already came with me in the shower this morning, he will last longer this time around. Another unwelcome thought comes to mind when I picture their morning betrayal on repeat in my head. I don't think they were using a condom.

This pisses me off even through the haze of my devastation. Now I have to get myself checked for STDs. There's no telling what Trent has been up to for the past six years of my life. He's loving and attentive. He's never pulled away from me. The only issue we've had lately is him working so much. Now I know he's been leaving me in the morning to no doubt bang my best friend.

I may not be aware of all that Trent has been doing, but I'm well aware of the lifestyle my never satisfied best friend has. Knowing he's not been using protection with her, means I'll be at a clinic first thing Monday morning. I never had a problem with her love 'em and leave 'em lifestyle until just now, knowing Trent's dick has been in her, bare.

I drag the rarely used suitcases from the spare bedroom and set them up on the bed. Six years of my life has been spent in this house. I came straight from a college dorm room to Trent's house, so all I had were my clothes and a few other small personal effects. Everything I've obtained since has been with Trent. I need none of it. I want no reminder of the wasted years. I don't want to be reminded that while I've been hoping he would ask me to marry him and start a family, he's been sleeping with my best friend.

I grab my clothes, personal items from the bathroom, and the small photo album I have of my parents. My sad life fits in two suitcases with room to spare. Pitiful.

I tug the suitcases to the front door and take one last glance at the home I thought I'd eventually raise children in after Trent manned up and asked me to marry him.

Wasted time.

Wasted hope.

Wasted life.

I lift my hand to my neck as a single tear rolls down my cheek. The first tear, but I know it's far from the last. My fingers brush across the gold and diamond infinity symbol hanging around my neck. I cherish this necklace. He gave it to me years ago, at the same time promising me he will love me and protect me always.

Lies.

Every word that he's spewed from his beautiful mouth has been a lie. Every kiss, every *I love you*, and every unspoken ounce of satisfaction reflected in his glacial blue eyes has been a betrayal.

I tug the necklace until the chain breaks free and place it with a strangely calm hand on the table near the entryway. I turn and leave my entire life behind with no idea or plans for my future.

Living in the northwestern area of Great Falls, Montana has me on Interstate 15 heading north in a matter of minutes. An hour and a half later I'm pulling into a tiny gas station in Shelby. I take the time to fuel up and set my radio to the same playlist I used nine years ago when my parents died; the sad songs of loss and despair seem fitting.

I hit *Subway* for lunch and decide to go ahead and eat in the dining area. They have no drive-thru, so I had to get out of the car anyways. I pick a quiet corner and stick my headphones in, continuing to work through my grief while I eat.

It's early afternoon and in a hasty decision I've decided I'll head west toward Washington and possibly later will head to Alaska. Putting thousands of miles and a huge chunk of Canada between the people who've betrayed me seems like a good idea. If I continue on IH15 right now, I'll hit Canada, and I don't feel like digging for my passport. West it is.

While Rascal Flatts, *What Hurts the Most*, blares through the sound system I convince myself I'll allow the duration of this trip for my grief and anger. Once I come to the place I want to settle, I tell myself I have to be over it; I'll need to move on and begin again. I'm determined, but not hopeful, it will be that easy.

I begin my self-proclaimed pity party with memories of my parents, their car accident, and the future destroyed after their loss. Gut-wrenching grief washes over me when my mind takes me right back to Keira and how her family was there for me after their deaths. They gave me a place to live and helped me with all the paperwork to get into college.

Keira, my best friend. In less than a minute, well of what I saw, she managed to turn a lifetime friendship into seething treachery. Don't get me wrong, I love Trent with each and every atom in my body, but she's like a sister to me. I can't decide which betrayal is worse at this point.

Was. Loved. Past tense.

I want to cry and grieve for the loss of not only my lover and the man I was certain I'd spend the rest of my life with but also the woman who I was sure would be the godmother to the children Trent and I would have. Now I have no one.

Rather than giving into the heartache and misery that is trying to creep up I focus on the anger and the hatred at their deception. I try to work my head around the last few years in an attempt to pinpoint where things changed; doing my best not to turn it around on me and give into the self-doubt I'm known to have.

I have a history of internalizing others mistakes and accepting blame, and historically punishment, for wrongs that altogether were never mine to begin with. With everything that's rushing and running through my head, I can't even concentrate on driving.

My phone has rang no less than a dozen times since leaving Shelby over five hours ago. The trip has been slow going in large part to the snow that has begun to fall; the fact that I'm on a two-lane blacktop doesn't help either.

I hit a gas station in Whitefish and decided to head south which will eventually shoot me over to Spokane, Washington. Seems like a place I could set down temporary roots. The population is high enough that work will be easy to find until I can make more permanent plans.

The goal for the day is to make it there by midnight, and from the looks of the road I should add in-one-piece as well. My Mini was not made for driving in the snow. Not the wisest decision considering I live in Montana. Lived in Montana as it were.

The roads are cleared pretty quickly in Great Falls, and this is my first winter in this car. It's becoming apparent very quickly that a vehicle change, although that will be another thing to break my heart, will more than likely be necessary.

Now Leaving Poison. Population 4,488.

Poison, Montana. Fitting to see the sign in my rearview, knowing I'm leaving behind more poison than a small town with the name. I grin for the first time since leaving my life behind at the prospect of starting over. That is until my phone chimes with a new voicemail alert. Reception must be bad out here because it didn't even ring this time.

Trent has called numerous times throughout the day, but he hasn't left a message until now. Not once did I want to pick up the phone when he called, but I struggle with indecision knowing he's left one this time. Unable to resist any longer I use the controls on my front radio display to play the voicemail he's waited hours to leave.

"London," he sighs loudly into the phone. "I…fuck." I hear papers crinkle, and I know he's still at the bar, sitting at the same desk he fucked my best friend on earlier. "I wish you'd pick up so I can explain. I've just been stressed out lately. I wasn't even thinking. Please, Kitten. I need you to come home so we can work through this. I love you."

"Fuck you!" I scream at the term of endearment that means absolute shit now. I see red at the three words he's always given so freely. I cut my eyes over to hit the end button, completely done with his ass and when I turn my gaze back to the road, I see the biggest fucking moose in the world, standing directly in my lane.

Hitting the brakes was the very last thing I should have done but, of course, it was the first thing that I did. Swerving back and forth, the only thing I could think of was my parents' tragic death. That involved a drunk truck driver, not a moose, but I just knew I'd see them soon, my fate inevitably aligning with theirs.

The car jumps and bucks, twists and turns, but thankfully never becomes airborne or flips over. I hit the ditch on the side of the road and somehow manage not to die. I watch with wide eyes as the huge moose huffs a breath of frigid air from his nose and walks away from the resulting puff of thick steam, absolutely unfazed by the near death collision he just caused.

I need to get out and assess the damage, but it's freezing cold and that oversized mammal may want to eat me. Fat chance of me getting out of this damn car with the hell-beast out there stalking me like prey. I have just over a half a tank of gas, and the functions of the car don't seem to have been affected.

I put the car in reverse, planning to get out of the ditch and spend the night in Poison until I can gain my composure and make sure the car isn't damaged too badly. I gently hit the gas with a shaky foot, not fully calm yet from the near death experience I just had.

The tires spin and the car doesn't move. I give it more gas, and the same thing happens. I try to convince myself not to panic but as the tires spin and spin that notion is becoming impossible. I put the car back in park and engage the emergency brake. I turn the hazard lights on for good measure, knowing I'll need someone to stop and help me.

I follow my cell phone charger cord and find my cell phone lodged between the passenger seat and the console. This situation will end quickly if I can reach a tow truck. Just my luck, there is not one bar indicating any level of reception. NO SERVICE mocks me from the top left corner of the screen.

I'm fuming as anger over the entire day hits me. I would ask 'what's next?' but fate or karma or whatever's been acting against me recently has been one vindictive bitch, and I don't want to press my luck. The last thing I need is for a logging truck to plow over me while I sit helplessly in my car.

I crank up the heat and sit back, praying someone happens to be just as crazy as I am and is out driving in this weather. That thought also scares the shit out of me. What kind of person will I encounter out here? All of the sane people are at home, warm in front of the fire.

Three

Kadin

Even though this 'vacation' has been somewhat forced, I'm grateful to be here. It's just the push I needed to take that next step; the outcome I've been mulling over for months. Not exactly what my uncle and the other guys had in mind when they told me to get out of town and get my shit together.

It took just over a week, but I have in fact 'gotten my shit together.' My condo is clean, the refrigerator empty so there are no nasty surprises for whoever is given the job of taking care of it. More importantly, my will has been updated. Everything is in order.

I try not to think about my parents, Kegan, and the note left on the dining room table at my condo as I start making a mental list of things to email the guys about as I put away the several weeks' worth of groceries I bought on my way out here. I don't know how quickly I will execute my plans, but I don't want to starve to death before I do; that's not exactly the way I see things ending out here in this cabin. Well, you can't really call a nearly four thousand square foot monstrosity a 'cabin' but it's made of logs none the less.

Weather predictions for the next week include what they are referring to as Iceapalooza. The wind is already whipping around the house and sending howls through the surrounding trees. It won't be long before the storm hits and leaves the property and roads in and out covered and impassable.

I pull out my phone and open a new note page as I walk through the house. I'm doing my best to make sure the place will be easy to sell after it's served my purposes. My interior design people did an excellent job making the house inside look rugged and lived in, just like I'd requested. I'll need a secondary wood holder. The one they put in the main living area looks great, but it's not practical for anyone who doesn't want to run outside for wood every few hours. I add it to the list.

Thinking of the storm and the real possibility that I'll be on the backup generators before it's said and done reminds me that I need to make sure the satellite phone is fully charged. I hit the stairs two at a time and dig the phone out of my suitcase, plugging it in to charge. I have no idea why I even worry about it. I have no intentions of calling anyone.

"Shit," I grunt out loud as my mental checklist has me realizing I never shut the gate to the property. I cuss myself thoroughly as I make my way back down the stairs and begin layering my flannel and jacket. Even a few minutes of exposed skin out in this weather could lead to frostbite.

Sliding my gloves on last, I pull the door closed behind me and quickly make my way to my truck. I consider turning back and just saying fuck it, but I know it needs to be closed, if anything, to deter anyone from bothering me over the next several days. *Discovering what you've done is more like it.* My mind once again goes back to my family.

I've only been here an hour or so but my truck has completely cooled down, and the only light around is the porch light and the faint gleam of my headlights as they attempt to slice through the dense layer of snow that is currently falling. I put the truck in gear and roll forward, activating the four wheel drive. I have no intentions of getting stuck in this shit; once again not part of the plan. The mile long hike back up the driveway would sure suck balls. *They say freezing to death is very peaceful.* This old work truck crunches over the snow and ice like it is made for off-roading.

The gate comes into view, and I steel myself, preparing to go back out in the freezing cold to close the gate that should be working from a manual button on my cell phone, but the storm has covered the area so thickly, cell phone reception is practically nonexistent.

I jump out of the truck and quickly shut the door, an attempt to keep the heat inside the cab. Grabbing the edge of the gate, I plant my feet and struggle to pull it closed. Keeping my footing and making progress with the gate is like trying to tow a car through quicksand.

A faint flashing glow catches my eye about thirty yards away, the gloomy orange glow reflecting off of the heavy snowflakes that have continued to fall. I release the gate and trudge across the road to investigate. The further I walk the easier it is to tell that a small car has slid into the ditch. I look around and wonder how long it's been there since there's no sign of skid marks or tracks on the road, having already been covered with a thick layer of snow.

I can see a steady trail of exhaust heat coming from the back of the car, and I hope that the people who were in it when it slid into the ditch were smart enough to have stayed inside.

I walk up to the driver's side door and knock on the fogged up window. No answer. Just as I bend down to put my nose to the glass in an attempt to see if anyone's inside the window slides down an inch.

"Yes?" asks a shaky feminine voice.

Seriously? Like you're just out here hanging out? Like you're answering the door after ordering a pizza?

"Need some help?" I respond.

The window rolls down further and a woman's face, lit by the dash lights, comes into view. *She has magnificent green eyes.*

She just stares at me, assessing the situation.

"Can I help you?" *Freezing my ass off here lady.*

"Can you pull me out?" I can't stop the laugh that rushes past my lips. She narrows her eyes at my reaction.

Fuck this is not how I saw my evening going. It's the last thing I need considering how I was sure my night was going to end.

"No way to get this car out of the ditch until the storm passes and they can clear the roads a bit," I inform her.

"Can you take me into town?" Her voice is pleading like I just signed her death certificate.

"We'd never make it. Come on. You can wait out the storm at the cabin," I offer and attempt to open her door for her. It's locked.

"Ummm," she replies. She's unsure about getting out of the car, but my patience is fragile seeing as I've been standing in the freezing downpour.

"Listen lady. I'm just trying to be nice here." I glance inside at the dash. "You have less than an eighth of a tank of gas left. You're lucky I showed up when I did. If you stay out here, you'll be dead by morning." I turn my back to her and begin to make my way across the street.

"Wait! Please!" I knew that little tidbit of information would get her ass out of that car.

"Kill the ignition but leave the hazards flashing," I yell over my shoulder as I reach the still open gate. She walks toward me, her entire body shivering. "Jump in the truck while I get this gate closed."

She doesn't wait another second, leaving me to work the gate closed as she hops in the truck. Just what I need on my forced vacation, playing host to some woman I don't even know. I need her out of here as soon as humanly possible. I'm an asshole on a good day, but there's no way I would leave a stranger responsible when I off myself.

My anger over the change in plans assists in getting the gate closed easier than before. I climb up in the truck and spend a minute with my gloved hands held toward the warm air rushing from the vent.

"How'd you end up in the ditch?"

"Moose," she says through her trembling lips.

"Elk," I say.

"Huh?" she asks in confusion.

"It was likely an elk. Moose populations have been dwindling recently. Haven't seen any around here." I cut my eyes to her and watch her nod her head in acknowledgment. *Like she has any damn interest in Montana wildlife trivia.*

Once my fingers are warm enough to actually operate the truck I put it in gear and turn back toward the house. I watch as she pulls out her cell phone and looks at the screen.

"The storm is too thick right now, and reception out here is spotty on a good day," I tell her. "I have a satellite phone at the cabin you're more than welcome to use."

She sighs and looks out the window. "I just need to call a tow truck."

Who wouldn't need to call a friend or family member after sliding into a ditch?

"You can do that, but they won't be able to get to you any sooner. I can pull you out when it clears up enough." *The minute it's even a possibility.*

"Thank you," she whispers softly and peers out the window again.

I wonder what she thinks because I know she does not see anything but a wall of white as we trudge slowly up the driveway. *Not your concern, Kadin.* I park with my side near the door.

"It'd probably be best if you slide over here and get out of my door." She narrows her eyes at me skeptically. "So you don't have to walk all the way around the truck." She scoots a little closer to me but stops just short of our bodies touching. "Ready?" I ask as I turn off the ignition.

She nods her head, and I open the door against the frigid wind and icy snow that is raging in all directions. I move out of her way and point toward the front door telling her to head that way. She walks past me quickly. Closing the door to the truck, I stay close to her back as we fight our way to the front door.

The process is slow and arduous, and I'd like nothing more than to pick her up and carry her because it would cut our time out in the cold by at least half; I don't, however, think she would appreciate a stranger putting his hands on her, especially with the way she looked at me when I suggested something as simple as climbing out of my side of the truck.

She steps aside for me to open the door as she crests the top of the stairs. *Is she trying to determine if I'm a gentleman or does she suspect the door is locked?* I stomp my boots on the mat to get the majority of the sludge sticking to them off and open the door, standing out of the way so she can enter first.

In the light of the foyer, I'm able to take her in. She has to be absolutely freezing. She's wearing a thick coat and gloves, but her legs are only covered in a thin pair of running spandex.

As much as I want to bawl her out for dressing so scantily during a blizzard in Montana I keep my thoughts to myself. I have no business getting in her business.

I turn to the left and enter the small mudroom. I shrug my coat off and hang it on a hook just inside the door and kick off my boots.

"I'm going to light a fire," I explain to her as she begins to shrug off her outer layer as well. Paired up with her thin pants she's also wearing a thin Henley type workout top; that's it.

I bite my tongue as I head to the den to make a fire. I stop by the thermostat on my way and crank up the heat another five degrees as well.

I throw several more logs into the already raging fire and jab at it with the poker, making sure all the logs will burn consistently. I feel her presence when she soundlessly enters the room. I frown at the sound of the crackling fire when my heart rate increases slightly in acknowledgment. I cut my eyes briefly to the drawer of the small table across the room that houses my demise, a bottle of pills and a glock; my mood being the only thing to determine which is used.

I turn to her and watch as she rubs her arms briskly with her hands. I push my tongue to the roof of my mouth to once again keep from chastising her for being out in the middle of a damn blizzard in what would easily be considered less than some people wear to bed.

"I've turned the heat up in the house. It seems you're stuck here so let me show you where you can sleep." I say instead. I need to get away from her. The sooner she gets settled, the sooner I can start in on the whiskey. I won't allow her to derail my plans; this little hiccup is no more than a short postponement. She can sleep, and I can begin my nightly ritual of drinking myself stupid.

She nods and follows me up the stairs to the guest bedroom. I open the door to one of the rooms I actually haven't made it in yet since arriving. The interior designer did a great job in here as well. She kept with neutral colors on the walls and gave it a modern feel without detracting from the rugged aspect of the home as a whole. The large bed is against the exposed logs which serve as the accent wall. Every room in the home that is on an outside wall has the same.

"Your room?" she mutters.

"Hardly," I say with a huff. "This is the guest bedroom. The bathroom is right through there." I point to a door on the far wall. "Should be fully stocked. If not? Well, we're in the middle of a fucking blizzard." *See, the asshole has arrived.*

"I appreciate it," she says and slides past me making sure she doesn't touch me.

She doesn't seem like the shy type but more uncomfortable with the situation she's been tossed into with no control. She walks further into the room and the sinful shape of her luscious ass does not go unnoticed.

I clear my throat. "I'll be downstairs." *Like she gives a shit.* I pull the door close behind me and take the stairs down two at a time.

I scrub my face with my hands and then run them through my overly long hair. I know getting drunk with a stranger in the house is not the best game plan, but it's going to happen none the less. I'm here with very strict instructions to 'get over my bullshit and don't come back until I do,' and that's my game-plan, well the first part at least... It starts with the whiskey.

Four

London

What the hell have I gotten myself into?

I'm in this big ass house, in a room larger than most hotel suites. I'm more concerned about the man wearing flannel driving a beat up old clunker. I can't keep my mind from wondering if he broke into this place and he plans to chop me into tiny pieces and burn me in the fire.

He's been courteous and respectful if a little put out by my being here. I sit on the side of the enormous bed and look around the room. It's like something out of a home décor or Crate and Barrel ad. The bed is made up of expensive covers and sheets, including a thick duvet I'd love nothing more than to snuggle up in.

Actually, that's the best idea I've had for a while. I use alternating feet to kick my shoes off. A glance at the door confirms there is a lock, but it's not engaged. I push myself off of the bed and walk to the door.

Just as my hand reaches the knob, a thunderous boom echoes into the house from outside and the lights go out, throwing the room into pitch black nothingness. I stand stock still, terrified as my other senses try to account for my loss of vision. Several minutes of standing in the pitch black of the room reveals nothing other than the sounds of the storm outside.

Shouldn't a backup generator kick in? It never does. The chill in the air from the heat not rolling through the vents is immediate, like icy fingers of death licking at the skin on my legs which are covered by only a thin layer of fabric. If I stay in here, it's going to be just as bad as sitting in the damn car.

I turn the door knob and do my best to make it to the stairs from memory, praying I don't tumble down them and snap my neck. Nothing says thank you for rescuing me from the car in the ditch like a snapped neck at the base of a flight of stairs. Keeping my hand on the banister and taking subtle, focused steps I make it to the bottom unscathed.

I want to call out to the man in the house, but I realize we never even told each other our names. Why wouldn't he ask? Hell, why didn't I ask?

I follow the faint glow of the fire through the house. A noise to my right catches my attention, and I turn my gaze just in time to see him coming back in the house and stripping out of his cold-weather gear. He's grumbling and cussing, no doubt from the severe weather outside.

He walks back toward the fire and stops short when he notices me standing in the shadows.

"The damn generator isn't kicking in," he says as he rubs his hands together near the hearth.

No shit Captain Obvious.

"Can I…I mean is it okay for me to stay down here? The room upstairs was already getting cold again." I give a weak smile because it's the most I can manage after the day I've had. I shiver and rub my hands up and down my arms.

"Of course. Shit, let me get you a blanket." He walks down the hall, and I hear a door open. Less than a minute later he walks back in and hands me a thick fleece blanket.

I wrap it around my back and settle on the couch in the spot closest to the fire. I should probably let him have his pick of places to sit seeing as this is his place, but he's got at least fifty pounds or more on me so I figure he won't get as cold as easily as I will.

He walks to a table just out of reach of the fire's light, half of his apparently muscular body hidden in the shadows.

"You don't need a blanket?" It's the best I could come up with as far as conversation is concerned.

"Why? Do you plan on sharing with me?" I smirk at him and give him my best not-in-your-wildest-dreams look. He laughs. It's deep and husky and even though I've had one of the worst days of my life I can still appreciate the sex appeal this man has rolling off of him in waves. "I have this to keep me warm anyways."

I watch with wide eyes as he brings an exceptionally large bottle of whiskey to the small table in front of the couch and sets it, along with two tumblers, down on the wooden top.

I grin from ear to ear at his presumptuousness.

"Can you tell I've had a shit day?" I ask nodding toward the other glass.

"We're stuck in a blizzard together, and we don't even know each other's names. Nothing says pleased to meet you like Jack Daniel's." I have to agree with him.

"London," I tell him.

"No, I think this is made in the States," he says turning the bottle at an angle so he can read the side.

I laugh. *Did I just giggle at him?* "No. My name is London."

"Ah! Nice to meet you London. I'm Kadin." He holds his hand out, and I shake it but pull away abruptly.

"Your hands are freezing," I explain and tuck my hand back into the safety of the fleece blanket, pretending I didn't feel more than just the cold of his fingers when we touched.

"Hence the whiskey. Would you like some?" He holds up a half-full tumbler.

I reach out and take it from him, making sure not to touch him again. "Thank you."

He pours himself an equally full glass, and I'm sure the leaving off of the cap is an indication of his plans for the night. I take an overly large gulp of the golden liquid and close my eyes as it burns a path down my throat.

I hold the tumbler with both hands near the bottom of my chin, in close range for my next sip. I watch the fire crackle and burn. The flames are shooting up and finding no respite, endlessly burning with nothing further to take hold of and destroy.

Nothing left to destroy. A perfect example of my life right now.

Another sip out of my glass tells me I've been drinking without realizing it as my latest attempt leaves me with an empty mouth. I cut my eyes back to Kadin and find him smirking at me.

"More?" He holds up the bottle.

Without a word, I hold my glass closer to him and watch him fill it fuller than he did the first time around.

"I don't usually drink. I've had a super shitty day." I explain as to why I'm throwing back whiskey like a marathon runner does water after a race.

"No judgment here," he says and tosses back the last of his own drink. He begins to pour himself another. "Story of my life these days."

I've never been the type to talk about my problems. Well, with anyone other than Keira, but for some reason I want to speak to this man. The silence around us is not uncomfortable, but I have a craving for his voice.

I realize I'm buzzed from the alcohol when I almost ask him to say the Pledge of Allegiance, so I can close my eyes and listen to his deep, husky voice as he recites it. I laugh at the ridiculousness of it.

He smiles slyly at me even though I'm certain he has no idea what I laughed for.

I clear my throat as he continues to watch me. The firelight makes his eye color appear almost black, in a soothing dark chocolate kind of way and the shine reflecting off of his mahogany colored hair would make any woman jealous. It's either tousled and messy from the hood of his jacket when he was outside earlier, or he's accustomed to running his hands through it repeatedly.

I turn my focus back to the fire when I catch myself staring at his full lips, chiseled cheeks, and strong jaw that's covered with a day or two of unshaved growth. My fingers itch to touch the coarseness of it.

Shit, I need to quit drinking. I bring the glass to my lips and take another long pull.

"You have a beautiful home." I look around the room that seems more romantic and less eerie than it did fifteen minutes ago. *Thank you, Jack.*

"Thank you," he answers giving nothing away.

I look back to the fire, suddenly feeling awkward and unable to think of anything else for small talk.

"Where do you call home?" I close my eyes at the rumble of his question.

Then I realize just what he's asking. "I used to live in Great Falls, but I'm moving."

"You were moving today? I don't recall seeing that much in your car." *What are you a damn detective?*

I shrug my shoulders. "I don't have much."

My hope that he would keep within the boundaries set by social norms in regards to what's considered appropriate topics among strangers is broken when he asks, "What are you running from?"

I whip my head to face him and find him watching me with a raised eyebrow. *You wanted to talk to him, don't get pissed when you're uncomfortable with the topic.*

"Boyfriend trouble," I answer honestly.

"Enough trouble to make you leave town?"

"Enough to leave the state," I retort quickly.

"Wish running was always that easy," he laments as he takes another sip of his whiskey and I notice for the first time the glint of the fire off of a wedding band.

Motherfucker.

I drain my glass without a second thought and mentally slap myself for ogling this married man's lips.

"When do you expect your wife to make it? After the storm?" I watch for his reaction, but his blank stare into the fire gives me nothing.

"She's not coming," he finally replies as he pours another glass and tops mine off.

I drink immediately. Trouble in paradise it seems.

He sets down his glass and stands; clearly I've said something to piss him off.

"I'm going to go get a fire going in your fireplace upstairs, so you don't freeze to death tonight." He clicks on a small flashlight he's pulled from his back pocket and makes his way out of the room.

I'm stuck with this man for the next God only knows how many days and a few hours in, and I've already pissed him off somehow. I toss back the remainder of my drink and close my eyes. Not like I have anywhere else to be or anywhere to go for that matter.

Five

Kadin

Although my legs and feet are steady, I can tell from the haze of my vision and the mild swimming in my head that the whiskey has already taken hold. Trudging up the stairs, I cuss under my breath at this whole fucked up situation.

When do I expect my wife?

I never imagined *that* conversation coming up and it sure as hell isn't a conversation I'm having tonight, with a complete stranger no less. I should never have asked the questions I did. I opened the door without even knowing it.

I hit my knees in front of the hearth in the guest bedroom and slowly begin to get the fire going. The wood supply is sparse up here as well. Another thing to add to the list of stuff to buy. *Not buy, add to the list to email. You won't be leaving here.*

Before long, the fire is raging, and I let the warmth engulf me even though nothing is strong enough to reach the iciness in my veins. I can't imagine anything in the world strong enough to return me to the man I was just a few short years ago. Knowing I can never go back is one of the nails in my coffin. Knowing I will never have what I once did is the catalyst for being in this cabin.

I sit for a while longer but realize, unplanned or not, I still do have a guest downstairs, and I'm in her room. From the way she was staring into the fire, I have no doubt she wants to get away from me as much as I needed to leave just a few minutes earlier. I climb to my feet and sway slightly; my time at rest allowed the alcohol to take a stronger hold of me.

Using the tiny beam of light from my flashlight, I make my way down the stairs and back into the den where I find London with her head back and her eyes closed. Thinking she's asleep, I reach out to pull the empty glass from her hands.

The movement startles her, and she gasps at my close proximity as her eyes snap open.

"I didn't mean to scare you," I apologize taking a step back.

She grins at me sheepishly and then…then she bites her fucking lip. Her green eyes sparkle in the flickering light of the fire and my hazy, alcohol-impaired mind uses this moment to remind me of her luscious ass.

I close my eyes briefly and try to convince myself that her reaction to me is in my mind, and my thoughts are only because of the excessive amount of whiskey I've consumed in a very short period of time. That, along with the crushing loneliness that always haunts me, is clandestine.

"Your room should be comfortable enough for you to sleep in." I take another step back from her and set her empty glass on the table.

She seems to be studying my face. "It's very kind of you to let me stay here."

I reach my hand out to her. "It's not like I could've left you to die in your car."

She smiles at me and takes my proffered hand. "I suppose not," she whispers as I gently tug her into a standing position.

The momentum of my actions and her alcohol intake leaves her ability to balance a little skewed as well. She falls against my chest and uses her hands to steady herself. The flex of her fingers against my shirt does not go unnoticed.

She giggles and sighs as she turns and sweeps her head back and forth; it's almost like she's already forgotten how to get back to the guest bedroom.

"Let me help you," I offer and steady her with an arm around her waist. I once again want to sweep her up in my arms, just like I did outside. Only, this time, the reason would be a little more self-serving because I want to feel her warmth against my body. I do know my limitations, though, and we'd both fall down the stairs if my drunken ass attempted that. In no way is a broken neck chivalrous.

I shake my head quickly trying to rid it of any of *those* thoughts.

"Thank you," she whispers and turns her head acknowledging me. The gust of her warm breath on my neck sends a quick shiver down my spine, and for the first time today it has nothing to do with the below-freezing temps that are going on outside.

I resist the urge to squeeze her hip with the hand that is resting there and take a step forward, gently propelling her to the stairs. We stagger and sway down the hallway and somehow manage to traverse the stairs without injury or damage to the house.

I'd closed her door behind me to keep the warmth of the fire in the room when I left earlier. Stepping up to the door, I use my free hand to turn the knob and push it open. As we clear the reach of the door, I use my foot to close it behind us. How I did that without toppling us both over I have no idea.

I'm trying to convince myself I'm not as drunk as I'd initially thought as I step up to the side of the bed. With London on my right, I reach out with my left hand and pull back the covers so she can slip in. When I feel her hot breath on my neck again, I'm convincing myself I'm too drunk to make good choices.

I blame the alcohol for parting my lips when she turns in my arms and presses her soft mouth against mine. I blame the alcohol for taking two large handfuls of her succulent ass and squeezing. I blame the alcohol for grinding my erection against her lower belly.

My erection.

An erection that I got from just this kiss. A typical response to a sexual stimulus. A response that hasn't happened in what seems like forever that didn't take an extremely assertive focus, namely long minutes of oral stimulation. In other words, it usually takes a focused blow job to get me this revved up. At least it has the last couple of years.

I groan when her cold fingers find their way under my t-shirt and caress the muscles on my back. I reach over my shoulders and pull the shirt over my head, tossing it unceremoniously to the floor. Grateful she broke the skin to skin proverbial ice, I slide my hands past the waist of her athletic pants, under her barely there panties and grip her ass.

Sliding her hands around, she begins to work feverishly to get my belt buckle undone. I step back and take over, unable to move fast enough with the whiskey haze. She watches me and begins to strip down. Not even bothering with her top half she hastily pushes down her athletic pants and underwear, kicking them to the side.

The second my jeans and boxers are free of my feet we crash back together. Her arms are around my neck, and my hands have once again gravitated to her ass. The skin to skin contact is electric, and I'm so greedy for her I lift her in my arms and position her on the bed, my erection pulsing against her hot, wet heat.

I nip her neck and release her ass so I can shove her shirt up. Pulling the zipper of her sports bra down, the most magnificent pair of tits I've ever seen are exposed in the dancing light of the flames from the fireplace.

Amazing. I've always considered myself an ass man until this very second when I came face to face with these incredible breasts. She whimpers when I strike at a puckered tip with my hot mouth. The grinding of her hips against my already straining length is all the permission I need to pull my hips back, lining the head up at her entrance and thrust into her.

She arches her back, pushing her magnificent breasts into my face. My mouth is hungry for her as I feed on every inch of her delicate flesh that I can reach without having to leave the incredibly tight heat of her body.

She's meeting every deep thrust of mine, rotating her hips on the downward stroke to grind her swollen clit against me, her body searching for release. The bite of her nails down my back urge me on, harder, deeper. I can't tell if it's her or the alcohol rushing thickly through my veins that's making this seem so euphoric. It feels too good to give even a second more of consideration.

I bury my face in her neck and breathe in the delicious smell of her flowery shampoo and clean sweat. She groans loudly and bites my shoulder as her body goes rigid and her core clenches me like a fist.

"Fuck!" I roar as she takes me over the edge with her into bliss. A perfect swan dive, head-first into sweet oblivion.

I kiss her lips briefly before pulling out and falling onto the bed by her side. I remember pulling the blanket up to cover us as the coolness of the air hits the sweat on my body. Then peaceful nothingness.

"Fuck," Kadin says gruffly pulling me from sleep. I feel his chest rumble against my cheek. My breathing hitches.

What the fuck have I done?

The only thing I can do is pretend to still be asleep as he shifts his weight gingerly out from underneath me. I can tell by his cautious movements he has no intention of waking me and facing what we so stupidly did last night.

Married.

You just slept with a married man. You knew he was married, and you let him fuck you anyways. Then, to make matters even worse you wrapped yourself around him like a vine and slept in his arms all night, just like you were back home with Trent.

The image of being in bed again with Trent makes me sick to my stomach. Holding each other all night. Falling asleep with him running his hand up and down the length of my spine. Just one more way he betrayed me. One more way he kept his cheating unnoticeable by never changing how our relationship has always been.

I squeeze my eyes tight and listen as he gathers his clothes and leaves the room almost silently. A tear rolls down my cheek before I can think to stop it.

Thinking of Trent and Keira leaves a disgusting knot in my stomach. Kadin is no better than Trent, and that makes me no better than Keira. I pushed all the warnings and the voices screaming at me last night to the back of my mind, used the alcohol as reasoning, and carried on with base instincts and primal need, using Kadin as vindication that I'm desirable.

The result? I helped a married man cheat on his wife.

Keira was my best friend, and that makes her sleeping with Trent way worse than what I did, I reason with myself. It does nothing to keep the guilt of my actions from settling in my stomach.

Once I'm confident he's not returning, I roll out of bed and instantly hate the tenderness between my legs. The reminder is a penance for the horrible things I did last night. By horrible I mean the fact that he is married. The sex was above and beyond. Even in my drunken stupor, I was amazed at how incredibly capable he was in that department.

His wife is a lucky woman. The thought hits me unbidden. Ugh. Maybe not. Even being a great lover is not worth having a man that cheats. Trent never left me unsatisfied and I never even took that into consideration as I packed my bags and left him yesterday. Some things you just don't tolerate no matter how incredible the sex is.

I'm in full castigation mode as I sweep up my yoga pants and panties I just tossed away last night. Never more than this moment right now do I wish I could have been so drunk that I woke up today with no memory of what happened last night.

I reach my hand up to the mildly irritated skin from where his beard abraded it last night. I touch it tenderly as I walk into the en-suite bathroom. If I thought the bedroom was amazing, it has nothing on this bathroom.

When I cleared the threshold last night, I asked if this was his room because it is so over the top I couldn't imagine it not being the master. The bathroom is opulent, top of the line, and beautifully decorated. Oatmeal colored marble countertops with dual sinks accent the multihued wooden décor perfectly. No way a man decorated this. I think of his wife once again.

I look in the mirror. My intentions are to chastise myself one last time before moving on. What's done is done, and there's nothing I can do about it now, even though I regret my choices from last night.

I don't find what I'm looking for. A disappointed woman, full of regret is not what peers back at me. Instead, I find sated eyes and lips still swollen from last night's kisses. The redness on my neck makes me wonder how the same irritation would feel on my inner thighs.

"Shit!" I slap my hand on the countertop as the sudden thought runs through my head.

You're raw and heartbroken. You have to stop picturing not only what happened last night but also what could have been. He's not available to you or anyone else. Let his lack of morals be on him and move past it.

I tug off my t-shirt and slide my already opened sports bra off my shoulders. It's not until I'm standing in front of the mirror completely naked that I realize the slickness between my legs is a combination of Kadin and me.

No protection. As if this situation can get even worse. What if he gave me an STD? Shit! What if *I* gave him an STD?

I rush to the shower even though I know whatever potential damage that could have occurred has been literally brewing all night. I turn the shower on full blast waiting for the water to warm. It never does. The generator that wasn't working last night is apparently still not working. No hot water. No way to fully wash away the physical proof of our sins.

In addition to the red skin and the soreness to my lady bits, I can now add a frigid cold whore's bath to my atonement. I run a wash cloth under the freezing water from the sink faucet and commence to cleaning myself as best I can.

I redress in my clothes from yesterday and make my way back out into the main bedroom area. The fire has burned down to mere embers, but I refuse to leave the sanctity of this room. I crawl under the blankets on the bed and bury myself as deep as I can.

Another method of torture? The bed smells like him. The earthy scent of rugged man and the slightest hint of the liquor we consumed last night assault my nostrils in the most heavenly way. Clearly there's no getting around or forgetting about what I did, what *we* did last night. I'm not the only one to blame here. He's the married one. He should have stopped what happened.

It only takes ten minutes of shivering under the Kadin-smelling blankets before I've had enough. I'm done freezing. I'm done feeling guilty and shouldering all of the blame from last night.

I throw the covers back with more bravado than I actually feel and head downstairs. I'm not a confrontational person, hence the reason I just packed my belongings and left Great Falls. It's also the reason I never answered one of Trent's calls the dozen times my phone rang yesterday. I'm hoping Kadin's feeling just as guilty of our indiscretions as I am and he avoids me all day; like I plan to ignore him.

Walking silently, I make my way into the den, sighing in relief at the blaze in the fireplace. Still as a statue, I stand near the fire, warming my hands and listening to determine if he's near. I'm met with the silence of the house and the intermittent crackle of the logs in the fire.

I settle back on the couch in the same spot from last night and wrap the now cold fleece around my shoulders. As if my presence in the den beckons to him, the outside door into the mudroom flies open, and he appears. From my vantage point, every inch of his soaking wet body is visible.

He's going to kill himself if he keeps going out in this blizzard.

I sink lower on the couch and watch as he strips out of the soaked outer layer of jacket and coveralls. Momentarily forgetting my shamefulness of last night I watch as he doesn't stop with the outer layer of clothes. He's soaked through, and the layers just keep getting ripped off and cast aside.

He's grumbling and cursing to himself, but I can't make out the words. I notice a streak or grease or dirt on his cheek as he flings his gray t-shirt to the floor. My fingers tingle slightly with the urge to wipe it away. He's standing in the mudroom in nothing but a tight pair of black boxer briefs and my mouth waters.

His chest and etched stomach muscles are covered in a well-groomed layer of dark hair several shades darker than the mahogany colored hair on his head. How did I miss that last night? My gaze follows the dark hair to the waistband of his boxers, and there's no missing the growing bulge in the front of his underwear.

He kicks at his pile of clothing and runs his hands through his hair in frustration. He squeezes his eyes closed and raises his face to the ceiling, muttering something with a pained expression on his face. His reaction to the situation and events I have no idea about drag me out of my shameless ogling. Apparently he's struggling with what we did also.

The sight of his regret makes me want to cry, and I'll be damned if I allow him to see that. I haven't been broken in a long time, and the last man who fixed me years ago is the same man who destroyed me yesterday. I'm done with this shit.

I slide off the couch, keeping the warm fleece wrapped around my body and run up the stairs to the room and close the door harder than I'd meant to. I know he had to have seen me, but he made no effort to stop me or call out to me. I know it's for the better, and it confirms he has no desire to see or speak to me either.

I have to get away from here as soon as humanly possible but from the view outside the window and the still raging snow storm it's apparent that won't be anytime soon.

Seven

Kadin

How it is possible to be frozen to the core and still be alive, I'll never know. I can't get my drenched clothes off fast enough. My jacket and then my coveralls start the sodden pile of laundry on the floor at my feet.

I misjudged my ability to stay dry in this weather. Feeling like a champion after fixing the generator, my dumbass thought it would be no big deal to trudge down the long ass driveway and get London's things out of her car. I never gave a second thought to the possible condition of her car. It took me, at least, twenty minutes to remove enough snow away to open the damn door and another fifteen to clear the trunk.

I glance at the two suitcases as I shrug out of my shirt, adding it to the ever-growing pile. Maybe she'll take it as an offering and forgive me for taking advantage of her last night. Granted she kissed me first, but that's still no excuse. Less than an hour after telling me she's running from man troubles, we're ripping our clothes off, and I'm slamming into her.

Fuck she felt so good.

I should just build an igloo outside to stay in. I have no idea how I'm going to keep my hands off of her if we're in the same house. This blizzard is honestly turning into the bane of my existence right now. I'm here because I can't handle being around people back in Spokane- *You're here to kill yourself, asshole*- and here I am thrown into a situation I just made, even more, awkward by sleeping with the stranded woman.

I crack my neck to try to relieve some of the stress I'm feeling and drop my wet pants in the pile with the other clothes. Out of frustration, I kick the soaked clothes. It doesn't help. Nothing helps. I can't work through in my head why last night is bothering me so much. It's not the first time I've slept with someone other than my wife. It doesn't even come close to being as fucked up as some of the other situations I've put myself in recently.

I can try to explain it away. I can once again blame the alcohol I drank in abundance last night, but I'm not the type of guy to make excuses and I sure as hell don't lie to myself. So why was last night the first night in as long as I can remember that the demons that haunt me never showed? Why the absence of pain and regret?

The answer, although simple, is not one I even want to think about. *London*. The sparkle in her moss green eyes flashes in my mind. The way her back arched when she orgasmed last night. No overproduction. No hint that she was performing for me. Just pure uninhibited bliss.

I grip my head in my hands and squeeze my eyes closed as tight as I can. Raising my face to the ceiling, I beg for forgiveness. I pray to a god who deserted me long ago to ease the pain in my chest and give me the strength to resist her, the strength that, as a man, I'm not sure I possess on my own.

When I open my eyes again, I see a flash of her as she runs up the stairs and slams the door to the guest bedroom. It's like He's taunting me for losing faith. He's throwing that temptation at me rather than helping me avoid it. I had no idea she was in the den. Here I am standing all but naked in the mudroom, not even taking into consideration where she may be in the house.

"Fuck," I hiss. I know she couldn't have read my thoughts as I just imagined sinking into her again, but there's no way to look past the half-erect cock jutting out, barely restricted by the thin layer of my underwear. This day just keeps getting better. She probably thinks I'm going to be trudging up the stairs any minute demanding sexual payment for her to stay here.

Oh God! Did she think she was obligated to sleep with me last night? My mind races, replaying the events of last night, trying to remember if in any way I may have said or done something that she misconstrued into sexual demands. I can't recall anything, and I try to justify it once again with the knowledge that she kissed me first, but I still feel like an asshole.

I keep my underwear on even though they're wet and sticking to my body and walk to the kitchen. Now that the generator is going I can make some coffee. This will warm me better from the inside than the whiskey I really want. Another way this storm is fucking me. I have to take my houseguest into consideration. If she weren't here, I'd tip the Jack back rather than standing here putting two scoops of Folgers into the machine. I have a feeling drinking the hard stuff before noon would be rather off-putting for her.

Come to think of it, maybe that's exactly what I should do. I shake the idea off, knowing the second my mind goes hazy from the liquor the first thing I'll want to do is get inside of her again.

Once the coffee starts to drip, I make my way to the den and toss several more logs on the fire. The waves of heat are hitting my skin, reminding me of the way London's breath felt on my chest when I woke up this morning. I turn my back to the fire, shutting that shit down as well as I can.

Another quick glance at the drawer in the den makes me want to scream. Nothing ever goes my way these days. I can't even kill myself in fucking peace. It's like the universe is cosmically against any plans I ever try to make.

I know it took me over an hour to make it to her car and back so the water heater should have warmed the water for showers. I grab her suitcases and set them outside of her door and make my way to my room for a quick shower.

Fighting the urge to stay under the hot stream in the shower, I wash quickly and get out. I know London will want to wash her horrible day from yesterday away, so I did my best to use as little hot water as possible. My consideration of her now doesn't take away the guilt from last night when her needs were the farthest thing from my mind. Regret for London, another thing I can take with me to my grave.

Wash it away. I wish it were that easy. I wish I would've taken the aftermath into consideration, given a second thought to the situation, knowing we'd be stuck in this house with no escape for several more days. I dress quickly and make my way back out into the hall. Her suitcases are still sitting outside of her door.

There is still a bit of coolness in the air, the generator having a lot of catching up to do since the power was off all night. She has to be freezing in there. I didn't want to wake her; *you didn't want to face her*, when I left this morning, so her fire has to have burned out by now.

I head downstairs to grab her a cup of coffee. I don't know how she takes it, but I make it girly with lots of sugar and creamer and hope for the best. My gentle tap on her door goes unanswered, as does the harder knock. I twist the handle and peer into the room. For a second, I think the room is empty until I see the lump on her bed move slightly.

I pull the suitcases from the hallway and leave them just inside of her door, sure to make noise because I don't want to startle her. I walk slowly to the side of the bed and set the cup of coffee on the bedside table.

"London?" Her body shifts again on the bed. "I brought you a cup of coffee."

I walk to her fireplace and put the remaining logs in and set it ablaze. The room is freezing still. I know things are going to be awkward between us. Nothing worse than the day after with a stranger when you can't just get up and leave.

I sit on the edge of the bed and tug the covers back, exposing her head and shoulders. She turns her head and makes eye contact with me. I notice two things. One she's freezing, and her entire body is shivering and two, there is no denying the regret in her eyes as they break their brief contact with mine. She sits up on the bed near the headboard.

My protective instincts are the first to respond, and I reach out to hold her, knowing she could use the warmth of my body. I frown when she wraps her arms tighter around her waist and scoots further out of my reach. She clearly doesn't want to be touched.

I nod at her in understanding.

"I grabbed your suitcases from your car." I tilt my head toward the door.

She cranes her neck, looking around me to the two nondescript cases. "You were able to drive down there?" Her voice is hopeful, and I know she's imagining she's going to get out of here quicker than she'd thought.

I can't help but laugh thinking about what I went through to get them back to the house. "No. I walked down there and got them."

She frowns. "You didn't have to do that."

"It's no big deal," I lie. I'm certain I may have frostbite on my ass from the experience. "Your car is practically buried, and it'll be a few more days until we can even attempt to get it out."

I'm surprised to find myself saddened at the way she drops her head, clearly not happy with being stuck here with me.

Eight

London

A few more days!

A few more days of being stranded with the Forbidden Fruit, a fruit that I'm well aware just how delicious it is? Like my life hasn't been bad enough lately?

"I'll get you more wood up here for the fireplace, but I was able to get the generators going. We should be good on power now." He stands from the side of the bed; giving me the distance my mind says it needs.

My body? That traitorous bitch is screaming for him to come right back and climb under the covers with me.

Married! The hand reaching out for me just a minute ago proved it in the form of a solid platinum band on his ring finger.

It's exhausting having to remind myself of that fact, a fact that is so blatantly evident right now as he twists his damn wedding ring on his hand. The act is subconscious like he's done it for years and doesn't even realize it.

"You should have plenty of hot water for a shower." He turns away from me and begins walking toward the door.

"Kadin?" My voice is soft and quiet, but he hears me and turns to face my direction, his hand just reaching out for the doorknob. "Last night." *Last night was perfect.*

He remains silent even though I'm hoping he will be the one to finish.

"Last night was a mistake." He shows no emotion; once again his face is completely stoic. "I think it was a bad idea."

Silence.

"I don't think it should happen again." I hang my head, the blank look on his face making me uncomfortable. "It won't happen again."

He nods and walks out, closing the door softly behind him.

"You're the one with the fucking wife," I mutter in his direction.

Now that we got that out of the way I hope things don't have to be awkward, but I know they will. After last night and seeing the tent in the front of his pants less than an hour ago I can't keep my eyes away from his crotch. Not a good sign of how the next few days of seclusion are going to go.

I close my eyes and take a calming breath, the faint smell of coffee invading my senses. I cut my eyes to the cup of heaven sitting on the bedside table.

Would he poison me?

I release a weak chuckle. *You slept with him last night; without protection.* My brain reminds me. *Now you're worried about your safety.*

I mentally shut those thoughts down and reach for the cup of steaming liquid. It's sweet and creamy, just how I like it.

Perfect.

Another item to add to the long list of irresistible things about him. Put that right under *body like a Greek god* and *fucks like it's his job.*

I need something to occupy my mind and as much as I'd love to go for a run and exhaust my body, that's not an option. I set the half empty cup of coffee back down on the table and get out of the bed.

I grab my smaller suitcase and roll it behind me into the bathroom. It has all the essentials I'll need for a long hot shower. Stepping into the bathroom for the second time today, I let my eyes dart between shower and the garden tub that's tucked away in the corner of the massive bathroom.

I have nothing but time, so I opt for a long hot bath rather than a shower. I didn't grab bath salts or oils when I packed my belongings so this will be a plain old bath, but with the tension in my body it will be glorious none the less. Well, this bath will be about as plain as a sunken tub with half a dozen water jets can be.

Clutching my shampoo, conditioner, and shower gel to my chest with one hand I turn the water on in the tub with the other. I pin my hair back for the time being with a clip from my makeup bag and step gingerly into the water that is steadily filling the tub.

I lay back and wait for the water to fill as high as possible before it would be considered too deep and would overflow onto the floor. I raise my foot into the stream of soothing yet near scorching water and frown at the condition of my toenail polish. Another thing to add to the list of stuff to get done once I get settled. The first being that visit to a clinic for bloodwork and a full STD panel.

I only have two things my mind seems to be able to focus on right now. The first being Trent, Keira, and their deceit. The second of course is the adulterer downstairs. Neither being something I want to have to think about right now.

I try to focus on moving forward and what I'll do once I leave here. Go to Spokane, find an apartment, and get a job. Seems easy enough. I have a vast array of skills and work experience that will quickly open doors in numerous markets. If I don't find work right away, that is fine too. I have quite a bit in savings, and that is one thing I'm grateful to Trent for. Had I known I'd be in this situation I never would've bought the Mini Cooper.

As I let the jets of hot water blast over my body my head takes me back to Trent and the years we spent together. Loving, dedicated, and attentive.

All of it *fake*. For a brief second, I wonder if I could forgive him. I question whether packing up and just leaving was the right thing to do. If throwing six years of happiness away is the right decision. Then I remember that I'm not throwing anything away. He is responsible for this outcome. My happiness was a lie. My happiness was an illusion that they wanted me to see, not an accurate reflection of how things actually were.

I stay in the bathtub until the circulating water begins to chill. Praying there's enough hot water left, I drain the tub and hit the shower to wash and condition my hair. I towel off quickly and wrap a towel around my hair. I slip on panties before making my way out of the bathroom to grab my hair dryer and more clothes from my other suitcase.

Looking down at the poor condition of my fingernails, a consequence of working in a fast-paced bar the past three months, I hear *fuck* in a husky voice, causing my eyes to dart up.

Standing across the room is Kadin with an armful of fire logs. He'd mentioned bringing some wood up, but I had no idea he meant he was going straight down to get it. I also didn't bother to lock the door behind him when he left earlier.

I screech at his intrusion and try to hide my exposed body, not missing the sweep of his eyes over my topless form. Whipping off the towel from my head, I do my best to cover my body. He looks confused, standing there glancing from the wood in his arms and back to me, like he doesn't know what to do with them but feels the need to escape.

Snapping out of his trance, he quickly gives me his back as he drops the wood into the log holder and turns to the door. "Sorry," he mutters and shuts the door roughly behind him.

I don't know how long I stand in the middle of the room staring at the closed door. So much for thinking the awkwardness would go away. I'm more affected now with him seeing my breasts in the full light of the day *sober* than I was last night drunken in the dark. Combine that with the bulge that couldn't be denied in the front of his pants when he turned sideways to leave the room and my head is all mixed up again.

Sighing, I lock the bedroom door, preventing any further surprises, grab my suitcase and roll it into the bathroom. I'll keep everything in here until I leave to avoid another ambush by my host.

With nothing else to do I stay in the room and fix, to the best of my ability, my toenail polish. I wish I could say I just didn't pack all of my things but hot pink nail polish is all that I own. So that's what my toes got. Unable to charge my now dead phone since I left the charger in the car, I stand in the bathroom and tap my foot, trying to figure out something else to occupy my time.

Over the next couple of hours, I've painted my toes and fingernails, straightened and then curled my hair, and I've even put on a light layer of makeup, which I promptly take back off. Well, mostly. All I had was waterproof mascara, and it'd take an hour to clean my lashes of that mess.

Just as I climb on the bed to take a nap, my stomach growls reminding me that I haven't eaten anything all day. As much as I'd love to avoid Kadin, I'm not going to sit in here and starve. I'll have to make sure to leave him some cash when I leave, repayment for his hospitality and use of his amenities.

Once in the kitchen, I notice a small note on the counter written in an apparent male hand. *Sandwich in the fridge.*

Shocked, I look in the fridge and, sure enough, there's a sub sandwich on a plate with chips. I slide the plate off the shelf and look around, thinking he's lurking in the shadows somewhere watching me take his offering, all the while I'm wondering why he bothered.

I sit gingerly at the breakfast bar with my prepared meal and eat as slowly as possible, hoping he will show so I can thank him. Honestly, I'd like to have some form of human interaction. I know being around him is asking for trouble, but I'm lonely and not used to spending time with only myself. I need a distraction from my thoughts.

With a full stomach, thanks to Kadin's thoughtfulness, I carry the plate to the sink, wash it, and return it to the cabinet with other plates of its kind. He still hasn't shown. The house is completely silent, and I can't tell if he's even inside the house.

I make my way to the den, stopping by the open door of the mudroom. His boots are in there, but the pile of clothes he discarded earlier is nowhere to be seen. I shrug my shoulders and continue my journey to the den.

I've spent enough time in the room upstairs and can't stand the thought of going back up there with nothing to do so I park it on the sofa and stare into the fire. The flames are small, and it's clear that he's not been down here recently to feed it.

I lay on my side watching the flames and listening to the crackling and popping, doing my best not to think of all the coulda's, shoulda's, and woulda's that are racing through my head. It's almost an impossible task since the sight of Trent plowing into my best friend from behind is all I see when I close my eyes.

Nine

Kadin

Her breasts last night in the light of the fire, while she was lying down, were incredible. Standing, in full unobstructed view with the lights on? Without a doubt, no contest, the best set of tits I've ever seen: in person, on TV, or in a movie.

I could tell I shocked her when she came out of the bathroom. Hell, it shocked me that she was topless. I stood there like a statue and just gawked at her perky, pink buds, taking notice that they tightened further under my scrutiny.

My cock seems to have a mind of its own around her and my attempts to control it have gone unnoticed. I'm sure she noticed my lack of discipline in regards to him. I was in full tent mode by the time I closed her bedroom door behind me, spontaneous erections being a recent rediscovery of my body.

Did I know she was in the shower? Yes. Did I know she was out of the shower? Yes. Did I slowly go about my business in hopes that I'd see her if even for a brief moment before leaving her room again? Yes. Did I ever, even for a minute, consider the possibility that she'd step out of there without clothes on? Never in a million years. One of her suitcases was gone, and I figured she'd grab clothes out of it already, a happy misconception on my part.

Then I think about the words she muttered to herself as I left the room earlier. *You're the one with a fucking wife.*

This is coming right on the heels of her shutting down any notion that I might have had about a repeat performance. I can accept that she feels like last night was a mistake. Hell, I felt exactly the same way when I climbed out from under her just a few short hours ago. Hearing it from a mouth surrounded by completely fuckable lips? Depressing.

What else besides fucking like rabbits is there to do for the next couple of days? *You could take a long hike outside without any desire to make it back alive.*

When she told me it couldn't happen again, all I could do was stand there and look past her. It was the only way to keep myself from arguing with her and citing all the reasons why I think sex would be the perfect way to pass the time until I can get her out of here and follow through with my other plans for this trip.

I have to tuck my erection behind the waistband of my sweats as I make my way down the stairs. Maybe her staying away from me and locked in her room is for the best. My constant state of arousal has me concerned about blood flow and circulation problems.

Since I'm not much of a cook, I decide on sandwiches for what would be considered brunch since it's later than breakfast and too early for lunch. My mother raised me with manners, so I make her a sandwich also, placing it at a setting across the dining room table from mine.

I tinker around in the kitchen washing the coffee pot from earlier, wiping down the already clean counter. After thirty minutes of her not showing her beautiful face, I sit down and eat, slowly. After I finish, I put her food in the fridge and leave a note so she can find it. She has to be hungry; she's not eaten all day.

Twenty minutes later I'm in a full speed run on the treadmill. The oversized home gym attached to my master suite was a must when building this house. At the time, I had every intention of moving here and becoming a hermit, however; these days I don't even like my own company. A number one complaint from family and friends back home, seems I'm hard to be around. Running outside is not the safest around here and a complete impossibility at the moment. An hour and seven miles later I hit the shower. Surely she's out of her room and bored out of her mind by now.

Maybe she'd be interested in a board game or something. Hopefully, the decorator stocked some. Wouldn't be a proper cabin near the mountains if there aren't any. Remembering the tiny size of the firewood holders makes me begin to doubt there are any here. It's becoming apparent the decorator was only going for looks and not practicality. She must not be from around here, an area where it is not uncommon to be trapped inside for days at a time during the winter.

I head straight downstairs after my shower. Her door is shut, so I keep my distance. The sandwich from the fridge is gone, and I notice that the plate is not in the sink. She must have washed it and put it away. Clean. I like that.

Hoping she's in the den, I head that direction. I find her curled up on the sofa facing the fire. Her gorgeous light brown hair is all over the place, and I resist the urge to reach out and touch the soft, graceful curls I never noticed until now. Her breaths come out softly over hands that are clasped under her chin. Thick eyelashes rest delicately on the pale pink of her cheeks.

Thankful I'm still tucked in the waist of my pants, I turn and leave her to nap. She didn't go into detail last night about the man problems she's having, and I didn't ask, but she whimpered several times in her sleep last night, so I imagine her dreams didn't allow for a very restful sleep.

I head back upstairs. The last thing she needs is to wake up and see me staring at her even though I'd love nothing more than to sit on the floor in front of the recliner and watch her sleep. I already ran my ass ragged on the treadmill so it looks like weights will be the way to go this time. At least if I exhaust myself, I'll sleep well tonight. *You'd sleep well if you curl in behind London.*

I slide my ear buds in and crank up the music, maybe the loudness of the death metal will keep thoughts of her away. It doesn't. My mind wanders back to last night. My mind wanders back to Spokane and the fucked up mess I've created there. My mind wanders back to my beautiful wife and a pair of soul-searching blue eyes I'll never have the chance to look into again.

I push my body and exert myself until I hit muscle fatigue and I practically have to crawl back into the bathroom for yet another shower.

I'm beating myself up over this whole situation, but it's not the way I've come to expect from having sex with a woman. My issue is stemming from not really having an issue with it other than her being upset that it happened. My concern is that I enjoyed it on more than a physical level. It was primal and instinctive. Raw and real, and even drunk it was the first time the guilt didn't slam into my stomach the second I pulled out.

My shower is slow and thorough. My body's exhausted, but my cock apparently didn't get the memo. I have every intention of hunting her down if only for companionship when I get out and this guy popping up every ten seconds will only make matters worse.

I lean my head against the tile in the shower and allow the water to rush off my back as I palm my erection. I sigh heavily and for the first time since high school I picture someone else other than my wife as I grip and stroke my length.

"*London*," I whisper as I explode against the shower wall. I continue to stroke until the surfeit of sensation is so overwhelming my hips jerks back of their own accord.

It's only a temporary fix. That's what comes to mind as I towel off and throw on some clothes.

I stop by her room and knock on the door. She doesn't answer, and there's no chance I'm going to open the door and walk in again without permission. Hoping to find her in the den I make my way downstairs.

At the landing, the smell of rich, decadent spices fills my nostrils. I breathe deep and moan as I head into the kitchen. She's standing in front of the stove stirring something in a saucepan. To her left I can see water boiling in another.

I stand in the doorway and just watch her. My grin grows larger as I hear her humming and occasionally belting out song lyrics. She doesn't have headphones in so she's singing from memory; poorly I might add. It's endearing and a happy change from her mood last night and again this morning.

I clear my throat, and she turns abruptly, dragging the spoon from the sauce in front of her. The movement causes some to dribble on the floor.

We both look down at the mess on the floor.

"Shit," she mutters, replacing the spoon back into the sauce. She grabs a paper towel and bends down just as I take steps further in the room.

"I'll get it," I tell her a second too late, as she drops to the floor quickly to clean up the sauce.

I look down at her and get the full effect of her on her knees. She looks up at me innocently, and I groan as my dick once again takes notice and twitches in my jeans. That's right I put on jeans, this time, knowing I'd grow hard at some point around her. The denim will be slightly more restrictive than the sweats I had on earlier. My self-love session in the shower didn't help one damn bit.

Once the sauce is cleared from the floor, I reach my hand down to help her up. She looks at it and back at me like she has to decide if it's a good idea or not. Reluctantly she takes it and stands. I take a few steps back, releasing her hand. I miss it immediately.

"You didn't have to cook," I tell her and make a show of looking around her at the stove.

"You made me a sandwich earlier," she shrugs and turns back to the stove. "I figured I'd return the favor."

"It's much appreciated. I haven't had someone cook for me since…well, it's been a while since anyone has bothered." I respond honestly.

"It's just spaghetti. I didn't know if you had any other plans for the ground beef, so I just made it vegetarian. Do you like Italian?" She still has her back to me. Wanting, *needing*, to see her face I step to the side of her.

"Spaghetti is perfect." I want to sweep the tendril of hair out of her eye so I can see her face unobstructed. "I'll put together a salad." I step toward the refrigerator.

"I already made one." She laughs like it's the funniest thing she's ever heard, and I can't help but smile.

"So I should just sit at the table and wait to be served?" I raise an eyebrow at her.

"Fat chance, Buddy. Grab some plates and silverware." *Feisty, I love it!*

She drains the pasta over the sink, and I do as instructed. We load up our plates at the stove and set them across from each other on the dining room table. We both head back to the kitchen. I grab a bottle of wine and glasses from the small wine rack, and she grabs two premade salad bowls from the fridge. I don't even drink wine, but it's here. I take it to the table since I don't think she'd be amenable to more whiskey after last night.

I'm almost giddy at the sight of him. Spending practically the entire day with very limited human interaction was horrible. I never do that. I seek others out, either at the bar or at the gym. I don't have to talk to people necessarily but I seem to gravitate to situations where there's a chance of holding a conversation should I feel so inclined.

I don't say a word to him as we sit at the table, and he pours me a glass of wine. I'm not much of a wine drinker but it's courteous, so I thank him and take the glass.

I clear my throat. "I want to apologize about last night." I keep my eyes on my plate, hoping the lack of eye contact will make this less awkward. "I shouldn't have…" why is this so hard? "I never should have kissed you."

He doesn't answer so I look up at him. He has an eyebrow raised at me.

"What?" I ask not sure I want to know the answer.

He shakes his head slightly. "It's a little insulting. Sitting here and having you tell me you didn't want to kiss me."

I laugh softly. "I didn't say I didn't want to kiss you," I qualify. "I said I shouldn't have done it."

"Not much difference from where I'm sitting."

Do I tell him what I'm running from? Would he even care?

I feel the need to explain why I jumped his bones last night without so much as a hint from him that he wanted it. He didn't argue or hesitate even for a second, but that doesn't mean he was interested until my lips hit his.

"I had a seriously bad day yesterday." I'm purposely vague, so I don't just lay all my shit at his feet if he's not interested in hearing it.

He nods, agreeing that yesterday wasn't one to add in the plus column.

"I walked in on my boyfriend fucking my best friend," I blurt out.

He drops the fork that was an inch from his mouth, and I watch as it clatters back down to his plate, leaving speckles of sauce on the table top.

"Worst fucking day ever," he finally says.

I wish. "At least in the top five."

"Rough life?" He asks with evident concern on his face.

"Last decade has held some pretty disastrous shit." I look down and twirl spaghetti noodles absently around my fork.

"Like I was saying," I begin after a long silence. "It was a shitty day, and I never should've thrown myself at you like I did. Especially considering you're...you know," I nod at his wedding ring.

I cut my eyes back to my plate and continue the pasta twirling even though my stomach is too knotted to even think about eating another bite. The silence drags on for what seems like forever. I put my hands on the table ready to stand and get away from the discomfort I'm feeling from my admissions.

His voice stops my momentum. "You have it all wrong." I look up at him. "I'm nothing like," he nods his head at me.

"Trent?" I offer.

"Is that the asshole that cheated on you?" I nod. "I'm nothing like *Trent.*" He says his name with disdain like Trent personally wronged him somehow. "I never cheated on Savannah. Never even thought to turn my head in the direction of another woman. Not once."

I feel like I'm in the Twilight Zone as I watch him twist his wedding ring around his finger. I feel the need to remind him where his dick was last night.

"Until last night," I whisper and drop my head. I'm the succubus that caused this dedicated man to break his vows.

"She's," his voice hitches. "My wife passed away in a car accident almost two years ago."

My head jerks up just as his chin hits his chest. He's broken.

I reach my hand across the table and place it on his, stilling the incessant twirling of his wedding ring. I don't know how to feel right now. I wish I could say that I feel better knowing that I didn't help him become an adulterer, but I don't. If possible, I feel even more like shit because I threw myself at a broken man. A man that is apparently not over the death of his wife.

To have a love like that, I think with jealousy.

I'm too far away to reach the tear that rolls down his cheek and mixes with the hair on his jaw.

"I'm so sorry for your loss, Kadin. I can only imagine how difficult that is."

I can in a roundabout way. My parents died which was horrible but not the same. This man lost his future, one that obviously he wasn't prepared to live without her. I lost Trent, and Keira, but that was by his choice not the consequence of a traffic accident.

"My parents died in a car accident," I share with him, hoping maybe the commiseration will let him know that I have some idea of the pain he feels.

"How long ago?" He doesn't raise his head but shifts his hands, causing me to let them go. I watch as he wipes his face on the back of his arm clearing away the rogue tears that dared to fall.

"Almost ten years ago," I tell him when he brings his head up to look at me.

"Rough decade."

"Rough decade," I answer in agreement.

"How long were you and the Idiot together?" He says, idiot, like its Trent's new name. I like it, very fitting.

"Six years." Best six years of my life if I'm honest. *All lies.*

"Long time."

"How long were you and Savannah together?" I hope he doesn't get upset talking about her, but he asked me, so I figure maybe the conversation is safe.

He looks past me and smiles at her memory. "I met her at Freshman Orientation."

"So college. That's a long time."

He laughs boldly; the sound reverberates around the room. "High school actually," he corrects me.

"Wow, that is a long time." He grins.

"We were together for a little over seventeen years. If you count the on-again-off-again months our junior year in high school." He chuckles again at a memory I'm not privileged to.

His face lights up when he starts thinking about her. His chocolate eyes shine, and they crinkle at the corner. This man is gorgeous.

"She was a lucky woman," I say out loud before I can stop myself.

He winks at me but otherwise doesn't respond, changing the mood in the dining room completely.

"Tell me about her?" I rise from the table and take our plates so he doesn't feel like I'm scrutinizing him.

He waits for a few beats before he starts to respond.

"She was as perfect as a woman could get. Blond hair and the most amazing pair of blue eyes I would have given my left leg for just the chance to stare into the rest of my life. She called me a jerk the very first time she spoke to me, and I think I fell in love with her then." He laughs again and gets up from the table bringing the wine glasses with him.

We somehow begin the process of putting the food away and washing the dishes, him drying. We move around the kitchen almost as one unit rather than two separate people.

"How do you go from being a jerk to marrying her?" I laugh.

"I followed her around like a lost puppy. I'd do anything and everything she ever asked of me."

"That's stalking," I say honestly.

His laugh rings around the room again. "That's what she said." He shrugs. "So one day I just stopped. She must have missed me because after two days she was at my house wanting to know why I didn't walk her home anymore."

"And the rest is history," I whisper.

He nods.

To have a love like that.

He hands me the towel after I drain the water in the sink.

"Want to play cards or something?" He asks as he turns and walks out of the kitchen.

I follow him. "Sure."

"Strip poker?" He asks teasingly. I stop in my tracks and stare at his back. He turns and smirks at me. "Too soon?"

I laugh. "Listen, Kadin." He holds his hand up to stop me.

"I heard what you said the first time." He says and turns back to a beautiful wooden cabinet tucked into the corner of the den, rifling through it looking for playing cards I assume.

I did tell him it was a mistake, and it was. Knowing now that he is a widower and not an adulterer shouldn't change things in my mind, but for some reason I feel myself gravitating to him in more than just what I'd originally intended when I set out making dinner. I'd wanted a little companionship. I didn't want to sit in the room alone going stir crazy.

I tell myself to get my hormones in check because this man is hurting and I only complicate things.

He sets the pack of cards down on the table in front of the fire and makes his way over to the table with the half empty bottle of Jack Daniels on it. He holds it up in offering. I shake my head back and forth, and he laughs but doesn't say anything.

"I wouldn't want to get drunk and jump you in the hall again," I say only half joking because I sort of do.

He doesn't respond, just pours some of the golden liquor in a tumbler and sets the bottle on the table by the cards. Seems he has different plans for the evening.

"What do you want to play?" I ask as I open the cards, removing the cellophane from them along with the other random cards they throw in there, and begin to shuffle them.

"Rummy?" I nod and continue walking.

It's incredibly late by the time I give up on cards with Kadin. He's won at least four games to my one and the more he drinks, the better he gets.

I yawn and cover my mouth. "I'm going to call it a night." I hand the stack of cards to him and stand from the sofa.

"Good night," he says and tilts his whiskey tumbler at me.

We talked about everything under the sun: our lives and childhoods. I laughed like I haven't laughed in years, and it came easy not forced.

I smile as I enter my room and head straight to my bed. Even with my nap from earlier, I'm tired. I kick off my sweats and slide in between the sheets, snuggling as far as I can go in the thick blankets and before I know it I'm drifting off to sleep.

My sleepy mind barely registers the hot, massive form that slides behind my back and wraps its arms around me. My mind does, however, register the gentle kiss to my shoulder just before he nuzzles his nose in my hair.

"So warm," he whispers against my neck as sleep drags me down once again.

Eleven

Kadin

Day two of waking up with London. I tossed and turned for hours last night before finally giving up and crawling into bed with her. I had planned just to head downstairs and drink some more but when I passed her door, I noticed it was cracked. I saw it as an open invitation.

I crawled in behind her and held her in my arms. Her only reaction was the release of a soft sigh in her sleep. Now that I'm sober and still wrapped around her back this morning, the idea seems more like a poor choice. If she wanted me in bed with her, she would've asked me to join her. Now I'm the creepy guy, taking liberties with a houseguest I've known for just over forty-eight hours.

I came in here straight from my own bed across the hall, so I'm only wearing my underwear. I'm doing my best not to move too much but from the warmth coming from under the covers, she's either naked or only wearing panties with her thin tank top. I could stay here all day and just lay against her, but eventually she's going to wake up and not only wonder why I'm in bed with her, but I'd also have to explain the erection pressing against her ass.

The sun is just beginning to shine through the window, so I know it's still relatively early. I wiggle and scoot backward gently. Once out of the bed, I give her one more glance and freeze as I watch her bury herself deeper in the covers, groaning slightly. I smile at the thought that she misses my warmth. We were in the same position we were in when I first came in last night so hopefully she won't even realize I was in here.

I leave her room, making sure to leave her door cracked open like I'd found it last night and shuffle across the hall to mine, closing myself quietly in my room. I shower quickly, taking care of the more-than-morning-wood issue before throwing on a pair of jeans and heading downstairs.

I purposely make as much noise as I can in the kitchen, hoping she'll wake up and join me for coffee. Once it's brewing, I crack open a can of cinnamon rolls and preheat the oven.

She has perfect timing as she shuffles into the kitchen just as I'm pulling the pastries from the oven. My back is to her, but I hear her walk in. "Coffee's ready," I tell her and set the cookie sheet on the stove top to cool.

Another ten minutes and these babies will be ready for the packet of cream cheese icing that came with them.

She didn't bother to pull her hair back before coming down this morning, and it's all over the place and down her back. Just a few shades darker than honey, it hits her in the middle of her back, which is facing me as she makes her coffee.

She's still wearing the soft pink tank she had on last night, but her legs and luscious ass are now covered in a pair of thin cotton pajama pants with pastel stripes. She turns with her coffee cup in her hand, cradled under her chin, blowing on it to cool it faster.

I stand across from her leaning on the opposite counter. I watch her eyes rake over my body. I'm shameless this morning and came down with no shirt on, my broad chest bare and loving the attention it's getting from her eyes. I can't keep my eyes off of her nipples which are practically visible in her thin shirt.

Perfect fucking tits.

I clear my throat, and she snaps her eyes up to mine. "How'd you sleep?" *Do you know I was in the bed with you?*

She grins at me. "Like a baby. Didn't wake up once."

"I made cinnamon rolls." *Thank heavens she doesn't realize my level of crazy.*

"They smell delicious," she says with a grin. She sets her coffee down on the counter behind her and takes a few steps closer to me.

I grip the edge of the counter to keep from reaching out to her. She brushes my arm as she reaches beside me into the cabinet for a few plates. "Want me to pour you a glass of milk?" she offers in a husky voice near my ear that makes me wish she was asking if I want something else.

"I'd love one," I return in a voice just as husky.

She moves toward the fridge, and I turn to add the icing to the cinnamon rolls. I put one on each of the plates she left near the stove and carry them to the table, making sure to put them perpendicular to one another rather than across the table from each other like last night.

She smiles at me as she carries in the glasses of milk but frowns when she looks down at the plates. I immediately think she's not happy with the proximity of our plates. "Let me guess? You plan on eating that with your hand?" She laughs and shakes her head, turning toward the kitchen to grab forks.

She hands one over to me, and I make sure my fingers brush hers as I take it. She doesn't jerk away this time and her hand actually lingers near mine.

I clear my throat again. I seem to do that a lot around her.

"The snow has stopped, for now," I say as I cut into the soft pastry and take a bite.

She lowers her head and nods, clearly not happy with the news, a huge change from her reaction to being snowed in yesterday. Interesting.

My fingers tingle with the urge to reach out and tilt her chin up so she can't hide her eyes. "What's that look for?" I ask trying to sound as nonchalant as possible and pop a bite in my mouth before I say something, even more, ridiculous.

She fiddles with her breakfast but doesn't take a bite. She gives a sad laugh and raises her eyes to mine. "You sure you want an invite to my pity party?"

I grin back at her. "I don't mind listening if you want to talk or work through some shit." I shrug my shoulders and take another bite. *Just don't expect me to share.*

"Remember you asked for it." She smiles.

I love her smile and how it makes her eyes close slightly.

"I told you last night I found my ex with my best friend." I nod. "I just went home and packed all of my things and left. I haven't even spoken to them since."

I narrow my eyes at her. "You didn't confront them?"

"Not really my style. There was nothing to say. No way to confuse what I saw, so I just left Trent at the bar inside my best friend, packed my stuff and left."

"You have more control than I do." I set my fork down on my empty plate and take a sip of the cold milk she brought me.

"I think I was in shock."

"Do you plan to go back?"

"Not a chance and that's the problem. I have no plans. Nowhere to live and no job prospects. I didn't really think any of it through. I just knew I had to get away." She holds her mouth in a straight line.

"What did you do back in Great Falls?" I finish my milk and set the empty glass back on the table.

"The last three months I've been at Trent's bar, waitressing and bartending. Before that, I worked as an administrative assistant for the president of a bank." I raise my eyes to her.

"You left a position at a bank to work at a bar?" Surely there's more to it than that.

"Trent and Keira both convinced me to come work at the bar. He never said it in so many words, but he acted like he was afraid for me to be alone with my boss." She finally takes a bite of her breakfast

"Was he afraid he'd hurt you?" I wouldn't want my girl around a creep either.

She chuckles. "Nothing like that. He was handsome, super successful, and flirty. I think he was afraid I'd leave him and end up with my boss." She grins like the idea, even now after being cheated on, is utterly absurd.

Loyal to a fault it seems.

"What about college?" I wait while she swallows her food and takes a sip of milk.

"That's an even longer story and an even bigger pity party." I raise my eyebrow to her. "I won't go into all of the details, but I had to leave college my last semester. I never went back."

"What degree were you working on?" Only a semester left, and this shithead of a boyfriend of hers didn't encourage her to go back?

"General business," she answers before taking another bite of her food.

I bite my tongue to keep from telling her about the position that's opening up soon at my job. Not that I won't mention it later, but I don't know if this woman is even going to want to see me once I'm able to pull her car out of the ditch, more importantly, I don't know if I'll want to be with her once I've returned to reality.

Why are you even considering any type of future? You're not going back.

"Where were you heading?"

"I was thinking of going to Spokane. Figured the city is big enough and there'd be more options for work." She finishes off her last bite and washes it away with her milk.

"I bet it all works out in the end." I stand and take her plate.

She follows me into the kitchen and just like last night we wash and put away the dishes.

"Dominos?" I ask as we head out of the kitchen.

"Sounds good." She settles on the couch as I head over to the cabinet that, to my surprise yesterday, is loaded with all sorts of bad weather games, cards, and miscellaneous forms of entertainment.

My eyes once again are drawn to the drawer with the pills and gun, and for the first time since arriving at my plan to off myself, I feel a twinge of shame and if I'm honest a small hint of hope.

After a couple hours of dominos, we've both grown bored of the game.

I begin to put them away, and she yawns. "I think I'm going to go up and take a nap. Get all the rest in I can before having to try to start my life over once you kick me out of here." She winks at me and stands.

"Okay. I should probably hit the gym anyways."

She glares at me. "You have a gym?"

I smile at her. "The room is connected to the master upstairs. You wanna see it?"

"See it? Do you have a treadmill?" I grin at her.

"Wouldn't be a home gym without one would it? Come on I'll give you the tour." I leave the box of dominos on the coffee table and head up the stairs.

She follows close behind, and I can feel the vibrations of excitement rolling off of her. Who would have known she'd get so animated over workout equipment.

I push the door to my room open and angle my arm toward the open door of the workout room. I don't bother with the lights in the bedroom since so much light is coming in from the other room. I walk behind her as she makes her way to the doorway and don't even try to resist looking down at the pajamas she never bothered to change out of. I'd love to see that ass bouncing as she runs on my treadmill.

"This is amazing," she says. "I can't remember the last time I went three days without working out. Would you mind if I use…" She turns her body, not realizing how close behind her I am and runs right into my chest.

Her warm hand is against my bare skin, and we both groan at the same time. I smile at her and begin to step away but when her eyes drop to my lips, and she begins to run her tongue over hers, I lose all power.

"London," I whisper, my mouth less than an inch away from hers. "Tell me to stop."

I'm sober. I haven't slept with another woman sober since Savannah. I've always wanted, needed, the booze to make it through.

She shakes her head slightly, and my lips crash against hers. My tongue darts out and coerces her to part her lips, allowing me to sweep my tongue into her mouth. Hot, heavenly bliss. I moan into her mouth as her tongue battles mine and pull her closer to my body.

"Kadin," she pants against my lips and pushes gently on my chest.

I open my eyes and peer down at her. I'm about to voice my opinions about the hot and cold routine, but she begins to speak. "I'm all kinds of fucked up right now. I'm not expecting anything from you, but you have to know I can't do any of the heart shit."

I know what she means, and I'm on board with that but I look down, and her hand is on my pec, right over the same muscle she's talking about. It beats louder, harder than it has in some time. I refuse to analyze it right now. She's being honest and telling me she doesn't want more than this. It can't be more than sex. It stings for some reason, another thing I don't want to address right now, not when my cock is throbbing in my pants and my mouth waters at the notion that I may be able to taste her sweet pussy.

"Don't worry about any of that shit sweetheart. I love my wife with every piece of my heart. There's not room for anyone else." She flinches slightly but then nods her head in understanding.

The hand over my heart slowly glides down my stomach, the light touch of her fingers tickling the thin layer of hair covering my abs. She runs the tip of her finger just barely an inch into the waist of my jeans. I close my eyes and let my arms hang, giving her full control of the situation.

I feel her hot breath against my nipple just before she licks then bites it.

"Fuck," I hiss, and my hips jut forward unprovoked.

She keeps her mouth locked on me as she unbuttons my jeans and begins to lower the zipper, the seductive rasp of it lowering the only sound in the room.

I clasp her hands before she can pull me out. I'm quickly losing control, and I'd rather not fuck her against the wall or the floor. I tug her hands and walk us closer to the bed.

I reach for the bottom hem of her tank top and pull it up only slightly so I can run my hands over her flat stomach, my thumbs grazing the underside of each of her breasts. She whimpers and lowers her hands back to my jeans, pushing them off my hips.

"Commando?" she looks down and giggles.

I raise my hands slightly higher and sweep my thumbs over her puckered nipples. Tired of having to compete with the fabric covering her, I pull her tank top off and simultaneously step out of the jeans pooled at my feet.

I take a step back and look at my large hands. They can barely handle the size of her perfect tits.

"They're too big," she says shyly.

"They're fucking perfect," I praise her lowering my mouth to one breast while manipulating the other with my hand.

I love the feel of her hand in my hair as she grabs a handful. Her body is in turmoil which is evident by her tugging me away one second and pulling me closer the next.

I release her nipple with a pop and work my mouth up her breast, over her shoulder, and up her neck. I close my eyes losing focus on her skin and lean my head back when her hand wraps around my cock.

Goddamn! The sensation difference without being drunk is more than drastic.

I drop my hands back to my sides as she looks down. We both watch as her hands slowly pump me from base to tip, forcing the slit to glisten with precome.

Slowly she sinks to her knees. *Did I just win the fucking lotto?*

She looks up at me, her green eyes catching the limited light from the open gym door. Opening her mouth slowly, she reaches her tongue out and takes the first hot swipe of the most delicate skin a man possesses, right under the head.

I touch her cheek gently with my hand. "Suck it slow," I command.

My balls draw up the second her pouty lips wrap around the head. The heat, unlike anything I've ever felt before, engulfs me as she takes me sinfully slow to the back of her throat. She manages to get about two-thirds of my length inside before she gags slightly and backs off, only to take a breath and do it again.

I groan loudly and grasp a handful of her hair, tugging gently to keep her from moving too fast. "Go slow." The words sound more like a plea than a command at this point. She either can't go slow or is flat out refusing as she ignores my gentle hand in her hair and continues to run her mouth roughly over my length.

I don't know how the rest of her stay is going to go, and I refuse to let today end without my mouth on her. Blowing down her throat is the very last thing I want to do right now but if I continue to let her have all of the control the result is imminent.

I grip her hair tighter, preventing her from being able to move her head. Her eyes dart up to mine, and she smiles around my cock. Yeah, she knows exactly what she's doing. I ease my hips back, dragging my cock down her tongue and then slowly easing it back down her throat.

She hums and the vibration sails up my spine. "Enough," I pant and pull her completely off, tugging gently on her hair to raise her to stand.

I attack her with my mouth, my hand on the back of her head determining the angle and depth of the kiss. I'm on edge and close to just throwing her on the bed, ripping her pajama bottoms off, and pounding into her for days. When she reaches up and places both her hands delicately on my chest, the greediness coursing through my veins calms and my thunderous heartbeat becomes slightly less erratic.

I pull my mouth from hers and look down at her. "God you're beautiful," I tell her honestly. "Let me see you." I take a step back, breaking all contact with her body. "Take them off," I motion my head at her bottoms.

She bites her lip seductively and my cock twitches, remembering just how amazing her mouth felt. She keeps her eyes locked on mine as she pushes her pajama bottoms to the floor.

"I went commando too," she whispers as she kicks the striped fabric to the side.

I break eye contact with her and look at her body thoroughly. Golden brown hair around her shoulders, full breasts with tips so hard they look painful, and a curve at her hips that more than hints at the hardy shape of her ass. I lick my lips at the sight of the tiny triangle of trimmed hair just above the lips I'm dying to get my mouth on.

I palm my cock, trying to ease the ache at not being inside of her and close the distance between us. I bend my head down close to her ear. "On the bed. Legs spread wide. I want to taste that sweet pussy of yours."

She backs up agonizingly slow to the center of the bed, and I follow close behind her. I regret not turning on the lights when we entered the room, knowing the dimness doesn't give justice to the sight on my bed this very second.

She whimpers when I ease my hands from her knees, sliding them to her inner thighs, and spreading her wider to allow for the breadth of my shoulders. Just like when my mouth took her nipple, her hands shoots straight to my hair when my tongue swipes over her glistening slit.

"So good," I breathe against her wet flesh.

I flex my hips on the bed, grinding into the mattress. My cock is in complete agony; jealous at the allowances my mouth is taking on the flawless flesh between her legs. I use the very tip of my finger and rub it around the very edge of her quivering entrance, careful not to dip it in even a fraction of an inch. The first thing that will sink into that hot pussy will be my cock; that's if I don't come against the mattress.

I suck and bite her clit as my harsh breaths skate over her lower stomach. I'm torturing myself right now, but I need to feel her come against my mouth. She's writhing and moaning with every lick and nip, but the second I bite harder on her hardened bud I feel her clench and convulse against my chin.

Enough fucking around.

I kneel between her legs and slam into her; her orgasm, still in full effect, grips me repeatedly. I thrust through it. If I don't focus on moving my hips, I'll come in seconds; my body revved from the blowjob and mattress humping.

I lift her up slightly; gripping her hips and sliding her up and down my length, I use her body to fuck my cock. I grit my teeth and have to squeeze my eyes shut when she starts grasping at her breasts, pinching her own nipples. Fuck that's hot.

I push into her hard. Deep. My body static and my arms doing all the work. All I can hear are her moans and the cadence of my own heart thumping loudly in my ears. The sweetest symphony.

"Need you to come, London." I grind my hips against her roughly.

She reaches a hand down to the apex of her thighs and sweep two slender fingers over her hard, pink clit. The sight is my nemesis, removing my control. I settle inside of her as her trembling inner muscles ripple and clamp down on me repeatedly, her head thrown back in wild abandon.

Fuck she comes like a queen.

A few more quick thrusts are all it takes, and I pull out of her warmth and watch as jets of hot come coat her stomach. I'm doing my best to calm my breathing when she reaches down, running her finger through the mess I made on her skin and brings it to her mouth. She sucks her finger, "You taste good too."

What the fuck have I gotten myself into?

Twelve

London

I flex my back and try to stretch which is an impossibility considering that I'm lying on Kadin's chest, and both of his arms are around me. I've never been held close to a man that had chest hair, but I love the way it tickles my cheek and nose when I breathe.

Further inventory of my body tells me that I'm just as tangled around him. I have one arm looped over his left shoulder, and my other one is across his lower stomach, dangerously close to his semi-erect penis. I'd only thought the sex with him when I was drunk was fantastic. Earlier? Absolutely no words worthy of how amazing he was.

I close my eyes and remember the way he commanded and tempted my body; how he easily made me feel sexy and utterly dirty all at the same time. *You licked his come off of your stomach!* I could easily spend the rest of my life with him inside of me. If only it were that easy!

Crazy how an incredibly superior sex session can warp your mind and alter expectations.

I love my wife with every piece of my heart. There's not room for anyone else.

It stung a little bit when he said it, but I fully understood where he was coming from. The devastation this man has been through being more than any one man should suffer.

After? Now that I'm sated and wrapped in his arms? The pain from his declaration is slightly more acute. I try to untangle myself from him, but my actions only make him grip me tighter. I'd love nothing more than to stay here in this bed in the dark with him, but the idea that he may be dreaming of holding his wife makes my stomach turn.

I push against his chest harder, and finally he relaxes his arms enough so I can slip out of them. I sit on the edge of the bed and shamelessly watch him sleep, his chest rising and falling peacefully, rhythmically. Even in slumber, there's no denying the hard planes of his chest and stomach, the dips and valleys covered with a surprisingly soft smattering of hair.

His cock lay heavily on his right thigh, thick and daunting despite it being only semi-erect. His leg is bent at the knee and raised slightly, the same position it was in when I was laying on him. I want to run my fingers from the side of his knee to the crease at his hip, but I'm certain it won't be well received.

I stand from the bed and immediately grab for my tank top on the floor as the results of our combined orgasms begins to flow down my inner thigh.

Son of a bitch!

I waddle to his en-suite, holding the chunk of fabric between my legs, and close the door quietly behind me. I was confident he pulled out before coming, but apparently he let loose inside of me as well. Discarding the pseudo-towel, I turn on the water in the shower, hoping I can get cleaned up and back to the guest room before he wakes up.

After rinsing his incredibly masculine smelling shampoo out of my hair, I turn my face into the water and let the drops mingle with the tears that have started to fall. I'm so lost. Jumping in bed, twice, with a man I don't even know is so out of character for me and a sure warning sign that I've lost my damn mind.

I feel a cold draft from the opening of the shower door, and I wrap my arms around myself and turn my back to Kadin as he steps into the shower. I'm not sure if I'm hiding my nakedness or the shame on my face from my thoughts.

He steps under the spray with me and sweeps my hair off of my shoulder seconds before his mouth lands at the base of my neck. I roll my head to the side giving him more room for his mouth to manipulate my skin. His fingers move from my hair and trail down my back.

He stiffens behind me.

No.

No.

No, no, no.

His warmth leaves my back, and I already know what's coming. I already feel the shame I never thought I'd have to face again.

"What the fuck, London?!?" He bellows and his booming voice reverberates around the enclosed shower.

"Please leave." My voice is weak, and my body is starting to tremble.

"I'm not leaving until you tell me where you got these fucking scars from." His voice is calm but full of authority. Commands and expectations of obeying are something I cannot handle right now.

"Leave!" I yell with fewer trembles in my voice.

"No." He reaches for me, and I lose it.

"Get the fuck out!"

He growls but listens this time. I see him grab a towel from the rack, angrily wrapping it around his hips, and leaving the room as I sink to the floor of the shower and cry as my mind takes me back to a time it had taken years to forget.

"I think you do that shit on purpose because you like it when I get upset," Brian whispers in my ear.

I whimper against the gag shoved deep in my mouth. I want to plead with him. Beg him not to hurt me again, but he's gotten smarter about the abuse. My tears angered him the first time he saw them streaming down my face so now he ties a terrycloth lined eye mask over my eyes.

Tonight is the culmination of the perfect storm, a storm that seems to increase in frequency as the months pass. I set him off tonight by just saying hi to a male classmate that is also in his fraternity; that combined with the excessive amounts of coke he grew fond of over Christmas break. Well, the coke isn't the problem; the side effect of not being able to get hard is what angers him.

You'd think I'd be upset that he started the drug habit, but I'm not. The beatings will always be there, but at least now the rape has stopped.

"Are you fucking him?" He rages around the room knocking things over smashing things against the wall. I can feel the violent energy rolling off of him even though I can't see him.

I shake my head back and forth. I know he'd kill me if he ever caught me with someone else. I'd never risk that. Regardless of what people may think when a woman stays with her abuser, I don't want to die. I do have the will to live; I just see no other recourse.

This is my last semester. Hopefully, I'll survive it and then I can leave.

He grips my jaw in his hand and leans in close. I can smell the alcohol on the hot breath that is ghosting sickly over my face. My stomach turns, but I choke it down, not wanting to drown in my own vomit.

"Do you think of him when I fuck you?"

I sob harder and attempt to shake my head no against the grip he still has on my face.

"I'll kill him if he touches you. You're MINE!"

I'm strapped up, almost hanging from a set of eye-bolts he's placed in the ceiling of his bedroom. I'm topless, but thankfully he's left my jeans on this time.

"Don't worry, London. I'm going to make it so no one will want you when they see you."

I count over a dozen strikes before my world goes gratefully black.

I sit, arms wrapped around the knees bent against my chest until the water in the shower runs cold. Shivering, I finally stand and turn off the frigid stream of water. Kadin left the door slightly ajar, and the water has been running cold long enough that the steam has dissipated from the room. There is not a layer of condensation on the mirror protecting my view.

My hair is a mess, my eyes are swollen, and my face is covered in red splotches. I'm quivering, and it's from more than just the cold. I'm raw. Mentally and physically I'm drained, exhausted. I grab two towels from the shelf, wrapping one around my hair and one around my body. I'm grateful Kadin is such a big guy because the bath sheets in here are huge, and they provide a much-needed layer of security.

I walk over and stand near the cracked bathroom door, listening for him. A quick but faint rhythmic pounding is all I hear. Feeling as if I can make it out and across the hall, I grip my towel at my chest and slide out of the door.

The pounding grows louder, and I can see Kadin on the treadmill with his back to me. The stationary equipment in the room faces the scenic mountain view and even in my wrecked state I can appreciate the beauty through the large windows.

His hair is slicked back, damp with the same sweat that is rolling off of his bare back, his muscles bunching and stretching as he runs. His feet are pounding on the belt heavily, and his speed is familiar. I run almost as fast when I'm trying to outrun the demons when they are attempting to chase me down.

I could use a long run right now, but there's no way I'm going in there with him. I sweep up my pajama bottoms from the floor and make my way to the door. I hear the treadmill slow just as I remember my come covered tank top on his bathroom floor. I can't handle running into him and talking right now, knowing full well that he's not going to let me get away without an explanation.

I leave it abandoned in the bathroom and scurry across the hall to the room he's so graciously allowed me to stay in. *I bet he's regretting that generosity now.*

I stay in the room as long as I can with trivial things to keep my hands busy, none of which occupy my mind. You can only spend so much time applying lotion, combing out and drying your hair, and pacing around the room before you start to go stir crazy.

I need to charge my phone if only for the books, music, and games downloaded on it. Making up my mind to trek down the snow covered driveway, I layer on the warmest clothes I have, grab my keys, and head down the stairs.

Thirteen

Kadin

I'll kill that piece of shit. What kind of man hits a woman? How sick, twisted, and fucked up do you have to be to leave scars all over a beautiful woman's back?

Dozens. She had dozens of thin white scars down at least a six inch stretch of her back just below her shoulder blades. Sickening straight lines. What the hell did he use to do that kind of damage to her? Why would she leave him for cheating but not leave him for the horrendous abuse?

Filled with violent energy, I hit the treadmill when she screamed and demanded I leave the bathroom. My first pick, the heavy bag, is still leaning against the wall waiting to be hung. I forwent the music, in hopes that I'd catch her as she left the room.

Yet once again, I was too wrapped in my own shit bouncing around my head, and she slipped out unnoticed. I towel the sweat off of me and throw on a shirt, heading downstairs when I see her door closed tight.

I hope she knows she won't be able to avoid me for long. I'll give her a little while to get a better control on whatever the hell just happened in the bathroom, but I'm not going to pretend that it didn't actually happen. More importantly, I need information on this Trent fucker. He'll never be able to lay a finger on another woman after I'm done with his ass.

I'm pacing back and forth in the den like a caged animal waiting for a chance to escape when she comes down the stairs. I stop cold. She's fully dressed, and her keys are in her hand. Where the fuck does she think she's going? Is she so hell bent on not talking about this that she plans to leave? As comical as I would find that on any other day, I'm not in the mood for that wasted energy today.

She's mumbling incoherently to herself as she crosses in front of the den.

"Where are you going?" I try to keep my voice calm, without accusation. I manage, just barely.

Even though it's been over an hour since her breakdown in the shower, I can still see the puffiness around her eyes. I heard her in the shower; listened outside of the door as she sobbed and cried. As much as I wanted to go to her and hold her through it I know I have too much of my own shit to work through before I'd ever be a benefit to someone struggling with their past.

With sad eyes, she just looks at me as if she's trying to decipher my mood. I give her a weak smile, hoping that she can see my anger from earlier has nothing to do with her and everything to do with a man that would dare lay a hand on her.

Her lip twitches in the corner, a feeble effort at a smile that gets nowhere near her eyes.

"I want to charge my phone." She holds her keys up so I can see them clearly. "My charger is still in my car."

"And you were what? Just gonna walk down there and get it?" I smirk at her. "We still don't have reception out here. My offer for the satellite phone still stands. You can use it to call anyone you need to." *Except him.*

"I don't want to call anyone, Kadin." She sighs and takes a few steps further into the room. "I'm bored. I have games and books on it."

"The snow just stopped falling a few hours ago, London. It's over four foot deep out there, even deeper in some places because the wind created massive snow drifts. It's not safe for you out there."

"I can't sit upstairs. I'm going stir crazy so what do you suggest I do?"

I raise my eyebrows at her, knowing that it will be taken sexually, and I smile because for the first time in as long as I can remember my old personality is showing through just a bit.

She, of course, takes it just how it was suggested, not knowing why I smiled. "Keep it in your pants, buddy."

"We can talk," I suggest. I know I sound like I just grew a pussy, but I need information from her about the asshole ex.

"That'd be great!" She says with fake excitement. "Can I braid your beard?"

I laugh heartily and run my hands over my cheeks and down my chin. "Not quite long enough, but you can paint my fingernails if you want to."

She smiles at my playfulness and the emotion finally replaces the sadness in her eyes.

"You're not just going to let it go, are you?" I shake my head no and watch as she sits down on the sofa, in the spot she seems to have claimed as her own.

She stands abruptly and begins to strip out of layers of clothes since she's given up on the notion of leaving the house and braving the mile long hike to her car.

My mouth waters when the beautiful form of her body and her curves becomes more visible. I wonder how far she plans to go. She ends up in a light pullover and a pair of baggy sweats, honestly looking amazing and innocent. A look that will be in stark contrast to the story I'm going to make her tell.

"Would you like something to drink?" I walk toward the table with the bottles of whiskey on them.

"No thank you," she answers and sinks back down in her spot on the sofa. "I need to keep a clear head around you."

Not a drop of alcohol in your system when my cock was halfway down your throat earlier.

I pour myself a drink, but decide against it and leave it sitting on the table. She looks at me funny when I sit down empty handed. "I don't have a problem if you drink."

I grin at her and say the next sentence with honesty for the first time in two years. "I don't need to drink." *Don't look at the drawer.*

She keeps her eyes down and wrings her hands in her lap. "How do you want to do this?" I reach over and push the curtain of hair she's hiding behind away from her face.

"Do what?" she whispers.

"Talk," I answer and place a gentle hand on her back. "Would it be easier just to tell me or if I ask questions?"

"I'll tell you. I just don't really know how to start."

"Come here," I tell her. "This may make it easier." I slide my leg along the back of the couch and pull her back against my front, resting my cheek on the top of her head. "Help?"

She nods her head slightly against my face.

"Any chance you're going to tell me exactly where this fucker Trent lives?"

"Trent?" She turns her head so she can look in my eyes. "Trent didn't hurt me." I raise my eyebrows at her. "Trent didn't hurt me *that* way. My," she swallows loudly. "The scars on my back aren't there from Trent."

I narrow my eyes and look into hers, making sure she's telling the truth and not trying to protect that piece of shit.

"If I'm going to do this I need you just to listen. Don't interrupt; don't ask questions. Can you do that?"

"If I can ask any unanswered questions when you're done." She gives me a weak grin, apprehensive to agree.

"Okay," she finally answers. "Now where to start." She sighs loudly.

"Just start at the beginning." I resist nuzzling her neck but wrap my arms around her and hold her hands in mine as she begins her story.

She's going to expect you to share in return. Are you ready to open that door for the first time?

Fourteen

London

then

"Hey there beautiful," the 'stranger' says walking up to me.

I grin at his bluntness. "Hi," I answer and dip my head so he can't see the smile that spreads across my face.

"Don't do that," he says and lifts my face with the tips of two fingers under my chin. "Don't hide that gorgeous face from me."

I blush uncontrollably and curse the pale skin I got from my mother, which shows the flush on my cheeks and always makes red splotches pop up on my cheeks and neck.

I'd be a liar if I said I'd never noticed him before. He may be one of the hottest guys on campus, and he always turns heads when he walks by. My shock is from him standing in front of me. His finger having gravitated from under my chin to run lightly across my bottom lip.

I know he has a reputation around campus for being a playboy. That fact was brought to my attention a month ago when I first arrived at the University of Wyoming. I'm in awe that he not only noticed me but he's talking to me, touching me. I seem to be his only focus right now, and I'm drinking all of it in.

"What's your name, baby girl?" His thumb applies more pressure on my bottom lip, and it tugs down slightly when he lowers his hand.

His eyes are on my mouth, and it's possibly the most erotic thing that's ever happened to me. I was dealing with my parents' death my senior year in high school rather than worrying about boys, prom, and who's going to take me to the Winter Formal. I still don't think it's weird that I'm a virgin in my first year of college. My thoughts, especially right now in front of Brian Weston, are anything but virginal.

"London Sykes," I finally manage to answer.

"Nice to meet you London. I'm Brian," he says as he holds his hand out to shake in greeting like he didn't just have his fingers on my mouth.

I giggle at the absurdity of this entire situation. *What is it 'talk to a nerd day' or something?*

"I know who you are," I say with a sweet smile.

"You may know *of* me, baby girl. The question is do you want to get to know me?" He takes a step closer, and the heat off of his body is undeniable in the crisp morning air.

I nod my head more enthusiastically that I probably should've. He pulls me to his side, wrapping his arm around my shoulders, and walks me toward the cafeteria. I'm too excited at having his arm around me in public to mention I've already eaten, and I'm going to be late for class.

That's the first allowance I made for Brian Weston.

"I'm ready to go, Brian," I slur my words. He glares at me but then his face changes back to the Brian everyone loves. I don't want him mad at me, but I never wanted to come to this damn frat party to begin with. Now I'm drunk and too tired to keep up with it and his mood swings.

I still can't believe this gorgeous creature has picked me. We go out and party more than I like, but that's just part of dating one of the most popular guys at school.

We get in his car, and I close my heavy eyelids as he drives me home. I doze as the car drives on, the jostling rocking me to sleep. I know he shouldn't be driving since he's been drinking much more than I have. He always assures me that he's fine, and he can handle his alcohol.

"Come on, baby girl." I look up, and Brian is standing beside my open car door. Thankfully we made it to my dorm safely.

I stand and start to walk past him as he slides his arm around my back and leads me inside.

I look up and stop. "Brian? Why are we here?" We're climbing the front steps to his frat house, which is eerily quiet since everyone is across town at the other party.

"I want you to stay here tonight," he whispers in my ear.

I smile weakly. "I don't know if that's a good idea." My hands begin to shake mildly. I know what he wants; he's been begging for it since the first time we went on a date.

He wasn't actually mean to me, but he was confused and a little pissed off that I was a virgin. Well, he wasn't mad that I was a virgin; that actually turned him on. What he was mad about that first date and every time we went out since was that I wasn't willing to just sleep with him because he was in the mood. I'd let him finger me twice, and I even attempted oral sex with him once, but I'd never let it go that far.

Despite my objections, I still let him lead me into the house and up the stairs to his room. The slam of his door startles me.

He kisses me and, of course, I kiss him back. I love kissing him. I fantasize about his mouth all over my body daily. He grips my ass with both hands and squeezes. I wince because his grip is a little too tight. He moans at my reaction, getting turned on by my pain.

Sliding his hands up my dress, he begins to lower my panties down my thighs. This is different. The times he touched me before he always left them on, sliding his hand inside the fabric.

"I'm…I'm not ready for this," I tell him.

He releases me, but my panties are still on the floor around my ankles. He takes a step back, and I love the desire I see in his eyes. His eyes stare into mine as he tugs his shirt over his head and works the front of his jeans open.

I shake my head back and forth as he steps out of his clothes and stalks toward me completely naked. I hold my hands up in front of me, an attempt to ward him off. "Wait," I say with a tremor in my voice.

"Wait? Waiting is all I've done." I stumble back and realize my mistake as soon as the back of my thighs bump against the side of his bed. "I'm tired of waiting; I'm tired of being teased."

He takes the hand I'm pushing against his chest with and drags it down his stomach to his erection. I close my eyes as a tear rolls down my cheek. I jerk my hand away, and he snaps. I open my eyes and see the anger and rage on his face.

He rips the front of my dress open and yanks the cups of my bra down, exposing my breasts to him. I shove against him again as he reaches in and pinches one nipple painfully. I scream when he bites the other breast.

Shoving me down on the bed, he overpowers me and is in between my legs before I can stop him.

"Please, Brian. Don't do this. I'm not ready."

"You'll never be ready if we keep at your pace."

He slams into me, and the pain is excruciating. I try to claw at him to get him to stop, but he just grabs my arms and forces them over my head. He's so much bigger than me; every attempt I make to get away from him is met with an even greater show of force.

"You're hurting me!" I scream. My voice is the only thing I have left; he controls everything else.

"You feel so fucking good, baby girl." I buck under him trying to get away. "It's supposed to hurt your first time. This beautiful gift you've given me. I'm the only one that will ever be inside you like this."

He's crazy. He's lost his damn mind. He's stolen from me the only thing I had left to give anyone. I sob under him, unable to do much else. Finally, he grunts his climax.

Not moving from between my legs like I'd hoped he would he leans down to kiss me. I turn my head and his lips land on my neck rather than his intended target. The tears are still falling, and all I want to do is curl up in a ball and disappear.

"That was amazing, baby girl. I love you," he whispers against my skin before rolling off me to my side. "Fuck I'm drunk," he mutters just before his breathing evens out telling me he fell asleep.

I'd always wanted a man that loved me to take my virginity. This was in no way part of that fantasy. I stay quiet for a few more minutes before climbing out of the bed and away from Brian. Numb, I grab his t-shirt and pull it over my head to cover my exposed breasts and leave his frat house.

I knew when I woke up this morning what I had to do, but that didn't make it any less daunting. Brian has called twice already this morning wondering where I was and why I didn't stay the night. He was so calm, sweet, and loving on the phone that I'm wondering if in my semi-drunken state last night I might have blown things out of proportion.

I let the third call go to voicemail as I walk into the on-campus clinic, surprised they are open on Saturday.

An hour and a half later I'm leaving the clinic with a dose of Plan B and a year's worth of birth control. A condom wasn't used last night, and a baby is the last thing we need. They also gave me a brown paper sack full of condoms with strict instructions to use them the first month I'm on birth control.

I put my phone to my ear and listen to the message he left while I was in with the doctor.

"Hey, baby girl. I miss you already. I'll be by your dorm around noon to take you to lunch. I think that Chinese place you like over on Commerce sounds like a good idea. Can't wait to see you. I love you, London."

We both had too much to drink last night. I'm sure he didn't mean to be so rough with me. I can't make a really big deal about it since I was planning to give him myself eventually anyways. He loves me, and I love him.

I head to my dorm to get ready to see him with a smile on my face.

eighteen months later

"London!" Brian calls from his bedroom.

I'm in the bathroom putting on my makeup, getting ready for the party. "What is this shit?" I cringe at the tone of his voice as he walks into the bathroom and stands behind me.

I look down at his hand and freeze. Without responding, I quickly gather my things, stuffing them into my makeup bag and walk back to his room. I'd rather have this argument in here than in the hall. I'm tired of the sympathetic looks from the other guys in the house every time we argue.

I wince when he grabs my arm and swings me around to face him. I rub the tender area that's still bruised from the last time he grabbed me.

"Explain this shit!" He bellows, spittle shooting out of his mouth.

"Why were you in my purse," I ask stupidly, knowing it's only going to make matters worse.

The rage streaming off of his body is almost palpable. Suddenly he drops the packet of birth control pills on the floor and slaps me across the face. The fire from the contact spans half of my face and forces my head to swing to the side; my eyes are suddenly tearing up from the pain.

I hold my head to the side and cover my face with my hands in complete shock. We argue and fight all the time, but he's never hit me before. He may grab me and try to shake some sense into me when I'm stubborn, but he's never gone so far as to strike me with his hands.

"Fuck!" He screams and pulls me against his chest. I'm trembling and terrified. "Why do you purposely piss me off?"

I whimper against his shirt, not sure of how to respond, afraid that saying something will only make him angrier. He leads me to his bed and forces me to lie down in his arms. I keep my eyes clenched tight. I want to reach up and touch my cheek. It's still on fire, and I'm certain it's starting to swell, but I know ignoring it is the best course of action.

That's what we do. He does something he later forgets, and I act like it never happened.

"I shouldn't have hit you, baby girl. No more birth control. I've told you more than once I want you pregnant." I nod my head in agreement against his chest terrified of arguing with him.

We never make it to the party because I couldn't cover the hand print on my face enough to be seen in public. Instead, Brian made love to me all night and whispered apologies in my ear, vowing never to hurt me again. It was one of the better nights we'd had together.

I went the next day to the clinic and got the birth control shot. No matter what he says and no matter my reasons for not being strong enough to leave him, there's no way I'd ever bring a baby into our situation.

the breaking point

I wish I could say that things with Brian got better after he hit me the first time. Hell, I wish I could say that they stayed the same. The truth? The first year and a half we were together was the best part of the relationship. Shortly after he hit me the first time, he hit me a second time and a third.

I got really good at hiding the bruises. Brian became an expert on abuse and began only hitting me where I could hide the damage with my clothes. Unless he was really angry, then it was a free-for-all. After those times, he'd just keep me secluded away in his house for days. Those were the worst days; the days where I'd spend all day and night as a slave to his every sexual whim.

I've learned to keep my mouth shut. I don't argue, and I don't talk to anyone about my problems. I no longer have any friends. He controls every second of my life. I'm his only focus it seems. Well, that's not the whole truth. I've come across feminine items and things we don't use around his house that don't belong to me. What do I care about the foreign pair of panties tangled in his sheets or the empty condom wrappers that have ended up under his bed?

I do care actually, but not in a way that makes sense. Not in a way that makes me human. I wish whatever girl that had on the panties I had to throw in the trash last week would gain all of his attention. I wish he would get some other girl pregnant so he can obsess over her. I know that's a horrible way to think, but I was the girl tied to the bed and repeatedly filled with his sperm during Thanksgiving break.

I've been on the Depo shot since he made me throw out my birth control. He can't understand why I'm not getting pregnant. He's even gone so far as to use an app on his phone to track my cycles making sure he fucks me as often as possible on the days it says I'm most fertile.

What I thought was a reprieve at Christmas time when he went home to see his family, turned out to be the worst thing that could've ever happened. Brian has always had a taste for drugs. He's snorted coke socially as long as I've known him; even forcing me to party with him a handful of times.

When he got back from his parents' house, his habit was a full blown addiction. He admitted that he spent half his time down there on a coke binge, blaming his asshole dad as reasoning. New Year's also coincides with my fertile days this month, so we make no plans to leave his house. My three most fertile days have been spent in his bed for the last six months.

Brian snorts a line of coke off my stomach. "Just jump starting the party, baby girl. Can't wait to feel you from the inside."

I turn my head, too sick with my life to even look at him. I've grown numb to the abuse and forced sex. Wouldn't do me any good to tell him no. Last time I tried I ended up with two broken ribs.

"Fuck," he mutters, rubbing his flaccid penis against my entrance.

This isn't the first time he binged on coke all day and couldn't get a hard-on; it's actually been happening a lot lately. This is the first time during my fertile days that he hasn't been able to perform.

"I can't even get my dick hard looking at your fat ass anymore!" He pinches the inside of my thigh painfully and gets off the bed. He pulls his pants back up and heads to the living room to watch TV. I lay on the bed in the silence, waiting for him to come back, which he will eventually.

If I were brave, I'd tell him that I'm eight pounds lighter than I was when we met. I started running at the school gym shortly after he made a comment about the size of my ass, which come to think of it was not long after we started dating. The snide, hurtful comments have progressively gotten worse, as has the abuse.

The next day he seems different, happier as we walk across campus to my dorm. He's no longer in school. He told me he was tired of the bullshit and found a small house off campus since he couldn't stay in the frat house because he wasn't enrolled anymore. He thought it was a great idea; I knew from the very beginning it just meant he could hurt me more with less chance of getting caught.

I said hi to people I knew as we walked. Keep up appearances right? Always be courteous but never be available to do anything. That's how you keep people from asking questions, remain elusive.

His good mood seems to worsen with every step we take back to my dorm. He has me pack a bag to stay at his house since we are going into the President's Day long weekend. I can practically see the steam coming out of his ears by the time we make it to his house. I stay quiet and try to not get in his way by keeping to myself in the bedroom.

It doesn't work; he's too angry. Today is the last day that Brian hits me; unfortunately he causes enough damage that I'll be reminded of him each and every time I look in the mirror.

By the time she was done telling me about the scars on her back and how that piece of shit Brian used a thin wooden switch to whip her repeatedly until her back was laid open and bleeding, she was quaking and completely drained.

I rocked her gently in my arms until she fell asleep. She didn't have the strength to finish the rest of the story, and my stomach turns to think of how she may have suffered more than what she told me about. I can't even begin to comprehend how someone stays in an abusive relationship for as long as she did. It's unfathomable to me, but I know it happens often.

I feel like I need to do something to help her, but I have no idea what that could be. She told me about Brian, but she hasn't explained that douche Trent except for telling me that she caught him fucking her best friend, so I don't know where that entire situation was left except she packed her shit and left town. She may change her mind and go back. Cheating is not something I could ever get over, but she may be different. She did stay with the abusive prick for years. If Trent isn't hitting her, she may not see that situation as being just as bad.

I wrap my arms around her tighter, wanting, for some reason, to protect her from the world. I want to shield her from everything and everyone who may cause her harm or make her cry. She's had enough shit dealt to her in the last ten years to cover the grief of at least a dozen people. Why is it that some people just get handed so much shit to deal with, and others just skate through life without a care in the world?

I rest my cheek on the top of her head and glide my hands up and down her arms and smile when she snuggles deeper into my embrace. Things are so easy with her. I don't find myself having to force conversation or dig for things to talk about.

I peer down at my arms around her; I catch the light reflecting off of my wedding band. I have absolutely nothing to offer her even if I wanted to. I hated the pain I saw on her face when I told her as much before we had sex earlier. I wanted to take the words back instantly, but that would have been untruthful. I'm not the type of man to lead someone on just to get laid. I never have been.

That makes my mind wander to back home and the mess I created there. My eyes shift to the drawer across the room. My urge to protect her is beginning to outweigh my need to use the things in there, but I know deep down that nothing has changed. I know that the same misery waits for me if I go back. The long drunken nights without Savannah; the misery of losing the love of my life. I've been over all of this a million times in my head, only now there is another whisper in my ear that tells me things could be different if I only allow it.

London shifting in my arms pulls me from where my head was about to go. She's a welcome distraction.

"I fell asleep on you," she says but makes no move to leave my arms.

"You did," I admit and kiss the top of her head. I need to keep myself from doing things like that. It's very personal and doesn't exactly scream 'all this is, is sex.'

"You ready to finish?" I need to hear the rest of it, and I figure we might as well get it over now, rather than rehashing tomorrow or something.

"I don't want to talk about Brian anymore," she sighs.

"I want to know about Trent," I say matter of fact.

"What do you want to know?"

"Everything." She shifts in my arms so she can see my face. "Start at the beginning," I add.

Her eyes focus on the fire in the fireplace like she remembers the beginning of her relationship with Trent. She looks sad at the loss with no anger. This worries me that my earlier thoughts are true and that she may want to go back to him.

"Trent is the brother of the girl who was my roommate my last semester at college." She clears her throat to tamp down the emotion trying to boil up.

"Brian, for some reason, took me back to my dorm after he beat me the last time. Trent brought my roommate back from a visit at home for the long weekend, and they found me on my bed. I was lying face down and naked; my back all cut up from the switch he used."

I squeeze her tighter because I can tell she's struggling with the memory. Even though it happened over six years ago, it's very apparent that she's still not completely over it.

"I was barely conscious, but I heard Trent ask her 'is that what you were talking about' and I knew then that even though I tried to hide the abuse as much as possible that people still knew about it. They cleaned up and bandaged my back, and Tina helped me get dressed. They wanted me to go to the police, but I couldn't. Brian had told me more than once that he'd kill me if I ever tried to get him in trouble. He said they'd blame me because if I acted right, he'd never have to punish me."

My rage is bubbling like lava in a volcano, and I hope the calming breaths rushing in and out of my nose are going to be enough to keep me from erupting. Blame the victim to justify his actions. Sounds like something a piece of shit boy who likes to hurt women would do. I have every intention of tracking his ass down when we're able to leave this cabin. He will know what it's like to be abused by the time I'm done with his pussy ass.

"I had met Trent a couple times when he came to see Tina, but I wouldn't consider us friends. He offered to take me back home with him so I could heal and as a chance to get away from Brian. I turned him down at first because I knew Brian would come after me. He had Tina take pictures of my back. I knew it was bad because it hurt worse than even the broken ribs he'd given me before, but when I *saw*." She swallows roughly. "When they showed me what I looked like and I had to face the fact that he would end up killing me if I stayed, I knew I had to leave. They helped me pack, and I left later that day with Trent to Great Falls and never looked back. Tina told Brian when he came to the dorm the next day that she hadn't seen me, that she'd gotten back from the long weekend and I, along with my things, were gone. Tina and I weren't close at all; mainly because he wouldn't allow it, so he really didn't have a reason to think she was lying."

I rest my cheek on her head and wait for her to continue. I have a million questions I want to ask her, but I'm hoping she wants to tell me what I'm dying to know rather than having to pull the information from her.

She's going to ask you next.

After a few more minutes of silence, she begins again. "We were completely platonic for the first couple of months. I wanted nothing to do with men in general and Trent," she chuckles lightly. "Well, Trent was very patient. Eventually, it turned into something more."

"Did he treat you better?" My voice is husky and clouded with the anger from her continued story about Brian.

"Trent treated me like a princess. He made me go to counseling. He helped me find a job. He gave me everything I ever needed and never asked for much in return. He held me when I cried and reminded me how special I am when I began blaming myself for what Brian did to me. He was my rock."

"I had assumed that things were bad, and then he cheated on you." I don't know why I said that out loud but if things were perfect why would he cheat on her?

She sniffles loudly. "Nope. No signs that I can think of; there were no arguments or problems. Trent made me whole and then shattered me worse than Brian ever did with his physical abuse."

I hold her tighter as she begins to sob quietly. This beautiful broken angel.

"I thought we'd get married eventually, have babies. Apparently I have really bad luck with men. Brian was my first, and I jumped straight from him to Trent and now…" Her voice trails off, but I get her point. Brian, Trent, and then me.

Third try's the charm, sweet girl.

Where the hell did that come from?

"You've only been with three men?" Not the best change of subject but it's all I can think of right now.

"Yes, including you," she whispers.

"Same here," I share.

"You've only been with three men?"

I laugh heartily shaking her on my chest. "Three women smart ass. Well, two and a half."

"Care to explain the half?" *Why the fuck did I say that shit?*

"Not a chance," I say flatly. Why I open my mouth and can't control what comes out when I'm around her, I have no idea.

"I shared my story with you," she pouts.

"There is a huge difference in being a survivor and creating your own personal shit storm."

"Will you tell me about your wife?" She changes the subject, and I can honestly say I don't know if this one is any better than the one we're leaving behind.

"I've told you a little about how we first got together. It just went from there. We went to the same college. Got a house together before we finished sophomore year. We wanted to spend every second together, and that was the only way. Her dorm was very strict and my roommate? Well, let's just say he was creepy and made her feel uncomfortable. We were spending so much each month on hotel rooms so we could be with each other; we just decided to rent a house instead." I laugh at the memory. "We actually saved money with renting."

She laughs too but doesn't speak.

"I went to work for my father after college. She went to school longer than I did. She was an LPC at a children's advocacy center."

"LPC?" She asks.

"Licensed Professional Counselor," I answer. "She spoke with and counseled children who had been abused, both physically and sexually."

"You guys didn't have kids?" Her question is just that, a question. She's not grilling me or trying to put me on the spot, but that doesn't change the fact that it does. I feel like the spotlight is shining right down on me.

"Savannah didn't want children. She said she saw such pain and horrendous stuff at work. She couldn't imagine bringing a child into the world where it could be victimized."

The silence seems to stretch on forever. "But what did you want?" she whispers.

"I wanted Savannah," I answer.

In truth? I always wanted children. We argued about it more than once. It was a conversation we'd had on more than one occasion. Before we got married, she couldn't wait to have my baby. Then she started her job, and all talks of children were off the table. She'd never consider it again.

If we'd had a baby, I'd still have some part of her left, and maybe life wouldn't be so hard right now.

Don't even try to pretend that you aren't taking other liberties to keep her memory alive.

I shift my weight under her, so she knows I want to get up. She sits up but stays on the couch beside me. I turn my body on the couch, placing both feet on the floor, and stare into the fire.

"I didn't mean to upset you," she says softly at my side.

"You didn't, it's just…" I run my hands roughly through my hair. "I got a lot of shit I have to work through. I haven't really been successful at dealing with all of this shit."

She just nods gently and looks back into the fire. "I'm going to go to bed. It's getting late." She stands and turns toward the stairs.

"Yeah, I think I'll turn in too," I say and stand beside her.

We walk up the stairs and linger briefly outside her door. I want to grab her hand and take her to my room with me and just hold her all night, but I can't tell if it's something that she wants.

"Goodnight, London," I say softly as she reaches for her door knob.

"Goodnight, Kadin." She closes the door behind her without another word.

I feel like I fucked something up between us but have no clue how or what it even was. I got to my room and made sure the door is cracked in case she wants to join me later, and I pray she does. I sleep better when she's near.

I don't know why he freaked out when I asked about kids. It was a simple question. It flowed easily into the conversation. He's in his thirties. Don't married people usually have kids by this time?

It felt so good lying in his arms, and I never wanted to get up. Life seems simple here with him, no other outside influences. I know it can't last forever. He's not mine; he made sure I knew that. *Why am I even thinking that?*

It's your MO. My mind answers.

Jump from one guy straight to the next. No pause in between. No time on my own to see if I can even make it by myself. The thought terrifies me, almost as much as sleeping with a man I have no future with; a man who has been nothing but upfront about what is going on.

I didn't miss the brief pause at the top of the stairs like he wanted to join me or ask me to join him in his room. I did the only thing I could think to do at the time, and that's to run. Get away from him to avoid whatever happened downstairs and tomorrow I will just pretend like it never happened. *Classic London.*

Today has been one of the most emotionally draining days of my life. I'm exhausted yet I'm tossing and turning in this bed and sleep is evading me at every turn. Frustrated, I get out of bed and pad quietly to the door. Opening it slowly I look across the hall, and notice Kadin's bedroom door is cracked.

I wonder if I can slide into his bed and then leave by morning time like he did and him not notice.

Deciding to do it even if he does catch me I tiptoe across the hall and stick my head in his door. His room is extremely dark, but I feel my way along from memory of being in here earlier.

"Hey," he whispers just as I draw my knee up to climb on the bed.

I freeze, like a kid caught with their hand in the cookie jar. If I pretend to be invisible then maybe I will be.

He chuckles softly. "Come here," he says huskily.

I climb on the bed and under the covers he's holding up for me. I lie across his chest without even being invited and wrap my arm around his waist.

"I couldn't sleep," I explain.

"Me either," he acknowledges and begins to run a calming hand up and down my spine.

I almost tell him that I'm so used to being in bed with someone and that's why I'm having trouble falling asleep, but I don't think that would be well received. I don't want him to think I miss Trent because I don't. Well, not as much as I probably should considering we'd been together for six years.

I'm not surprised how fast I settle into him and how quickly I grow relaxed, my eyes fluttering closed and my breathing calming.

I'm right on the cusp of sleep when he whispers, "I don't miss her as much when you're in my arms."

I smile against his chest and welcome unconsciousness.

I wake to the feel of Kadin's fingers grazing my sex over my panties. I didn't even bother getting dressed last night when I snuck in here. A tank top and a tiny pair of panties are all I have on, and if the feel of Kadin's thick, bare cock against my thigh is any indication he went to bed with even less than I did.

"Is this okay?" He asks softly, noticing that I'm no longer completely asleep.

I smile and nod. Then I stretch as inconspicuously as possible to increase the pressure his fingers have on me. He chuckles lightly; obviously not as inconspicuous as I'd hoped.

I watch him with heavily lusty eyes as he slides my panties to the side and sweeps his large finger over me, coating his digit with the arousal he must have conjured before I woke up. He bites his lip, and it makes me moan.

"So fucking beautiful," he murmurs to himself. I smile hearing the words I'm not sure he meant to vocalize.

His head sweeps down, and his wicked tongue lashes out at the nipple straining against my tank top. This man is sex personified and almost has me coming in a matter of minutes with very little effort. As much as I'd love to come apart right now, I also want to please him just as much.

My center clenched at the memory of him in my mouth yesterday. I'm nearly drooling to do it again.

I shift out from under him and push him onto his back. I know he's allowing me to do it. There's no way I'd ever have a chance to overpower him. He falls to the center of his bed and smirks at me. A look that says 'now what are you going to do with me?'

I nip his chin with my teeth then run my tongue from his ear to his shoulder, stopping my mouth periodically to taste his skin with a closed mouth, gently sucking at his skin but making sure not to mark him. He's gripping the sheet with both hands like he's fighting the urge to take control of the situation, but he also turns his head and moans slightly.

Closing my lips, I run them over the softness of his chest hair, flicking my tongue out at his nipple as I inch lower. He jerks slightly, and it makes me smile. Feeling adventurous, I nip at it with my teeth. His moan is louder, this time, so I lick and bite him exactly how I like my nipples to be stimulated. It seems he's a fan of it too.

I work my way further down his body, making sure to drag my highly sensitive breasts over his skin. I line them up perfectly and tilt my head down to watch his thick erection peeking through the top. The friction of his hot skin on mine is glorious. He groans, loudly, when I open my mouth and take him to the back of my throat from the very first contact. I'm rewarded with a quick burst of precome, and I swallow it down like it's a lifesaving liquid. I groan at the taste as I drag my suctioned mouth to the tip of him.

I make the mistake of looking up at him on my next downward stroke. I grow still on him when I see the lust in his eyes. They're heavy and hardly open; his lips are parted slightly, and short puffs of breath are escaping from his mouth. He's clearly just as hot for me as my body is for him. The cold air on my wet, overheated center is reminding me of what I'm missing. *What I need.*

I pull my mouth off of him, and he looks momentarily disappointed until I lick up his shaft and begin to lick my way back up his body. For the first time since we got started, he releases the sheets and reaches for me. I watch with fascination on my knees as he stands himself up at my center. I'm entranced at the sight, knowing that such an amazing piece of him is fixing to plant itself inside of me.

His other hand grips my hips. "Please go slow," he begs.

His words draw my attention away from our imminent connection and up to his dreamy chocolate eyes. Slowly I lower myself onto him and watch his face as I take him inside. He hisses loudly, and I smile with feminine triumph at his response.

I place my hands on his wide chest for leverage and raise myself back off of him agonizingly slow, only to sink back down even slower. Delicious torture.

Unable to do as he wishes I arch my back and begin to bounce my hips, sliding him in and out of my aching core faster. I groan; so does he.

"Fuck, London," he gasps.

I take his praise appreciatively by increasing the speed of my hips. Both of his hands are on my hips and I can tell by his grip that he wants me to slow down, but I just smirk down at him.

"No," he pants harshly and before I can squeak in surprise he has me flipped over on my back and pinned to the mattress by the weight of his body.

I bite my bottom lip and flutter my eyelashes at him. He laughs which causes his cock to jerk inside of me. I moan in response, closing my eyes.

He lifts some of his weight off of me, and I whimper at the loss. "Are you okay?" He whispers, and I nod marginally. "I don't want to scare you." I know he's afraid I'll freak out after telling him about the assaults I suffered from Brian. I could never confuse the two, but he doesn't know that.

He withdraws a fraction, and I close my eyes at the sensation. "Look at me," he begs. "Know that it's me pleasing you." I groan when he drives in deep and swivels his hips, rubbing perfectly inside and out. "Know that I'm the one inside of you." He shifts back a few inches only to slam back in. "Say it, London."

I whimper in pleasure. "You," I whisper.

"My name," he grunts, sliding slowly in and out from tip to base. "I want to hear it when you come."

He reaches between us and masterfully flicks his rough fingers against my clit. He's holding my eyes hostage, daring me to look away.

"Oh please!" I bite my lip in complete blissed-out appreciation of his skills.

"Come for me, London." It's a command, not a simple request.

My body obeys immediately. "Kadin! Oh God!"

My core spasms around him, gripping him uncontrollably, simultaneously begging him to continue and stop all in one.

"London," he groans, rewarding me with his praise for my body and what I'm able to do for him.

He wrenches from my body and releases on my stomach. I smile down at the hot jets of come as they splatter on my body. I'm honored that I can please him.

"Jesus," he mumbles as he strokes his cock, squeezing the last bit of his orgasm from the tip.

He leans over me on knees and elbows and takes my mouth in a passionate kiss, whispering praise against my lips. I smile as he begins to nip at my chin and neck. I groan when his thickening length grazes my clit.

As much as I'd like for round two to start immediately on the heels of the first round, I'm covered in come and a sticky mess.

"Shower," I whisper in his ear.

He grumbles, but backs away, pulling me up as he goes. Never releasing my hand, he walks us into his en-suite and turns on the shower. We kiss gently outside of the glass and wait for the steam to rise, informing us that the water is warm enough for us to get in.

He grabs a natural sponge from the built-in cubby and squirts a generous amount of manly smelling shower gel in the center.

"Turn around," he says huskily, no doubt still ready for round two if the full erection jutting from his hips is any indication.

I falter in my actions, knowing what he's going to see.

"Turn," he gently commands. He doesn't touch me, and I inwardly smile that he's allowing me to make the choice.

I take a deep breath and turn to face the wall, placing my hands on the tile for support. I wait for the coarse feel of the sponge in his hand, but it never comes. Instead, I feel his hot breath first then the touch of his tender lips as he kisses my shoulder. He trails kisses down my spine until he reaches my scars; then his hands graze gently over where I know the worst of the damage is.

"You're beautiful." Kiss. "And brave." Kiss. "Your scars, they make you beautifully flawed. They make you perfect."

Tears of happiness stream down my face as this man tells me exactly what I never knew that I needed to hear. Standing in the shower of a cabin, with a man I've only known for a few days, I heal completely from every wrong that I've suffered. I am whole. I am complete.

Seventeen

Kadin

With the exception of food, showers, and an amazing round of sex against the wall, we've spent the past twenty-four hours in this bed. London's warm body is wrapped around mine like a second skin. It feels too good; too familiar for only having known her for a handful of days. I know I could stay like this for the duration of my vacation, and that's exactly why I'm slowly sliding out from underneath her.

Waking up thinking about her? *Bad.* Waking up wanting her? *Bad.* Waking up needing her? *Extremely dangerous.*

I throw on a pair of sweats and head downstairs to make coffee. We should probably stay as far away as possible from any beds today. *Didn't need a bed when you took her against the wall, or when you bent her over in the shower.*

My dick twitches in my sweats and my balls grow heavier at the memories. I groan and open the fridge to get some fruit out. I don't think I'll ever come back to this cabin and not think about London and the things we've done. We both confirmed that sex is all this is, but holy shit is it beyond amazing. I find myself praying another blizzard hits, and we're stuck here for a month.

The more I hope for that, the more I wonder if she's only staying because she can't leave. There's only one way to find out, and as nervous as I am about it, I know she needs the option of being able to leave. I can't imagine loving anyone besides Savannah, but I'm also not looking forward to watching London walk away.

It's bad enough I've already started comparing London and Savannah. London cooks, whereas Savannah couldn't boil water. London doesn't even take half the time getting ready for the day as Savannah did; I explain this away because London knows she is only going to be around the house and not going out into the public. Savannah snored, and London sleeps very quietly, with only the occasional whimper, but I chalk that up to her abusive past and some things just don't ever go away.

I shouldn't compare them at all and every time so far the thoughts have come unbidden. I understand why it does. Savannah and London are the only women I've slept with, well sober. The other woman. Fuck, that's a mess. Maybe knowing I have to go back home and clear that shit up is another reason why I want just to stay here and get lost in London.

It hasn't snowed now for almost two days, and I know what I have to do even though the outcome may not be what I particularly want.

Picking up my cell phone, I notice that I actually have reception and won't have to go back upstairs and disturb London to get the satellite phone.

I dial the office, and it's answered on the second ring. "Hello, Mr. Cole. How can I help you?"

"Hey, Lisa. I need you to arrange a snow plow to come clear the driveway at the cabin and get a car out of the ditch by my front gate." I hear her typing the note, and I wait for her to finish.

"Time frame?"

"Immediately," I answer.

"Budget?"

"No matter the cost, Lisa. I just need it cleared."

"Yes, sir. Anything else?"

"No, Lisa. I think that's it."

"Should we expect you back before the next storm hits?"

"Next storm?" This sounds promising. "What are the predictions?"

"They're saying the next will be much worse than the one you got last week. Information online expects it to hit Monday evening." She provides the information and then remains quiet after that.

"I'll inform you of my plans as I make them."

"Very well, sir."

I have one of the best assistants money can buy. Unfortunately for me, she's over eight months pregnant and doesn't plan to come back to work after the baby is born. Finding a new assistant. It's another thing that has been overlooked in my grief.

I smile as London makes her way into the kitchen. Her light brown hair is piled high on the crown of her head and sticking out all over the place. She even has a crease line from the bed linens on her face, but the sight of her legs under my t-shirt has me rock hard.

"You look great," I tell her honestly.

She laughs. "You don't have to lie."

I take a step away from the counter and look down, showing her how truthful my words were.

"Coffee first, big fella." She walks to the coffee pot and begins to pour her a cup.

Without even thinking, I'm behind her with my arms wrapped around her waist, my chin resting on her shoulder; the proof of my body's approval of her is pressed against her back.

"The snow plow will be here today," I tell her as she adds sugar and creamer to her cup.

"The city is coming out?" She blows over the top of her cup of coffee, cooling it down.

"Not exactly," I say. "I called and have one coming in."

Her shoulders fall under my chin. "You trying to get rid of me?" She says it playfully but I can hear the sadness in her tone.

"Hardly, but I also don't want you to stay only because you're stuck here." I release her and turn her gently in my arms. "I actually wanted to talk to you about coming back to Spokane with me."

Her face lights up, and her eyes begin to sparkle at my words. *Shit.*

"Yeah, I mean I have a guest room, and you don't have anywhere to stay. Figured you could stay there until you find a place of your own."

And her face falls.

"Oh. I see." She shrugs and pulls from my grasp, planting a half-smile on her face. "I'll think about it."

I refresh my cup of coffee and follow her into the den. She's upset, and that stresses me out. I glance over at the liquor cabinet and realize I haven't had a drink since the second night she was here. That's enough to keep her around right there. Three days, that's the longest I've gone without a drink since Savannah died. The drinking has been a huge part of all of my issues at home. It's also become my coping mechanism and my way to escape the pain and loneliness.

"How long were you planning on staying out here?" I watch her bring her cup to her lips and take a tentative sip.

"I didn't really have a specific timeline in mind. I figured I'd stay two weeks. That seemed like long enough to get the board off my back." There's no way I'm going to mention the fact that I hadn't planned on returning at all.

She tilts her head slightly in confusion.

I sigh knowing if she's going to come back to Spokane with me that I, at least, need to explain shit a little bit.

"Some of the guys at work thought it would be best if I took some time off." I run my hand over my chin, scratching the stubble I haven't even thought of shaving in over a week.

"Working too hard so they force a vacation on you?" I can't help but laugh.

"Not exactly. More like going to work drunk; if I even showed up to begin with."

She crinkles her nose. "That bad? Like this is more of an ultimatum than a vacation?"

"Exactly," I say taking too big of a sip of the boiling hot, black coffee in my cup. I wince as the scalding liquid burns my tongue.

"How long have you had a drinking problem?" She looks affronted like she can't believe the words came out of her mouth. Holding her hands up she says, "Sorry. Not my business. You don't have to answer that."

I can't help but laugh. "London," I say flatly. "You've had my cock down your throat, answering a few questions isn't a big deal."

I take another glance at the half empty bottle of whiskey across the room. "I started drinking after the funeral and never really stopped. Savannah's been gone a year and a half."

She frowns, but the look is more of sympathy and pity rather than disappointment in my inability to get my shit together. I don't know which one is worse. The pity over my situation is what I'm most familiar with, but I don't like it coming from her. I don't want to seem weak in her eyes. Maybe that's why I haven't been drinking.

You don't need the alcohol when you're around her.

The thought slams into my head, and now it's my turn to frown. Am I such a glutton for punishment and so used to my pain and grief that it unnerves me that another woman has the ability to make me feel less broken? I should be smiling and rejoicing that the last couple of days with London have been better than every single day of the last eighteen months since Savannah passed away.

Being happier feels like a betrayal. It shouldn't, according to the counselor I attempted to see shortly after the accident. Natural progression, she called it. The one session I went to came on the heels of one of the worst breakdowns I'd had to date. I nearly drank myself into a coma after I caught myself laughing at some dumb ass sitcom on the TV. What kind of husband was I if I could forget my grief even momentarily long enough to laugh at some shitty TV show?

I've practically maintained the drunken haze since, and I got rid of all of the TVs in the house. No sense in tempting fate. I've since purchased one, but I only have it on in the background for noise when I drink.

"I haven't seen you drink in a few days," she says, vocalizing my same thoughts.

We both look over at the liquor cabinet. I wait for the urgency that I normally feel when I see a bottle of liquor to hit. It never does.

"Haven't really needed it." I wink at her; she seems unaffected.

"So, Spokane huh?"

I guess now she's ready to talk about staying with me. I know she's upset from earlier. Her demeanor changed the second I mentioned the guest room. What was I supposed to say? There's no way I can explain to her that the idea of not just her but any woman staying in the room I shared with my wife makes my stomach turn. The more I think about it, the more fucked up I realize my whole situation is.

"Yeah, I mean I have a condo, and it is way too big for just me. You're more than welcome to stay there until you find something of your own." I attempt another sip of coffee, smaller this time. It still burns my already injured tongue.

"That's very generous of you, Kadin, but I don't expect anything else from you. Sheltering me during the blizzard goes above and beyond already."

Ouch, that unexplainably hurts a bit.

I chuckle and shake my head.

"What's that reaction for?" She asks and nudges my shoulder with her own.

"I was also going to tell you that I have a job for you if you're interested." I look sideways at her to check her reaction to the bit of information.

"A job?" She snorts. "Doing what?"

I shrug. "I need a new assistant."

She almost rolls off of the couch she's laughing so hard. I love her laugh. It's throaty and rough, not very feminine at all. I smirk at her reaction even though I have no clue why offering her a job would be considered hilarious.

"Is this when you tell me that I'll be bringing you coffee and sucking you off under your desk?" Her smile is from ear to ear even though her words aren't one bit funny. At least to me they're not.

"I'm serious, London." My voice is hard, and it sobers her up immediately. "My assistant is about to pop, and she has no intentions of returning to work after the baby is born."

"Oh," she says, and her cheeks pink as she grows embarrassed from her reaction.

"Now," I say to lighten the mood. "If you want me to fuck you over my desk it will have to be before or after working hours. Unless you're interested in a quickie during lunch." I nod at her teasingly.

"Oh, yes. Of course. No fucking on desks during business hours." She's grinning again.

We grin at each other for a long moment and the air around us grows thick with sexual anticipation.

"Seriously, London. The job and the room are yours if you want them. No pressure on either one. But I will say that I'd rest easier knowing you weren't at some hotel or shitty apartment while you looked for work and a decent place to stay." I set my coffee cup on the table and rest my back against the arm of the sofa.

She sets her coffee down also, and I prepare myself to take her to my chest. I frown when she mirrors my actions and places her back against the sofa arm opposite of me. We just watch each other. Studying the other in silence.

The silence I'm used to. I'm comfortable alone. It's only when I get around others, and the expectation of conversation sits heavy on my shoulders that I grow uncomfortable. London is the opposite of me. She loves to talk and be around others. She said as much herself once. Right now? Right now she seems just as content to sit here with me and not say a word.

Eighteen

London

I don't even want to contemplate the reasons I got upset when Kadin mentioned coming back with him then dropping the 'guest room' bomb. It shouldn't bother me. Sex. That's all this is. Tell that to my broken heart; the same muscle that Trent destroyed and has no signs of healing anytime soon.

I wish he would've said something about it before now. I wish he hadn't wrapped his arms around me and whispered in my ear, and more than ever I wish he hadn't been so wonderful earlier. The lines got incredibly blurry when he kissed and stroked my scars, telling me I'm beautiful and perfect.

I watch him warily from the opposite end of the couch. He's incredibly good looking. Nothing like Trent. Don't get me wrong, Trent is a great looking man, but he's not the type of guy when you see him on the street he makes you miss a step and dampen your panties at the same time. Kadin is the kind of man that makes your mouth hang open, and you forget basic skills like speech and breathing.

Trent is lanky and has long lean muscles. Kadin? Well, Kadin is a mythical wonder. He's just a tad shorter than Trent, but still much taller than I am. It seems every inch of his body is covered in hard, compact muscle. He's got wide shoulders and a strong back that tapers at his waist; all of that is awesome, but it's his gorgeous face and the way he carries himself that drew me in from the first look.

He seems cocky, and an air of indifference surrounds him, almost as a warning to others. The sunlight from the window glints off of his hair making it seem more auburn than the rich mahogany I know it is. His warm chocolate eyes focus on my face, and I wonder if he's trying to read me like I'm attempting to do to him.

"Your hair looks red in this light." My words are the first spoken for at least twenty minutes of our stare-fest.

He rolls his eyes up like he can see the hair on his head from that angle. "I was born a ginger," he says with a laugh. "My hair didn't start to get darker until Jr. High."

"I have a thing for gingers." I wink at him. "I bet you were adorable with red hair."

He huffs. "Where were you back then?"

I grin at him, clearly not the fondest of memories for him. "That bad?"

He nods. "No love for the ginger kids at Lincoln Jr. High."

"You turned out okay." I over exaggerate my motions as I run my eyes up and down his body and biting my lip for emphasis.

"Not all of us were born beautiful, London." He's grinning and the sentiment, albeit way off base makes me melt a little.

"I was the girl always in the shadows. No one noticed me, and I liked it that way." I point to my chest. "Virgin until college remember?"

His eyes grow dark, no doubt remembering exactly how my pesky v-card was cashed in. Change of subject needed very quickly.

"I would have noticed you. I'm certain." His voice is smooth and filled with sensual innuendo.

"You think so, huh?"

"Did you have those?" He raises his hand up and points back and forth at my breasts.

I look down at them and back to him, noting the mischievous grin on his face.

"Yes, those showed up super early for me."

"If you had tits like that in Jr. High I guarantee not one boy in that entire school didn't know who you were." His face is serious, so sure that what he says is fact. "You're lucky if they never said anything to you. The dickhead boys in my school were so horny all the time, raging hormones they had no clue what to do with; they usually picked on the girls they wanted the most."

"I wore loads of baggy clothes. I was embarrassed by them. I did my best to hide them," I explain.

"That's a damn shame." I notice his eyes are fixated on my chest. I clear my throat, and he's cognizant enough to raise his eyes to mine.

"What about you, Kadin?" I raise an eyebrow at him.

"What?"

"What did you notice first?"

"Honestly?" He reaches to the side and grabs my foot, massaging it over my sock. I nod. "You were in your car, so I noticed your eyes first. They're incredible, but I also saw pain. It's like even without knowing you, I felt like I knew you. That probably doesn't make sense."

"Makes perfect sense," I say honestly.

He smirks. "When you got out of the car I forgot all about your eyes when I saw that glorious ass of yours!"

I laugh at the animated way he uses his hands to cup upward in the air like he's got two hands full of my ass. "An ass man I take it?"

"All day long!"

I open my mouth to speak but his phone rings. I watch as he pulls it from the pocket of his sweats. Glancing down at it, he springs off the couch and is heading out of the den. "Excuse me," he says just before answering. "Hey, Lisa. I'm glad you called."

Lisa?

I begin to wonder if she's part of the shit storm he mentioned going on in Spokane, but stop my thoughts almost as immediately as they begin to rear their ugly little heads. None of my business. Except he's asked me to stay. He offered to let you stay, not asked you to move in. Big difference. The end result is the same. The last thing I need is to go back and be planted right in the middle of his drama. I have enough issues on my own; I have no need to go looking for trouble.

I get off the couch and leave the den, passing him in the hall. He stops talking as I approach. I place my clasped hands to the side of my head giving him what I hope he reads as the universal sign for going to sleep and hit the stairs, suddenly tired and in need of a nap. If anything, I need to gain a little distance from him.

I feel like I just shut my eyes when a knock sounds on the door. I wanted to climb into his bed and bury myself in the covers that smell like him, but I turned right at my room instead of left at his, forgoing his room and choosing the guest room. It's where he expects me to be in Spokane, might as well get used to it. I sound bitter, and I'm well aware of it. I don't love the man. Seriously it's only been like five days, but apparently I'm incapable of having sex with someone without the lines muddling themselves.

I ignore the annoying tap and turn over in the bed thinking he would take a hint. He doesn't. I didn't hear the door open, but I feel the bed dip at my back just a short time later. Then the breeze from the covers being lifted. I almost complain, thinking he's lifting the covers to annoy me, but then I feel the warmth of his body against my back and the ghost of his breath on the side of my face.

I almost break.

I know I'm the one who told him I couldn't get my heart involved. I said it first. He agreed, rather harshly, but the dense piece of muscle in my chest didn't get the memo.

"What are we doing?" I whisper.

He chuckles. "Staying warm," he coos in my ear, obviously not understanding the depth of my question.

"I don't mean at this moment, Kadin. I mean what are we doing?" I keep my eyes closed and my face straight ahead. When he rejects me and leaves, I don't want to have to watch him walk out.

He stays silent for a long moment. "This is all I have to offer you."

"Warmth?" I sigh loudly.

"My body," he says with a halfhearted chuckle. I don't see the humor he's feeling.

"I'll take what I can get." I hope he can't see the tear that just rolled down my cheek or hear the sadness in my voice.

"You deserve better," he whispers at my back; the heat of his breath tickles the tiny hairs on my neck.

Yes, I do.

Nineteen

Kadin

If I were a better man, I'd leave this entire situation alone. I'm not a better man, which has been established quite thoroughly over the last eighteen months. Plus, I love the way she feels under my fingertips.

"The snow has been cleared. Your car is parked in the garage." I pull her tighter to my chest. "You're no longer stuck here with me, but I'm hoping you still want to stay."

She doesn't respond right away, and I immediately think she's trying to formulate a way to tell me she wants to go. I close my eyes and wait for the words, not knowing how I will respond to them but sure that I'm not going to like it when she's gone. *The contents of the drawer still wait.*

"My assistant Lisa called and said there's another storm coming in. Weatherman expects it to hit the area late on Monday. I was planning on heading back Sunday afternoon." Silence. "I thought we could head into Poison and grab some junk food. Figured it'd be nice to leave the cabin."

Just like that, at this very moment is when I decide that life is, after all, worth living. I'd like to think that the guilt I've been feeling over how my death would affect my parents and my brother, but I know my will to live is because of her. London. Even though there is no telling how this will end up between us, knowing that there is, at least, one other person out there that makes me feel this way, gives me hope for life after Savannah, that knowledge makes things, at least, tolerable.

"I would kill for some Twizzlers right now," she mumbles more to herself than to me. "But I'm so comfy here."

She wiggles her body, burying herself deeper under the covers, her delicious ass rubbing me just right. I begin to thicken immediately.

"Keep that up, London and the only thing you're going to get is fucked." She wiggles again, and I do the only thing I can. I place my hand flat on her lower belly and pull her tighter against me. I groan, feeling my cock nestle right between her cheeks. I slide my hand lower; my middle finger is brushing her clit and the outside fingers roaming over her decadent lips.

Just as the tip of my finger dives into her wetness, she wiggles out of my grasp and jumps out of the bed.

"Twizzlers!" She exclaims happily.

Alright. Two can play that game.

Holding her gaze, I lift my finger to my mouth and lick the tip. Resisting the urge to buck my hips at her taste, I suck the wet digit into my mouth. Her eyes darken, and she looks like she's going to take a step towards me, changing her mind about being a tease.

I stand on the side of the bed and catch her eyes as they wander down my chest to the erection I have no luck of hiding, even if I wanted to. Her tongue snakes out over her lips when I reach down and adjust myself over the fabric of my sweats.

Clearing my throat, I turn toward the door. When she grumbles something incoherent, I turn my head back to her. "I'll get changed." A quick wink and I'm leaving the room.

"You're just fine naked," I hear her say as I close the door behind me.

Less than half an hour later we're bundling up to head outside to the truck. London looks annoyed, clearly not happy with how her teasing backfired. I'd love to tell her my cock is just as annoyed, but I hold off. Knowing it and thinking it are much different than verbalizing it. If I give it too much credit, we'll never make it to the store because I'll end up stripping her down in the truck.

"You ready?" I ask as she wraps a scarf around her neck.

I pull the door closed behind us and guide her with my hand on her lower back. I instantly hate the multiple layers of clothing that separate my skin from hers.

I tug open the passenger side door and stare at her ass as she climbs inside.

"Nice," I praise quietly.

Just as she was about to ask me what I said I close her door and make my way to my side of the truck.

I get in and shut the door quickly. Even with the speed we got inside the cold has crept in and obliterated the heat that had been building the last fifteen minutes. I rub my gloved hands together and hold them to my mouth, angling my hot breath over my chilled fingers.

I cut my eyes to London and see her raise an eyebrow at me.

"What?"

"Just thinking about how warm those fingers would be if I hadn't gotten out of the bed." She frowns playfully.

Trying not to think about the wet heat of her core, I put the truck in gear and begin to roll down the driveway. The plowing company did a great job, leaving the truck with an extra wide berth.

"Have you given any thought to my offer?" I finally speak as we turn right out of the driveway, heading into Poison proper. I told Lisa to make sure the plow driver left the gate open because the last thing I wanted to do was get out any more than I had to since I had no idea if the gate opening app on my phone would even work.

"I don't think I have any other choice at this point than to move....I mean stay in your guest room. As far as the job," she cuts her eyes at me, "I'd need to know more about it before I make a decision on that."

"I imagine it's just like any other office job." I shrug my shoulders.

I glance at her and see her roll her eyes. "Not all office jobs are the same, Kadin. What role do you hold at your company?"

Shit. I don't want to complicate things even more than they already are and for some reason I like her thinking I'm some regular old Joe. *Regular? Yeah right, you saw how her eyes bulged when she stepped foot in the cabin that first night.*

Avoiding the whole CEO conversation I give her the basics. "I work for a company that builds log cabins. They built the one we've been staying in."

She laughs; it rolls out of her mouth straight from the bottom of her stomach.

Her laugh is contagious even though I have no idea what she finds so funny. "What?" I ask with a chuckle.

"You're a lumberjack?!?" The laughing continues, "Like you use an ax and cut wood." She snorts in the most unladylike manner and abruptly covers her mouth with her hands, her eyes dancing.

"I use an ax to cut firewood, but we use machines and saws when we build." I turn my attention back to the road.

"It suits you. Especially with the beard, Lumberjack."

I raise my hand up and rub the scruff on my chin. "You have a problem with my beard?"

"Not one bit," she answers seductively. I glance over at her, catching her watching my mouth. "I've already told you how handsome you are. Are you fishing for compliments?"

Instead of answering I just wink at her. I had thought about shaving; change of plans.

The short trip into town ends when I pull up in front of a Mom and Pop store. It seems to be one of the only places open in town, which won't be a problem since I've only seen a handful of people since leaving the cabin.

London puts her hands in front of the vents, warming them before facing the cold once again. I just watch her, mesmerized by her beauty. Her bright green eyes shine behind the layers of her scarf and the hood on her jacket. Her cheeks are flushed from the cold, pinking them ever so slightly.

"What?" she asks eventually.

"He's a fucking idiot," I say without thinking. "Why on Earth would he think he could find something better than you?"

I watch the shimmer leave her eyes, and I immediately regret saying something so insensitive.

She turns her head and focuses out her window. "I've been asking myself the exact same thing the last few days."

I lift my hand twice to reach out to her; to comfort her somehow. I'm a complete asshole for saying what I did. I didn't mean it the way she apparently took it, and I feel like shit now. I want to beg her to come back to Spokane with me, let me show her how a real man treats a woman as precious as she is, but I don't. I'm just now considering not killing myself, and I know without a doubt that jumping from my grief to London wouldn't do either one of us any good.

"You ready?" she asks, breaking into the internal struggle going on in my head.

I look at her, and she has managed a small smile, so I take it and run with it, hoping I can actually make it become legitimate joy. I need to see the shimmer and sparkle in those amazing green eyes.

"You feigning for Twizzlers?" I wink at her. She grins just a bit wider, but it's genuine. "I hope they have dark chocolate," I say as I lean in closer to the windshield and look at the weathered sign, not feeling hopeful at all.

"Only one way to find out," she says and pops out of her side of the truck and runs into the store.

I do what any decent man would do when a beautiful woman runs away from him; I chase her.

Twenty

London

The more I'm around him, the more I want to be around him. We've been trapped in his cabin for days, and we spent less than an hour apart yesterday, yet it seems not to be enough. I crave him. I yearn for his touch. I covet every caress. The most alarming thing about this entire situation is that although the sex is out of this world amazing, it's the embrace after the orgasm that causes the wildest beating of my heart.

His hot and cold is giving me whiplash. Well, maybe not cold; he never just shrugs me off. Sometimes I wonder if it's only because we were stuck together and he knew there is no real way to get completely away from me. We hold each other all night yet we say that this is only sex. I'm just as guilty. I was the first one to bring up the fact that I can't get involved any more than just the physical. It needed to be said, but now I think I should've kept my damn mouth shut.

The smell of moth balls hit me the second I open the door to the little country store. The smell is not completely off-putting, but the muskiness causes me concern for the snacks they have. I remind myself to check expiration dates on everything I get. I grab a hand basket and venture in further.

The gust of frigid air at my back informs me that Kadin has made it inside. I don't acknowledge him; I just begin to wander up and down the aisles. The merchandise is as eclectic as the empty flower pots that were sitting on the small porch, and I do mean porch. This store has apparently been transformed from an old wooden house. The selections range from diapers and dog food to detergent and diamonds; that's at least what the sign on top of the glass case claims anyways.

I stop in the food section and immediately notice the lone bag of dark chocolate Kisses. I plop them in the hand basket. From what I can tell they don't have *Twizzlers* but they do have the generic 'Vines.'

"This will have to do," I mutter to myself, grateful to have anything remotely close to my favorite candy.

I turn down the next aisle and see Kadin crouched low looking at items on a bottom shelf.

He notices me, grabs items off the shelf, and stands. "What do you think?" He asks holding the boxes in front of him. "Barely there or ribbed for her pleasure?"

I gape at the merchandise in his hands and then look around the store for the clerk I saw lurking around earlier.

We both take steps toward each other, closing the distance between us. We should never have had sex the first time without condoms, but now is as good a time as any to begin.

I tap my finger on the bottom of my chin in contemplation. "I think the ribbed for her pleasure will be best."

"Are you disgruntled, lover?" He asks with a smirk. I raise an eyebrow at him. "Sex isn't pleasurable enough with me; you need ribs now too?"

I snort an unladylike laugh. "No, *lover*. The ribbed ones are magnums, and well," I cut my eyes to the front of his pants, "you have a big cock."

Now it's his turn to drop his jaw and look around for the creepy clerk. "Who knew you had such a dirty mouth, London."

I smile wide at him and his playfulness. He places the box we don't need back on the shelf and steps close to me, his body almost flush to mine. I can feel the heat coming off of his body and my thoughts suddenly run impure.

He drops the box into the hand basket I'm holding. "You sure that's enough," I whisper huskily to him.

"More?"

"You never know. Several days until we leave." *We can also use them when we get to your place in Spokane.* I don't say it out loud, and it's not until the thought comes to my head unprovoked that I begin to have concerns for what we will look like once he returns to reality.

Sarcastically he grabs the two remaining boxes off of the side-counter and drops them in the basket.

"Thirty-six may be pushing it," I huff playfully.

"You never know," he says, repeating my words and walking past me with a wink.

An hour later we are back at the cabin, both of us in his home gym. I'm on the treadmill watching him hang up an impressively large punching bag. I lick my lips at the sight of his back flexing and rippling as he picks it up and hangs it from the massive hook he installed into the exposed beam of the ceiling.

I offered to help him, and he laughed at me, which honestly pissed me off a bit. Truthfully I'd never be able to lift that bag, and now the anger has completely subsided at the image of him doing all the work. I'm grateful running is like second nature to me and requires no real thought; my body just performs from years of developed muscle memory.

Next, he wraps red, athletic tape around his wrists and palms and tugs on a pair of simple fingerless gloves. I nearly stumble and fall face first on the treadmill as he strikes at the bag. I wish I could see the pure beauty of the action, the training and strength it takes to make the enormous bag shift the way it did. Instead, my skin gathers a sheen of sweat that wasn't there a second ago, and I begin to tremble.

I know Kadin and Brian aren't the same persons, but seeing a man do something that my body reads as violent is unnerving. I quickly hit the red stop button on the treadmill and hastily exit the room. My pulse is fluttering harder than I know it would if only the exercise on the treadmill was warring in my body.

I enter the guest room across the hall from Kadin's and strip my clothes off, leaving a trail behind me as I make my way to the bathroom. I found some bubble bath at the store when we were out and sinking into a hot bath sounds perfect right now. I don't get the vibe from Kadin that he'd ever strike me, so I don't know why my body had the reaction it did earlier.

I'm naked by the time I reach the tub to turn on the water and pour in the bubbles. The water flow in this house is amazing, and the tub is ready within just a few short minutes. I slump into the tub and close my eyes the second I step in. Gardenias, which happened to be the only scent they had at the little store, is not my favorite smell, but it works in a pinch.

The faint touch of Kadin's hand on my face pulls me from my calming thoughts. My eyes go wide, and I audibly gasp, not hearing him come in. He holds his hands up beside his head in mock surrender.

"I didn't mean to frighten you," he admits.

I notice his hands are free from the tape and gloves and the thin layer of sweat glistening on his chest and arms is the only thing that even hints at his workout.

"I turned around, and you were gone. Did you get the seven miles you said you were going to do done that fast?" He stands from the edge of the tub where he'd perched when my eyes were closed.

"I kind of freaked out when you started hitting the bag," I confess, deciding to lay it all out there.

He tilts his head, momentarily confused; then understanding hits him. I love that he's paid enough attention to what I've told him that I don't have to explain my reaction. "Fuck, London. I wasn't even thinking about it." He looks like he wants to reach for me and I hate that he doesn't, unsure of where we now stand. "I'd never hit you. Fuck, I'd never hit any woman."

I reach my hand out to him. "Join me?"

He gives me a tentative look proving he's undecided about how to proceed. Finally after glancing from my hand to my eyes several times he kicks off his shoes and strips unceremoniously out of his sweats and socks. Even though his cock is soft it remains incredibly impressive; apparently he's a shower *and* a grower.

I scoot forward in the tub when I can tell his intention is to climb in behind me.

"No jets?" He asks as he pulls me back against his chest.

"I didn't want to deal with the mess the bubbles would make," I answer honestly.

He chuckles. "I never would've even thought of that." After a few minutes of silence, he says, "I seriously didn't mean to scare you earlier."

I squeeze his arms tighter around me. "You didn't frighten me. It was the situation for some reason I responded to. I honestly thought I was over all of that shit that happened with Brian. I never thought I could be triggered like that." I turn my head when I feel him dip his mouth closer to my neck. "I was watching you work, and it was incredibly sexy, and then all of a sudden it wasn't."

I feel him nip my shoulder with his teeth, then lick the pain away with a hot sweep of his tongue. I also feel him thicken behind my back which makes me want to squirm against him.

"Let me remind you what else these hands can do," he says unwrapping his arms from around my waist. One hand travels north to cup a breast, and the other slowly glides down my wet stomach, skating tenderly over my already swollen clit.

Twenty-One
Kadin

"Fuuuck," I hiss through my teeth, opening my eyes to find London's amazing mouth wrapped around my straining erection. My hand instinctively reaches out to grip a handful of her hair as her sinful mouth slowly glides up to the tip.

"Good morning," she whispers before she engulfs me again.

I can only nod my head in answer and smile like an idiot. That is until she forms a tight suction and her cheeks collapse, my throbbing cock getting the full effect of her amazing mouth. If she keeps it up, I will be the only one having a 'good morning.'

I sit up and sweep my hands under her arms, forcing her to release me from her mouth. I slide down as I pull her up until my face is at the apex of her thighs staring at her swollen cleft. It appears she's been awake and needing for much longer that I'd originally suspected.

She hisses and bucks violently at the first harsh swipe of my tongue. Holding onto the headboard, she looks down, meeting my eyes as she bites down on her lip to keep from whimpering so loudly. I want her out of control. I want her so lost in her pleasure that she doesn't have the wherewithal to even try to be considerate of the noise level. I get my wish when I suck her clit into my mouth and flick it with my tongue.

She reaches down with one hand and tangles it in my unruly hair, rotating her hips and grinding harder against my mouth. I close my eyes and welcome the sound of her moaning and erratic breaths.

"Oh God. Kadin!" I shift her forward an inch and sink my tongue into her heat just as the first convulsion of her core begins. I nearly come myself when her delicious pussy grips my tongue in waves of pleasure. She grows languid and relaxed as her orgasm ebbs, and she settles petal-soft onto my chest.

I wrap one arm around her to keep her from falling and shift my weight so I can reach into the open box of condoms on the bedside table. I'm thankful one is loose from the rest, and I make quick work of getting it open and rolled down my cock.

London is practically dead weight from her apparent earth-shattering release. I glide her further down my body, positioning myself at her entrance.

"London? I need to…" Before I can even continue to beg, she suddenly shifts her weight backward and takes me to the hilt. We groan simultaneously, and I'm thankful for the desensitization the condom provides because if I just went into her bare like this, I would've come immediately.

I grip her hips preventing any movement that she may have in mind. I keep my hips static, my cock buried deep and nuzzle her neck with my nose, licking at her pulse point which is surprisingly more accelerated that I would've imagined with her calm appearance.

I bend my knees and shift my legs up to allow my body the traction I'm going to need. With her laying on my chest, I hold onto her hips and slam my hips forward, impaling her further on my length. Her gasp turns to whimpers as I set a brutal pace, one I hope gets her off again before I blow.

I love the sound the bed is making as it taps periodically against the wall. The furniture in the room is all handmade and extremely sturdy, and I know just what kind of power is required to make it move. London and I found that out several days ago.

My balls draw up and just as I'm about to apologize to London for coming too soon she clamps her teeth on my shoulder, and her pussy grips me like a pulsing fist. It grabs me and pulls me over as well.

"London!" I gasp as my orgasm hits full force, both of our bodies clenching and pulsing together.

She releases my neck, and I moan at the feel of the blood flowing back into the damaged area.

"Sorry," she mumbles and kisses the tender spot.

"Did you draw blood?" I chuckle and trace her spine with the tip of a finger. She has perfect skin, I think even when my hand glides over the thin scars that mar her back. "I didn't take you for a biter, London."

"I didn't draw blood." She tilts her head back to the side looking again at my neck. "Close but not quite. I don't know what came over me."

"I'm not complaining, but don't pretend this is the first time you bit me. It's not."

Her cheeks flush further, and she rolls her lips inward between her teeth to keep from smiling. "I've never bitten anyone before," she admits shyly. She lies back down against my chest, and the tickle of her hot breaths against my neck sends a welcome chill over my body. "But then again," she whispers in my ear. "I've never come like that before either."

And my dick is rock solid instantly. Pleasing a woman is one thing; pleasing a woman better than her prior lovers? That is an incredible honor to carry.

I reach out to smack her on the ass, but remind myself of her past and stop before I follow through with the action. Instead, I grip her luscious rear in both hands.

"We need to get packed," I tell her.

She groans and mumbles a few cuss words but rolls off of me and heads into the bathroom.

Today is the ninth day we've been in this cabin together: eight nights of us being in her bed or vice versa and I don't want to leave. Things are too easy here with her. Life doesn't suck when we're tangled up in bed with each other.

Now I have to go back to a city, to a condo, to a job I had no intention of ever returning to. I almost mentioned my plans of suicide to her on several different occasions, but I don't want her to know just how weak of a man I really am.

I asked her to come back with me. I offered her a room in the home I shared with my wife and now that the day has come for her to be there I wish I'd never said the words. I don't want to get rid of her, but I know how difficult going back to my place is going to be. Bringing someone back with me? That seems almost impossible to me as I pack my clothes.

After making sure everything is unplugged and the bed is stripped, I make my way to the foyer with my duffle bag. I place it near the door and head into the kitchen to begin the process in there.

The doorbell chimes through the house and I'm fairly certain it's the first time it has ever sounded off of the walls. I set the pile of dishes I was pulling from the dishwasher down on the counter and make my way to the door. I pull it open and see a uniformed man there. He's here to transport London's car back to my place in Spokane. I'm signing his paperwork as London makes her way down the stairs, dragging both her suitcases down behind her.

"What are you doing?" I ask. Handing the guy his clipboard back and turning to grab her things. "I was going to come up and get those for you."

She smiles, and it nearly makes my heart stop. "I can handle them."

"Clearly," I say grinning back at her. I take both suitcases from her and collapse the pull bars, picking them up easily and walking them to the front door, setting them beside mine.

"Who was at the door, caveman?"

I laugh at her term of endearment. If she thinks helping a woman is acting like a caveman then she most definitely has been around assholes her whole life. "That was the transport company. They're here to load up your car."

I start walking back to the kitchen so I can continue the cleanup in there. "What do you mean 'load up my car?' I'm driving my car to your place."

"No, you're not. You're riding with me." I begin putting the plates and saucers in the cabinets where they belong. It doesn't go unnoticed that she isn't responding.

I turn my head in her direction to find her standing all indignant with her hands on her hips and her foot turned out. She's annoyed and angry and if she wasn't so fucking cute that way I'd be agitated myself for her making a big deal about such a trivial thing.

With my now empty hands, I stalk over to her and sweep my hands inside the crook created at her elbows. I bend my head close to her ear. "I thought the trip would be more enjoyable with a little road head."

She gasps. I laugh. I honestly didn't even think of getting my dick sucked until the words came out of my mouth, but suddenly it sounds like the best idea ever.

"Yeah, maybe for you since you have the dick," she says stepping away and slapping my arm playfully.

"Seriously, London. The roads are still shitty, and I don't want you ending up in another ditch when a large mammal walks out in front of you." I step forward and kiss the top of her head.

"You could have lead with that," she mutters.

I cock an eyebrow at her. "Seriously? You went all evil twin on me before I had the chance to." I wince at the evil twin part. The shit that comes out of my mouth.

I place the last piece of silverware from the dishwasher into the drawer and turn back to her. "Are you ready to go?"

"Yep. You need help with anything else?" She asks looking around for something to do.

"I don't think so," I respond and make my way out into the den. This and the bedrooms upstairs are practically the only places we've been the last week and a half.

My eyes dart to the tiny drawer across the room. The house has a great alarm system, but that doesn't mean someone still can't break in. I can't in good conscience leave a loaded gun and full bottle of prescription painkillers in the house.

"Hey, will you run upstairs and grab the sat phone for me. It's plugged into the wall by the lounge chair." I begin to straighten the cushions on the couch and fold the blanket that she's been using.

"Sure," she says and heads out of the room and up the stairs.

I calmly walk over to the drawer and tug it open. I reach in and pull the gun out, the feel of the cold metal in my palm causing a wave of eeriness to cloud my mood. I shake my head to clear the gloom that is trying to settle in my bones. Grabbing the pill bottle, I take them both to my suitcase and zip them up inside, telling myself I will flush the pills as soon as I unpack back at the condo.

London makes her way back down the stairs empty handed. "It wasn't up there."

I walk into the mudroom and grab it from the table on the inside wall. "Sorry," I tell her holding it up so she can see it. "Forgot I brought it down the other day."

I stick it in the pocket on the side of her suitcase, not willing to take the chance of unzipping mine again.

"So we're ready to go?" She asks looking around again for anything to do.

"Yeah. I'll have Lisa send someone out to make sure everything is taken care of. I had the transport people pull my truck up so it should be nice and cozy." I hold out her jacket for her to slide her arms into it.

Twenty-Two

London

I'm surprised when we step outside of the cabin to leave and a sleek, jacked-up Dodge was sitting in front. I was certain we were going to be taking the old truck we went to town in the other day. I don't know where this thing came from, but it's beautiful and perfect for driving on the roads in the horrible conditions we are certain to encounter.

I notice it's a quad-cab when Kadin hefts all three of our suitcases up and settles them on the floor board in the back. He turns around and holds out a hand; an offering of assistance into the cab. I smirk at him and take his hand. Surprisingly he doesn't cop a feel or even linger on my body like I'd expected him to. He just lifts me with economical movements inside.

The door closes with a soft whoosh, and he comes around to the driver's side. We sit up incredibly high, and I feel much safer on the passenger side of this truck than I knew I ever would have driven myself in my car.

I watch as the flatbed truck drives toward the gate with my sleek Mini Cooper strapped to it. So much, yet so little has happened since I drove that car into the ditch outside of Kadin's gate. My head is still spinning, and I have no idea what the future is going to hold, but I'm taking a leap of faith. Faith in what, I'm not even certain of at this point.

I noticed the change in Kadin's mood when I came back down the stairs after looking for the satellite phone. We're over an hour into the trip, and it just seems to be getting worse. He's not rude, but he's also not being very interactive either. Every question I've asked has been answered with as few words as possible on his part. I eventually gave up.

My phone has rang half a dozen times, and I grew so frustrated with it that I put it on silent, but I can still hear it occasionally vibrate in my purse. When it vibrates again, I reach into my purse determined to tell Trent to leave me alone and never call me back.

I press the answer button and begin to bring it to my ear when Kadin reaches out and grabs it from my hand. He looks at the screen, confirming it is who he thought it has been calling so much.

"Hello?" Kadin says.

Pause.

"None of your fucking business. Why don't you tell me why you're calling my girl?" *His girl?*

Pause.

"From what she tells me it ended with your ass the second she caught you with your dick in her whore of a best friend." I wince at the blatant crudeness as the truth spills out of his mouth.

"Don't worry where she's at fucker."

Pause.

"Say it again fucker and I'll track you down and make you wish you were dead."

Pause.

He pulls the phone from his ear and looks at the dark screen. Trent evidently hung up on him. He hands it back to me.

"Thank you," I tell him weakly watching his face for his reaction to the situation.

He winks at me and turns his focus back to the road.

"What did...?" I begin.

"Leave it alone, London." I slide my phone back in my purse and sit in silence until we pull up to a small store with a large sign on the front that reads nothing but "CAFÉ."

"Hungry?" He asks putting the truck in park at the front of the wooden building.

Lunch at the café went just as I figured it would with the way the first leg of the trip was. It was quiet and awkward, and Kadin seems, even more, somber as we drive through downtown Spokane, navigating the roads to his place.

Pulling up to what Kadin informs me is his building I can do nothing but stare at the tall glass and steel structure. It's sleek and elegant and somehow masculine at the same time. It's over a dozen stories high and looks incredibly regal with the late afternoon sun shining down on it.

I look back at him. "You live here?"

He grins at me, clearly finding my astonishment comical. "I don't own the whole building, London."

"And when you say you don't own the *whole* building you're actually saying you own *part* of it?" I turn my head back to my window and watch as we drive into a subterranean garage. He turns the corner toward an empty parking space, and I see my car backed into the spot beside the one we're heading toward.

A quick ride in the elevator brings us to; you guessed it, the damn top floor. I should have known with the opulence of the cabin that he was rich but it never honestly crossed my mind. He drove a ratty truck and wore flannel more than once while we were there, and the last thing he presents as is uptight and snobby. Exactly what I would expect from a man that lives in a place like this.

He opens his front door and strangely goes in ahead of me and drops the luggage unceremoniously at the front door. Thankfully the home is equipped with motion sensor lights so the foyer and living room to the right light up as he makes his way further in. I linger near the front door unsure of how to act, especially after the weird mood he's been in since we left the cabin.

I sit on the step leading into the sunken living room and wait until he reappears. It doesn't take long before he's walking back into my sight. His steps don't carry the same determination they had just minutes before when he strode into the condo with purpose.

He walks past me, and I lean back and watch as he sweeps up my suitcases, leaving his at the door. "If you want I'll show you your room." I stand and follow him down a hallway.

He's walking toward an open door at the very end, and I run right into his back as he stops at the threshold and pulls the door closed.

I take a step back, and he turns toward me. "That's…" He runs his free hand through his hair. "I don't want you in there."

I know my eyes go wide, but I just nod my head in agreement, allowing him to slip past me in the wide hallway. He opens the door farthest from his and sticks his head in like he's unsure of what he's going to find. Satisfied with the sight, he swings the door open and flips the light switch.

He walks into the room and sets my suitcases down at the foot of the bed. "I, uh. I've got some things I need to take care of."

"Okay." What else do I say? He's informing me of his plans but gives nothing away. I'd started to wonder in the truck on the way here if he regretted the offer to let me stay. With the way he's acting now, I'm certain of it.

"There's nothing to eat here. I cleaned it all out before I went to the cabin." He makes his way into the hall. "I'll grab something on the way back. Pizza okay?" I nod, and he walks away. Less than a minute later I hear the front door open and close, leaving me in a condo, in a strange city, alone.

I'm surrounded by complete silence. The walls here are thicker so I can't even hear the wind like I could at the cabin during the times Kadin grew reflective and wanted to be alone. I sit in the room for a bit, refusing to unpack any of my things. With the way he's been acting today, I don't know how long the invitation to stay here is going to last. I have the feeling it will be rescinded soon.

Growing weary of staring at the details of a room that has apparently been decorated by a woman, more than likely Savannah before she passed, I wander out into the common areas of the house. In the living room, I notice several framed pictures of a younger Kadin and a beautiful blond woman who I presume is Savannah. They look happy and ridiculously in love.

I do take in the fact that Kadin looks quite different that he does now. In the pictures, he has no facial hair at all. He's very clean cut, and I can tell that he has more bulk to him now than he did in any of the pictures presented in the frames. I wonder if he exercises a lot now to pass the time he would've normally spent with his love.

His love.

The woman he chased after as a boy. The woman who married him and promised him forever. The very same woman who took his heart with her when she died.

"What are you doing here, London?" I ask out loud holding a picture of Kadin, who has his arm slung over the shoulder of a younger man who carries the same familiar traits as he. I run my finger over the face of the Kadin smiling back at me. A look I was able to pull from him less than a handful of times in the nine days we were together. My guess would be a younger brother, which I find odd because he's never mentioned having one. Come to think of it, he never gave any details about his family.

Just another thing to add to the long list of things I don't know about the man I've agreed to live with. I place the picture back down where I got it from and head back to the room that has been designated as mine. Standing just outside of the door I glance down the hall. Every single one of the doors is closed. I respect his wishes to not enter his room. He was only specific about his bedroom, but I'll extend the same courtesy to the other rooms as well.

I step inside and close the door behind me. I'm frantically digging through my purse looking for my phone when I realize I left it in the trash in the bathroom of that café before we left. Trent tried to call twice more after

Kadin answered and I was just sick and tired of hearing it ring, disgusted every single time I saw his name pop up on the screen. I backed-up everything from it last night before packing my laptop, so it served no purpose. I didn't want him to be able to track me since my number was on his plan. I needed to sever all ties to him and Great Falls.

I lie back on the flowery comforter on the queen sized guest bed and stare at the ceiling. Less than an hour in Spokane and I've never felt more alone in my entire life.

Twenty-Three

Kadin

Thankfully I was able to get into the condo first and get the letter to my family off of the dining room table. Not knowing what else to do with it, I shoved it deep into the inside pocket of my jacket. Having London in this home is conjuring a wide variety of emotions, every one of them something I refuse to deal with right now.

I got out of the condo as fast as I could with no other explanation than I had some shit to take care of. The truth is I had to get away from her; more importantly away from her in the home I shared with my wife. I knew it was going to be hard for me, but I underestimated the shock it would cause to my system when it actually occurred.

Less than half an hour after I leave I'm pulling into the long winding driveway at my parents' home and just my luck my uncle's and my brother's trucks are in the drive as well. Sunday. Apparently they still have the family dinner, one I haven't attended in as long as I can remember.

I'm actually amazed I showed up here. I haven't been to this home in months. Avoiding people, including every member of my family and the friends I had before Savannah died has become part of who I am. Suddenly I miss them. Maybe it's knowing how close I was to ending it all and never seeing them again.

I stand on the front porch and ring the doorbell like a stranger. I don't know why, it just feels like the right thing to do. Like I need to be welcomed back into the fold rather than throwing myself back in without an invitation.

Without flare my mother tugs open the heavy door, her hand suddenly going to the base of her throat like she's seen a ghost. It hits me then the pain I've caused my family even without the extreme of suicide. It's almost like she'd already accepted that I was gone, my absence weighing heavy on her.

I don't say a word; I just cross the threshold and wrap my arms around her. She holds me tightly, and I return the embrace with fervor, letting her love sink in deep and wrap itself around my heart.

Eventually, I lean back from her, kiss her forehead, and wipe tears off of her cheeks.

"Are you hungry?" She asks. As always, the mom of two boys is concerned about my food intake.

I want to please her and sit down with a plate of home cooked food, but I know I told London I'd bring food home. Suddenly thinking of her makes me want to return to the condo. That thought makes me regretful for being such an asshole the five minutes we spent there together.

"Not tonight mom," I tell her and step to the side keeping my arm around her shoulder. "Where is everyone?"

"The guys went to your dad's study. Your Aunt Diana had a migraine, so she didn't make it this evening with Scott. Go say hello. I have to finish in the kitchen."

"Thanks, Mom." I begin to make my way down the hall toward the study.

"Kadin?" I turn back toward my mother. "Please come say goodbye before you leave?"

"Of course, Mom." I give her a genuine smile she hasn't seen in a while. Nodding at me, she heads in the direction of the kitchen.

The three men in my dad's study have seen much more of me that my mother has in the last eighteen months; probably more than they wished they had with the sourness of my attitude and self-destruction I've been displaying, so when I reach the closed office doors I swing them open animatedly.

All three heads turn and stare. Six eyes gawk at me like I'm a circus bear riding into an arena on a tiny little bike.

Kegan is the first to move, standing from his comfortable spot on the leather sofa and slowly walking toward me. He's the one I've allowed around me the most since my world fell apart. I grin at his timidness, and then my smile falters when I realize he's acting this way because he doesn't know which personality he's going to get.

"Brother," he says extending his hand for me to shake.

I slap it out of the way, and his eyes go wide at my action, clearly anticipating some outburst or aggressive intent, rather than what he gets. I pull him to my chest and hug him a few seconds longer than would be considered manly.

I release him and chuckle at the look shock still on his face. "Quit that shit," I tell him and walk further into the room shaking my dad's hand first then my Uncle Scott's.

They are both members of the board of *Cole International*, and even though I'm now the CEO of the company, ultimately the board makes most of the decisions. It was the board's decision to administer the ultimatum that landed me at the cabin. They have to look at the best interest of the company and its stockholders, as well as the several hundred employees who depend on the Cole name to feed their families and pay their bills. I can see now why they did what they did and respect them for it. When it was issued two weeks ago, I wasn't as understanding.

My father and uncle know I'm here to give them my answer. They want to know whether or not I'll step down and allow the vice president, a man who is not a Cole, take over the company, or if I will man up and treat the business as the family legacy that it is.

"Son," my dad says motioning his hand to the side as an offering to take a seat.

I settle onto the leather couch at his right and Kegan sits down beside me, silently watching all of this unfold. He's anxious to hear my answer as well. My dad tried to get him to agree to take over for me if I decided to step down, but he refused, said he had no intentions of spending his life behind a desk. Most days I wish I could be just like him, but being the first born son I have been groomed most of my life for this position. A position I always took pride in until my world fell apart.

"You get it together, boy?" My Uncle Scott has evidently been hitting the scotch heavily already. He struggles to control his mouth when he's been drinking. It has led to more than one altercation in the past.

Normally I would stand and rise above him, becoming as imposing as possible and tell him to go fuck himself, but today is different on so many levels. The first being, I'm not drunk myself. It's a very different change of pace.

I chuckle at his gruff question and shake my head without looking at him. Thank the Lord my dad has the most invested into this company because if I had to deal with Uncle Scott directly more often, my decision would probably be different.

"I'm far from having my shit together, Scott." I look at my father so he can tell how serious I am. "But I finally understand that I need to. I want to."

I look down at my hands briefly and then back into my father's eyes. "I haven't had a drink in a week." I want to tell him more. I want to tell him that I plan to reach out to the counselor I saw right after Savannah's death, but it's not something I'm going to say in mixed company. I know if I do and Scott pops off at the mouth I'm going to end up laying him out cold, and that is the behavior I'm trying to prove to my dad that is in the past.

My dad nods, understanding the significance of my admission. Alcohol has been my closest relative recently and the only thing I felt like I needed in my life, other than my grief.

"When do you plan actually to start getting some work done?" My uncle slurs.

I raise an eyebrow at my dad. He grins at me and shakes his head slightly. "Shut your mouth, Scott or I'm going to send you home and have the board force you to dry out as well."

We all laugh while my uncle huffs and mumbles unintelligible things under his breath. I'm grateful to my dad for deescalating the situation.

I pat both hands on my thighs and stand. "Well, I'm going to get out of here. I'll be at the office first thing in the morning."

I lean over and give my dad a quick hug. I merely nod at Scott as I leave the study making my way back to the kitchen to tell my mom goodbye.

"You leaving already?" She asks as I wrap her in another one of her famous hugs. The type of hug that makes you feel hope, like you can face anything in the world so long as you stay in her embrace. I can't of course. There are so many things I have to fix; wrongs I have to right.

"I won't stay away as long this time; I promise." She kisses me on the cheek, and I make my way to the door only to find Kegan shrugging into to his coat.

"You leaving too?" I ask reaching for the doorknob.

"Yep. Going with you." He begins to button his coat, not paying much attention to me.

"You sure as fuck are not," I answer before I can stop the words from coming out of my mouth.

"Yeah, I am. We can watch the game. I'll crash in your guest room, and we can head into work tomorrow together." I shake my head back and forth.

"Not possible, Kegan." I'm not trying to hide London, but honestly I still feel a wave of shame, knowing eventually people will find out that she is there.

"I stay over there all the time, Kadin. It's no big deal."

"The room is occupied."

This gets his attention. He tilts his head to a slight angle.

"Occupied? You have a roommate now?"

His assumption, not mine, so I go with it.

"Yes." Simple answer right? Well, it won't be a simple explanation when he sees her. I don't feel like getting into it right now in the foyer of my parents' house.

"Okay, so I'll go home after the game. No biggie." He slaps me on the back and walks out the front door, seconds later he's climbing into my truck.

Motherfucker, this is not how I had anticipated introducing London to my family.

Twenty-Four

London

I've fallen asleep with my eReader on my chest; it's not the first time it's happened, and I'm sure far from the last. I'm thinking it is the lights still on in the room that have kept me from falling into a deep sleep but then I hear noises in another part of the condo.

I stretch and grunt in a very unladylike manner and make my way out to the living room. I stop dead in my tracks when I see a man crossing the end of the hallway. My first instinct is to run because I have no idea who the hell he is or why he's even here. This could be some sort of robbery. If people who break into other people's houses are relaxed enough to walk around without shoes drinking a beer.

He notices me, no doubt from the loud gasp I released when I first saw him. Slowly he lowers the bottle of beer from his lips revealing the most amazing smile. In his smile is the evidence of who he is. This is the man that is in the picture I was looking at earlier. Kadin's brother.

"Sweet Christ," he mumbles, his eyes taking me in from top to bottom and back again.

Just then Kadin comes into view, and I cut my eyes to him. He looks from the man to me several times, the jovialness I caught a glimpse when he first rounded the corner quickly fading.

"Where are my manners," the man says as he wipes his right hand on his jeans and stretches it out for me to take it. "I'm Kegan, Kadin's younger, more handsome brother."

I take a few steps forward and reach my hand out to meet his. Surprisingly he pulls me forward another step and raises my hand to his warm lips were he kisses it delicately, his eyes never leaving mine. This little devil is quite charming.

I grin at him until I hear Kadin growl. Seriously, he growled, like a territorial animal. I smirk with satisfaction. A feeling I know I shouldn't have but can't deny even if I wanted to.

"Nice to meet you, Kegan. I'm London. Kadin's…" I cut my eyes to Kadin unsure of what to say, unsure of what to call myself.

Registering my uneasiness Kegan cuts in. "Roommate. He said he had someone in the guest room, but he failed to mention it was an incredibly gorgeous woman." He turns his head toward his brother. "Now I know why you didn't want me to come over."

Kegan releases my hand only long enough to swing his arm over my shoulder, guiding me to the living room where a baseball game is playing on the enormous TV.

"That's enough," Kadin says slapping his brother on the back of the head and tugging his arm off of my shoulder.

I look back to Kegan to apologize for Kadin's rudeness but when I meet his eyes he just winks at me. I can't help but smirk at his blatant flirting. I have no idea what Kadin has told him about me, but I'm guessing it was minimal if anything at all considering the genuine shock on his face when I walked down the hall.

"Let me get you some pizza," Kegan offers. "Beer?"

I look over at Kadin and see a bottle of water in his hand.

"Water please," I tell him.

He nods and leaves Kadin and me alone in the living room.

I look back to Kadin. "You didn't tell me you had a brother."

He shrugs his shoulders like it's no big deal or even more disturbingly like we aren't on a level with each other that would require him to mention his family. It gets my hackles up immediately, annoyance coursing through my veins.

"Careful," he says without enthusiasm. "He's likely to charm the panties right off of you."

And again with the shit that comes out of his mouth, assuming I'm the type of person that would spend a week with someone and then jump to his brother the first chance I got.

"Well," I said just as rudely. "Good thing I'm not wearing any."

I sit on the couch and cross my arms over my chest. I know I'm acting immature, but he's been distant all day and now he's resorting to snide comments. I want to tell him that if he doesn't want me here, then I'll leave, but I'm afraid he'll agree and then that leaves me with nowhere to go. I'm impulsive but not that crazy.

"London," he sighs and takes a step closer to me, and I can see the apology in his eyes.

Kegan reappears before he can say another word. He hands me a plate with a huge slice of pizza on it and sets a bottle of water in front of me on a coaster on the table.

"Thank you," I say and place the plate on my lap, looking up at Kadin as his brother settles in right beside me on the couch.

He rolls his eyes at his brother and walks out of the room.

"So you and Kadin huh?" His brother is obviously pushing for information Kadin hasn't given him.

"Roommates," I answer refusing to tell him anything his brother hasn't already disclosed.

"So you're single then?" I smirk at Kegan and take a bite of my pizza. I can tell he's only trying to irritate his brother, and I refuse to play along with whatever game he's getting at.

"Back off, Kiki," Kadin says coming back into the living room with his own plate of pizza.

"Don't call me that, KayKay," he sneers playfully.

I roll my lips between my teeth in an attempt not to laugh. Kadin sits down on my other side so close he's practically sitting on my lap.

"Kiki? KayKay?" I say looking back and forth between them.

They look past me at each other. "Truce?" Kegan asks.

Kadin narrows his eyes in contemplation. "Truce," he agrees and they bump knuckles in front of me.

He places his hand on my thigh, an apparent show of possession. I hear Kegan chuckle beside me.

With the battle over and both parties back in their own corners, we watch the baseball game and eat pizza. Well, the guys watch the game. I sit there and wonder just what in the hell is going on. Here I am, the meat in a Cole sandwich, and I have no idea how to act.

If we were back at the cabin, I would be snuggled in his arms, but other than the hand that remains chastely on my thigh he's made no other attempt to welcome me closer.

"I'm glad you finally got a TV, man," Kegan says before taking a ridiculously large bite of his pizza slice.

"Got tired of watching the game on my laptop," Kadin says with a shrug.

They begin talking back and forth about the teams and how their seasons have gone, and I eventually block them out. Instead, thoughts of employment and apartment hunting are running through my head. I haven't agreed to take the position Kadin so kindly offered me the other day.

The way things are looking already in the few hours I've been here in Spokane with him, it may be best to find my way on my own and not rely on him. If things go any further south, I know I'll have to leave.

I made the decision before I even ended up in the ditch that I was done being run over. I was through with not following my gut and allowing people to walk all over me; to make decisions I should have been making for myself. I need to gain every ounce of independence that I can muster.

I honestly don't know what I want from Kadin and if anything with Kadin is even an option, but it's a conversation we need to have. One that's not possible with his brother here.

The deep timbre of Kadin's voice calms my nerves and settles my thoughts without purpose on his part. Without thinking, I place my hand over his and lay my head on his shoulder.

"Don't say a fucking word," I hear Kadin tell a laughing Kegan before my eyes flutter completely closed.

Twenty-Five
Kadin

"Care to explain?" my brother says angling his head toward London's sleeping form that's nestled into my side on the couch.

"I told you not to say a word." He won't listen. I don't know why I even waste my breath on him most days. As the youngest, the baby of the family, he knows if he pries long enough most people around him will just cave and give him what he's asking for.

I want to talk to him about her, but I have so many unanswered questions myself I don't even know where to begin. Savannah is everywhere I look in the condo, and I honestly feel guilty with her snuggled up to my side on the sofa.

"Why didn't you just say your girlfriend moved in with you?" He cuts his eyes back to the TV.

"Roommates," I say flatly, not giving into him.

"I wish I had a gorgeous roommate who clings to me in her sleep."

I move my hand from her thigh and place it around her back. "You should get one. It's really nice." I'm trying to annoy him, just like I know he was doing when he was flirting with her.

My brother is childish most days, but he knew there was more to her and me when she walked down the hall in a tank top and skin tight yoga pants. Even in her rumpled state with her brown hair piled messily on her head, he could tell how beautiful she is.

It took everything I had not to grab her by the arm and force her back to her room to get more clothes on. I knew that would throw up a red flag to Kegan, hinting at what we've been up to, so I didn't. Not leaving well enough alone he flirted with her anyways; I'm certain just to get a reaction out of me.

It worked; incredibly so. I almost threw him out on his ass and carried her over my shoulder to her room like a caveman; somehow I managed to restrain myself, attempting to act as nonchalant about it as possible. He saw right through me like he always does.

I shouldn't toy with him, especially where London is concerned. I don't know where she and I are heading, but I can't forget that she's a large part of the reason I'm sitting in this room again rather than a corpse waiting to be discovered in the woods. She's more than a roommate, but how can I explain that to him when I'm not certain I know what it all means myself?

"What's her story?" He asks and sets his empty plate on the coffee table.

"She ended up at the cabin after driving her car into a ditch."

"And before that?" I can tell he's trying to act casual, but he forgets I'm older than he is and I've seen every trick he's ever tried to use to get information when the person is less than willing to give it to him.

"That's her story to tell you if she ever feels the need." I raise my eyebrows at him.

He huffs, and I smile, loving the fact that I can still get on his nerves.

"You sure you're ready to get back to work?" He asks changing the subject to one he may feel like is safer.

"As I'll ever be," I answer. "I got a lot of shit I need to clean up. Quite a bit of stuff has been neglected. Smaller things completely ignored when I lost focus even on the larger issues."

"Someone has been handling business up there. The crews are happy, the projects keep coming in, and my checks aren't bouncing." He winks at me.

I smile at him, appreciating his support and acknowledgment that I haven't fucked things up completely at work. I think about the other non-work related issue I have to clean up and put an end to, and I hope that I can have at least a few days to deal with current issues before that rears its ugly head.

"Some days I wish work was as simple as showing up, reading schematics, and working with my hands building all day." I look down at London, asleep on my side. Simple. I wish things were simple. I wish decisions were easy, and grief was less difficult to overcome.

"Well, you make the big bucks, so your job is supposed to be harder," Kegan says in reply.

I huff. "Well, I have enough money to last several lifetimes. I just don't want the company to end up in someone else's hands. Dad has worked too hard to let it fall into the hands of a man who is not a Cole."

Kegan holds his hands up near his head. "Don't look at me. I've got no desire. That shit will make a man age too fast. I'm having fun as a young man."

I grin at him. "It will catch up with you Kegan. Besides twenty-eight isn't all that young. You ever plan to settle down instead of breaking a million hearts?"

He smirks at me. "Imagine how many hearts I'd be breaking if I picked only one. You're a bachelor too, lest you forget." He stills and his eyes go wide.

I shake my head slightly and give him a weak smile. "I never forget that I'm single, Kegan."

"Fuck, man. Shit." He runs his hands over his baby face roughly. "I wasn't even thinking. I'm always saying stupid shit."

I shrug my shoulder with more force than I'd planned and I feel London jerk beside me. She raises her head and looks around, confusion marking her brow.

"Hey," I whisper running my hand down her back as she pulls away from me, sitting up straight. "Why don't you go get into bed?"

She yawns and stretches clearly without thinking about being in mixed company. I watch my brother watch her perfect tits as they rise gracefully and jut forward in her tank top as she stretches her arms over her head.

I cough to get his attention and glare at him. He raises his hands in surrender once again and mouths that he's sorry. I can't blame him really. She's incredibly gorgeous, and he's not quite a dog but very permissive in his sexual proclivities. I can't expect more from him around her. It would be unfair to his abilities.

"Night," she whispers, placing her hand on my chest, leaning toward me. I was going to let it happen, needing her lips on mine more than I realized until she started to shift toward me; then Kegan shifts his weight on the cushion beside her, and she suddenly remembers he's here. I see her eyes go wide at the realization. She pulls back suddenly and stands from the couch.

"Nice to meet you, Kegan," she says quickly without meeting his eyes and disappears down the hall. Seconds later I hear the door to the guest room close.

I avoid Kegan's eyes as long as I can, but I know there's a point to his silence. When I reluctantly raise my eyes to meet his all I get is a pair of raised eyebrows.

He full-out laughs, head thrown back; the sound is reverberating off of the walls. Finally, he calms enough and rises off of the couch. "I see how you're going to play it."

"Roommates," I say again, knowing he believes it about as much as I do.

I walk him to the door and shut it on him as he's still laughing and trying to get his coat on.

I've been lying on my bed for hours tossing and turning, unable to go to sleep. Giving up on sleep, I roll over and turn on the bedside table lamp. The room is covered with a faint amber glow from the soft light. I look at the framed picture of Savannah that has taken up permanent residence beside the lamp.

I'd give anything to have her back. It wouldn't be the first time I've attempted to bargain with the devil for one more day. Every negotiation with God and Lucifer himself has gone unanswered. I think back, once again, about the means I was planning to use to arrange the meeting between myself and whichever one I ended up in front of. It seems like a lifetime ago that I loaded that glock and met that dirty dealer in that back alley on Main.

I know what I need to be able to sleep, and she's in the other room. I told my father I'd be at work on time, and I plan to keep my word. The last thing I need is to break another promise to the man who's been nothing but supportive of me my entire life.

"I'm so sorry, Savannah," I say to her picture and stand from the bed. My mind is battling between the pain at leaving the bed I shared with my wife and the excitement I feel heading into the room where my lover sleeps.

After a brief stop by my suitcase to grab a condom, I'm sliding into the bed behind London and pulling her against my chest.

"I didn't think you'd show up," she says groggily.

"Never doubt that this is right where I want to be," I whisper against her neck. She doesn't respond, and I'm thankful that maybe she didn't hear my vulnerable admission.

Twenty-Six

London

Kadin crawled in the bed with me last night after hours of wondering if he'd ever come to me again. I'd contemplated going to him, but he was very specific about not wanting me in his room, so I lay in bed practically questioning my existence for hours.

He showed up at some point. I even remember him muttering something beautiful and sweet while I was near sleep. This morning I can't recall his words just that they made me smile and caused my restlessness to calm almost immediately.

The sun isn't even up, but he's grinding his erection against my ass cheeks. I know he's doing it to try to rouse me from sleep, but I'm not playing the way he wants; rather I'm pretending to still be asleep. Or at least I was until he slid his erection between my legs and brushed my clit with it. There's no denying I'm awake now since I just let out a ridiculous moan.

"If you keep pretending to be asleep, you're going to make me late for work," he groans and cups my breast, rolling my already hardened nipple between his fingers.

I hum at the pleasure he's causing. "You could've gotten started already." I shift my hips back and forward, stroking his length deeper between my legs.

"Forgive me for wanting permission before I thrust into you." He says it playfully but I can tell he's thinking about what I told him about all of the times Brian took me by force, without permission. He nibbles on my neck, and it causes a wave of tremors over my body. I forget the past immediately.

"So I overstepped the other morning when I sucked you into my mouth before you woke up?"

He pinches my nipple slightly harder, enough to elicit another moan from my mouth.

"No. Of course not. Consider this as the verbal consent of all future morning blowjobs *and* sex for that matter. If you're ever in doubt, the answer is always 'yes' where this pussy is concerned." He slides his hand from my now tender nipple to the apex of thighs.

"Good to know," I pant and then groan loudly as he sinks into me from behind.

I lift my leg and shift it backward over his leg, opening myself up further so he can thrust harder, deeper. His hand continues to explore my cleft with almost debilitating accuracy. Less than two weeks I've known this man, and he is already playing my body like a musical instrument he's been manipulating since early childhood.

I'm slick and needy; my core is rippling, grabbing at him, begging for more. He answers the call with expert finesse as he thrusts forward and grinds against me in circular motions. His fingers match the perfect symphony.

"You're so deliciously wet for me, London."

I close my eyes and let his praise wash over me. I arch my back, tilting my hips at a better angle, one that allows him to plunge deeper than ever before.

I'm right on the cusp of orgasm when he wrenches his hips away, pulling his thick cock from inside me. I whimper at the loss. He repositions his weight and flips me fully on my stomach, raising my hips up and leaving the top half of my body on the bed, my back in a severe arch.

I cry out into the pillows when he thrusts back into me without warning. The tiny bite of pain from his initial thrust subsides immediately turning into pure erotic pleasure.

"Look at me," he demands.

I respond without hesitation and turn my head so I can see him over my shoulder. He's got his lips clamped between his teeth, and his eyes are heavy with pleasure, the look on his face almost pained.

"Come for me, London." My body obeys before I can open my mouth to tell him I'm not ready.

All I can do is tremble and watch his face as his body responds in kind to mine. I feel the wild throbbing of his cock deep inside me as my eyes once again grow heavy with exhaustion.

He leans over my body and kisses my cheek which is still turned over my shoulder, my eyes watching him, almost like I'm waiting for his next command.

Just as he eases out of me, his cell phone alarm begins to chime on the bedside table.

"Perfect timing," he says as he slides off the bed and pulls off the condom.

I turn around, so I'm sitting cross-legged on the bed facing him. It is then that I realize my tank top is still on, just pushed up over my breasts. My yoga pants are nowhere to be seen, and I can't believe he got me out of them without waking me.

He grabs his phone and turns off the alarm; leaning over, he kisses me softly on the lips. "I've got to shower and get to the office."

He's almost to the door when I finally speak up. "When were you expecting me to start?" *Why am I suddenly nervous?*

"I figured next week would be soon enough. Gives you this week to get acclimated to Spokane." He lowers his eyes. "Figure out what you want to do."

"Okay," I whisper to his back as he leaves the room. Seconds later I hear his bedroom door shut and just like that he closes me out of his life once again.

I'm almost certain 'figure out what you want to do' is his nice way of telling me I have a week to make plans for alternate living arrangements, at least, that's how I'm reading things.

I roll out of the bed and tug on the yoga pants Kadin had taken off of me this morning and head into the kitchen. During my snoop session last night I discovered that coffee is literally the only consumable thing in this place.

I set about to making an entire pot, knowing I'm going to need quite a bit to keep me going for the entire day. I was restless for the hours before he climbed into bed with me and I'm already feeling the tiredness sneak up on me. That in combination with the energy spent on this emotional rollercoaster means a second pot may be needed by midday.

I'm pouring Kadin coffee into a travel mug I found in the cabinet when I feel him enter the room. The air seems to change around him, growing denser, and this morning I can't even determine if it is a good thing or a bad thing. I resolve myself to act just as he told his brother my station is. If a roommate is what he wants, then a roommate is what he'll get.

I also remind myself I need to go to the store to grab a newspaper so I can start to look for a job, knowing it would never work out with me working for Kadin, the time outside of the bedroom with him is too stressful here at the condo. I can't imagine what it would be like if he were in a position of authority as my boss.

"You didn't have to make me coffee," he says as I hand him the lidded travel mug.

"I made me some," I tell him turning back to the coffee pot to pour myself a cup. "It's the least I could do."

Sensing my somber mood he closes the distance between us and I watch as he sets his cup of coffee on the counter near my arm and rests his body gently against my back. He leans his face down and nuzzles my neck, and I let him, even though I know I should confront him on the whiplash he's giving me.

"Please bear with me, London." He kisses my neck softly. "I'm struggling more than I thought I would with you here."

"If you want me to go," I begin.

Suddenly he turns me in his arms. "That is *not* what I want." He cups my cheeks in his hand and closes his eyes briefly. Swallowing roughly he says, "I never thought I'd come around the corner into the kitchen and be happy to see a woman other than Savannah standing at this counter."

Whoa!

I never for a second thought about how he was dealing with me being in the same space that had been previously occupied by his late wife. Now, I feel like a total bitch for thinking he's only toying with me. This once again goes so much deeper than I realized.

"Tell me what you want; what you need me to do to make things easier for you." I close my eyes and nuzzle my cheek in his hand.

"You're already doing it," he whispers before he kisses my lips.

Well, it wasn't a declaration of love but sure wasn't walking papers either.

I had mentioned to Kadin before he left for work that I'd planned on going grocery shopping today. He shut me down immediately and said he will call a list in and to expect them to deliver later in the day. I told him I wanted to get out of the house, and he showed me on a map where the gym in the building was. The storm was blowing in later today, and he didn't want to have to worry about me being out in it. I promised to stay inside the building.

Another surprising request he made was to box up all the liquor in the dining room as well as the living room. An easy task I was certain of until I began and realized just how extensive his supply was. Currently, three rather large boxes sit on the dining room table, waiting for him to do with them what he wishes. They're too heavy for me to lift on my own.

I let my mind wander back to the way Kadin looked when he left for work this morning. His three piece suit is a stark contrast to the jeans and t-shirts he's worn every day since I met him. I wanted to rip them off of him more than once before he finally left me in the apartment alone. The dark gray suit fit him like it was tailor made for his amazingly fit body. I know I'm going to fantasize about the turquoise colored tie for weeks to come.

I'm sitting on the couch, unable to concentrate on the book I pulled up more than twenty minutes ago on my tablet with the doorbell chimes through the condo.

I get up off the couch and make my way to the door, opening it for the food service delivery people. I gasp when a leggy blond saunters inside instead of a delivery boy with bags of groceries.

I notice her perfection the second my eyes land on her. Bone straight blond hair, super thin body, and a huge bottle of Jack Daniels in her hands. She mustn't have gotten the memo on his drinking.

"Can I help you?" I ask. My hand is still on the open door.

She turns suddenly as if she's just now noticing me for the first time. Her eyes skate up and down my body dismissively. Suddenly I wish I had opted for less comfortable clothes; my leggings and t-shirt are obviously not meeting her approval.

Although she's sneering at me, there is something familiar about her I can't place.

"Who the fuck are you?" She spits out like I just walked into her residence unannounced.

I smile at her sweetly, knowing just how to handle women like her.

"That's not how this works. Who are you?" I stand with one hand on my hip and the other still on the doorknob.

She places the heavy bottle of liquor on the entry way table and focuses her attention on me.

"Where's Kadin?" She asks making her way further into the condo.

"Not here. You're more than welcome to leave a message with me. But I'm not entertaining today, so I'm going to ask you to leave." I walk a few steps ahead of her and get in her path, praying she doesn't attack me or anything.

"You've got to be kidding me, right?" She says, her voice rising several octaves.

"Afraid not," I answer. "I will let him know you stopped by…" I wait for her to give me her name, but she doesn't. She huffs a few more times and makes her way to the door.

"Show him that," she points to the bottle of Jack. "He'll know who it's from."

Just as I'm reaching the door, she holds her hand up like she just realized I'm in Kadin's home.

"What are you doing here anyways?"

"I live here," I say and close the door in her face.

It isn't until I cross over into the threshold of the living room and look around when I realize exactly who she looks like.

Twenty-Seven

Kadin

I could say I have an unexplainable skip in my step as I make my way to the office, but I know exactly why it's there. Even if seeing her standing in my kitchen like she owned the place almost stopped my heart this morning; I'm glad that she's there.

"Good morning, Lisa," I say as I pass the front reception desk.

"Sir," she says with a disbelieving nod, unaccustomed to seeing me in anything but a shitty mood.

I push open my office door and find Kegan already inside leaning on my desk; a planned attack apparently.

"Hey, man," he says and goes in for the manly hug, back pat move.

"Whew! You smell like sex," he says backing away quickly waving the air in front of him with his hand.

I reach down and smell my shirt. "I took a shower," I say before I realize the setup.

"I fucking knew it!" He's bouncing up and down like an idiot, looking more like a toddler than a grown man.

Busted.

"Would you settle down? There's no sense in spreading your joy all over the office first thing in the morning." I advise him before sitting down in my office chair.

He's grinning from ear to ear like he's just won the damn lottery at my slip up. I may know most of his tricks but every once in a while even I'm outsmarted, and he catches me slipping.

"What?" I ask when he sits down in the chair across from me and doesn't say a thing.

"Are you going to spill it about London?" He looks hopeful; he shouldn't.

"Do I look like the type of man that would sit here and give you details about anything that happened between a woman and me?" I raise an eyebrow at him. He doesn't respond, but his smile falls just a bit. "Just because you want to tell the world every time you dip your stick in someone doesn't mean I'm up for sharing."

"But you do admit that you dipped your stick, right?" I glare at him and don't respond.

Is this normal brother conversation? Kegan was so young when Savannah and I got together, so we never had sex conversations with each other. Well, he's shared every detail anyone was willing to listen to since he became sexually active, but he knew better than to ask me questions about my wife. Why he feels like I'd share now is beyond me.

The thought strikes me that Kegan has never been serious about a woman before, and maybe my lack of detail sharing is due to the fact that I know I see London as more than a piece of ass which is all Kegan ever sees a woman as. Maybe it's easier to guy talk about one night stands and quick fucks; my limited experience doesn't allow for it.

"In no way shape or form am I going to discuss London with you; so you can stop trying to dig for information." I reach over and hit the power button on my computer and wait for it to boot up.

"You seem happier," he observes with a more serious tone.

He was the last one to see me before I left for the cabin with no plans to return. Even with our age difference we've always been close and leaving my parents a note was an incredibly horrible thing to do, but I couldn't leave without seeing him. We had spent the day before I left working out in the gym at his apartment complex and the evening was spent in the bar of the hotel next door. He called me an idiot when I hugged him too long before he went home for the night.

That's another reason I'm glad my plans have been diverted. I know he'd feel guilty and blame himself for not realizing what was going on with me if I'd followed through. It would be misplaced, but it wouldn't make things any easier. I knew my suicide would hurt people I love and it's one of the reasons I took so long actually to come to the decision to follow through, but I was more focused on ending my own suffering than being concerned for everyone else. I hoped that eventually they'd understand my actions even if they could never comprehend the level of suffering that comes with losing a spouse; I pray they never did. I wouldn't wish it on anyone.

"I've gained," I pause doing my best to think of the best way to put this, "some perspective."

"Have anything to do with that hot brunette at your condo?" He's taken a seat in the chair directly across from my desk. He hooks his ankle over the other knee looking like he's getting comfortable and planning to stay awhile.

"I'm not talking to you about her, Kegan. You might as well leave it alone."

I turn my attention away from him and enter my password to access my computer. It doesn't work which isn't surprising, much of the last year and a half has been spent in a drunken haze. Looks like I'll have to have IT back up here to sort it out.

I look back at my brother and notice the look of patience on his face, a trait that doesn't show up often. Just what I need is a nosey brother with time on his hands.

"Don't you have a job to get to as well, brother?" I lean back in my chair; without access to my computer there's little else I can do until the issue is corrected.

He looks at his watch and back to me. I can see him evaluating my level of seriousness about sharing the goods on London. I raise my eyebrows in challenge. He folds. "I guess you're right." He stands from his seated position and grins at me deviously. "Wanna watch the game tonight?"

I feel like he's trying to test me once again and I don't know which way to go with my answer. Deciding just to tell him the truth, "I have plans this evening." I don't expound, but I watch his smile grown in understanding.

"London." It's not a question; it's a statement.

He's right; my plans do include London this evening. I know after spending all day away from her after being with her almost every minute for a week and a half is going to be an adjustment to my system. It is because of this I know I'm going to want to be inside of her the very minute I get back to the condo.

"Have a good one, bro. Talk to you later." I watch him leave the office and hear him say something flirty to Lisa on his way out, knowing he's joking. He may be a manwhore, but he'd never cross the line with a woman who is taken.

After speaking to Lisa about getting the IT guy up here to get things set straight with my computer, I call the condo, inexplicably needing to hear her voice. She's never given me her cell phone number so I can't reach her that way or I'd text her. I smile as I listen to the phone ringing, wondering if she'd give me her cell phone number so I can text her dirty things throughout the day. The phone call goes unanswered, and I'm sure it's because she'd feel weird about answering the phone in a place that doesn't belong to her.

The IT guy enters my office to get my password issue corrected. I can tell by the look on his face that he's not impressed one bit. I couldn't even tell you how many times this man has had to come in here and do this very thing. *This is the last time, buddy. I promise.*

I tried calling the condo several times, but each one was left unanswered. For a split second, I hate technology. What I wouldn't give for a good old-fashioned answering machine that I could scream into and beg her to answer, rather than the digital voicemail that accompanies the phone service at the condo.

I had every intention of asking her what she wanted for dinner. Since she never answered, I grab a couple of subs from the sandwich shop just down the road from my building. It's the fastest meal to get, and I want to get back to the condo. I have no reason other than unanswered phone calls to be concerned, which isn't a big deal, but that still isn't keeping the dread from settling in my gut.

I squeeze my eyes closed at a red light and try to keep the memory of what happened the last time my calls went unanswered as well as calls placed to a cell phone. That night I came home to an empty house, and the worst thought came to mind. Savannah had been spending so much time at the office recently, but she'd always answer when I called, even if the call was answered with mild annoyance at being interrupted.

After driving by her work and seeing that her car, in fact, was not there, I went back home and waited. I'm certain I wore a path on the floor of the condo that night from all of the pacing, my head raging with thoughts of my wife with another man. The anger grew with each step and every unanswered call. All of which was explained shortly after eleven that night with a knock on the door I knew I should never have answered.

Knock. Knock. Knock.

Who the fuck would be at my door at this time of night? I quicken my steps when I realize that maybe Savannah lost her purse which always housed her phone and her car keys.

The second I opened the door I knew that was not the answer. I knew what was happening the second I saw the forlorn faces of the two uniformed officers at my door.

I crumpled to the floor, my body wracked with sobs before they could even confirm they were at the right place.

The blare of the horn behind me snaps me out of the horrendous memory I've lived through a million times since it happened in real time, adding to my guilt the fact that I let the idea of her cheating on me snake its way into my thoughts when in fact her lifeless body was being cut out of a twist of metal by the jaws of life. Ironic name for the equipment considering there was no life left in the car by the time first responders made it down the ravine to the wreckage.

I shake my head in an attempt to rid it of the thoughts that have become second nature almost, trying to keep the demons from sneaking up on me once again. I let my mind wander to London and how I hope I find her on the couch reading a book on her electronic book device. I smile knowing I'll find her in tight-as-fuck yoga pants and a tank top.

I valet my truck when I get to the building because I just don't want to have to waste any more time getting upstairs; they'll park it right where I would've anyways. I drum my fingers on the top of the sandwich container as the elevator makes it slow climb to the condo. I make quick work of the lock and toss my keys down right beside an unopened bottle of Jack Daniels. My heart drops into my stomach because I know exactly what that bottle means. I thought I'd have more time before I had to deal with her.

I place the food on the breakfast bar in the kitchen on my way to search for London. The condo is cast in an eerie silence as I walk down the hall toward her room with dread in the pit of my stomach, afraid I'm going to find that she's left. That the calls all day went unanswered because the delivery of the bottle on the front table came with a gamut of information she wasn't prepared for and would refuse to deal with.

The gentle tap on her door remains as unanswered as the dozen calls I made early. I take a deep breath and slowly twist her door knob. Relief rushes through me as I see the lump in the middle of the bed. This may not be the best scenario to walk into, but, at least, she's here and I can explain the mess I've made. On better thought, I need to dig a little and find out what she knows first. Not trying to be an asshole but the situation I had created before I met her is not something I feel the need to go into explicit detail over.

"Hey," I say placing a hand on the back that's facing me.

She turns her head slightly in acknowledgment but doesn't fully turn over or even attempt to look at me. "You had a visitor today." The rough gravel in her voice tells me she's upset and has been for a while. When I don't add anything she continues. "Beautiful, blonde. Ring any bells?"

My pulse begins to thump heavier at the sound of jealousy in her voice. I don't even want to visit with the knowledge that I like it.

"Yes. Her name is Sierra. She didn't tell you who she was?"

"Nope," she answers. "She practically shoved her way in and tried grilling me about who I was and refused to tell me who she was."

"She's Savannah's twin," I explain, hoping she doesn't try to dig deeper.

"Is that all she is, Kadin?"

So much for hoping.

"Sierra's," I sigh, "complicated."

"She brought you a bottle of whiskey," she says quietly.

"She likes me drunk," I mutter shifting my weight on the bed so I can kick my shoes off.

I wait for another line of questions, but they don't come. "I'll talk to her," I say softly running my hand up her back and freeing the hair that is partially blocking her face.

"I'm not here to interfere with your life, Kadin." She sounds resigned as if she still feels like the situation we had back at the cabin has remained the same since we came here.

She won't know things are different for you unless you tell her where you're at with it. What if she doesn't want things to be different with me?

Unable to fight the battle in my head right at this moment I turn my body so I can lie behind her on the bed.

"Please don't," she begs weakly.

Shame hits me over the situation with Sierra and how it's affecting London, and she doesn't even know part of the clusterfuck it is.

"I want you here, London. Don't ever question that," I whisper in her ear and leave her room, closing the door quietly behind me.

Twenty-Eight

London

Even though Kadin left me in my bed alone yesterday evening, I still felt his body heat join mine late in the night. I welcomed the warmth and wanted to turn in his arms and hold him, but I didn't. I couldn't get a read on his emotions where Sierra is concerned, and it's not something I wanted to hash out in the middle of the night, knowing he had to get up early for work the next morning. He was gone when I woke up, and the spot behind me was cold as if he was never there.

I stay in bed until I hear the apartment go quiet and then go in search of coffee and something to eat. I couldn't even stomach the idea of food after the impromptu visit with Kadin's friend yesterday. I know it has to be more than that. The way Sierra acted was so much more than a woman upset that her twin's widower had another woman in his house. Her demeanor was territorial like she felt she had some sort of hold on him.

I round the corner into the kitchen and simultaneously gasp and clutch at my heart in surprise when I see Kadin standing in the kitchen eating a bagel. "I thought you'd be gone." Well, that came out exactly how I felt it.

He gives me a knowing smirk and instead of just letting it pass he says, "You mean you waited for me to leave and I shocked you by still being here?"

He places his bagel on a napkin on the counter and reaches out his hand tugging me to his chest. I go willingly because honestly it's exactly where I want to be. I rest my head on his chest and let the sound of his strong heart calm my racing one.

After a few moments of leaning into him and his hand stroking up and down my back, I feel his voice rattle in his chest against my cheek. "I was serious last night when I said I want you here, London." He gently grasps my shoulders and shifts my weight back a few inches so he can look in my eyes. "I need you here," he whispers.

His kiss is soft and gentle and if I'm reading it right, filled with more emotion than a man who just wants a fuck buddy. His hands don't roam over my body; they clutch me to his chest. His hips don't rotate against mine. This kiss is his way of affirming to me that I'm more valuable to him than I'd realized last night when he struggled to talk about Sierra.

"I want to spend the weekend with you," he whispers after reluctantly pulling his mouth away from mine. "I want to lock out the whole world and spend every second wrapped around you."

I swallow roughly, his words confirming my thoughts from just a minute go. "I'd love that," I answer with a smile.

Over the next four days, without thought or plan, we'd ended up with a routine; one should any other person see from the outside spoke of domestication. Mornings began with amazing sex, not the shower quickies I'd grown used to with Trent but passionate and sometimes borderline crazy sex. Our nights ended much the same way.

After showers, I'd make coffee and breakfast; see him off to work, just to have dinner waiting for him when he got home. We've talked about everything under the sun. The one subject he's brought up more than once is my employment. I finally had to tell him I had no intentions of working for him, which he said was fine, but I could tell he wasn't happy about. Savannah is a subject he always steers away from. I mentioned her once, and I regretted it I think just as much as he hated me asking. After seeing his eyes darken and his demeanor change I knew I'd never bring up the subject again.

I spend the middle of my days running on the treadmill in the apartment gym downstairs and searching the help wanted ads looking for a job. I've tabled the idea of searching for another place to live even though he still keeps the door to his bedroom closed. My concern over this is squelched knowing he only goes in there to change now since he's been showering in the bathroom in my room. I rarely see him going in there and when he does it's usually a quick in and out.

I think it was Wednesday evening while making out on the couch after ignoring the hockey game that I realized I was falling in love with him. He'd looked at me, for the first time since I crashed into his life two weeks earlier, like I was the only thing in his world that he could see. He'd stroked my cheek, and I got lost in eyes that said a slew of things that had never crossed his lips. That night we made love for hours not once feeling the need to rush to completion. I was certain things were progressing in our relationship even though we weren't giving a voice to it. I could feel it, and I was certain he could too.

"London." His voice holds something it never has before. He's cupping my cheeks and his eyes enrapturing me to him. I couldn't look away if I wanted to. I see pain, acceptance, and possibly even love in them.

Say it, *I want to whisper.* Say it and I'll say it back.

He doesn't; he's not ready yet. I bite my tongue to keep myself from blurting it out. The demons he's fighting are much stronger than mine. I can't open my heart to him completely until I know he feels the same way. I can't handle being the only one in love again. If I could, I would've stayed with Trent.

The feeling didn't last long when he woke up in *my* arms screaming for Savannah. I know there's no timetable for grief. I also know there is no way I can ever expect him to forget her. I'd never even ask. He loves her; he'd spent seventeen years of his life dedicated to her, but it didn't lessen the sting I felt when he left my bed that night and didn't return. The hurt was amplified when I woke up the next day, and he was already gone to work.

It's now Saturday morning, and since he got home from work Thursday evening, we've ignored the subject, acting like it didn't happen, and went right back into the routine we'd established. I'm not certain if that is the best thing or the worst thing that we can do, but apparently it's not something either one of us going to bring up.

"What do you want to do today," I whisper against his chest, loving the way the trimmed, crisp hair feels on my face.

I know we've slept in some, but the faint shadows cast by the sun through the window tell me either we didn't sleep in late enough, or the weather outside is bad.

"This," he whispers holding me tighter against his chest after gently kissing the top of my head.

"Mmm," I hum. "Great idea."

We spend almost every second together on Saturday. Even when we weren't in bed together, we always found ourselves looking for a reason to be in close proximity if not actually in each other's arms. It was exactly like the last few days at the cabin. We cooked together, ate together, and showered together. Our bodies met more times than I'd openly admit to anyone.

I'm certain we've christened every surface in the condo. When that thought struck, self-doubt and unworthiness accompanied it. I've yet to step foot in his bedroom, and I'm not the only woman he's made love to here. With that came shame knowing that I'm jealous of a deceased woman, knowing had he not lost her I wouldn't be spending my time in the arms of what I'm beginning to accept as the most incredible man I've ever met. At first, I was disgusted with myself but accepted that I'd give him up in a second if it meant he could have his one true love back. Realizing that was when I knew I was in trouble.

Twenty-Nine

Kadin

"Fuck, London. Too fast," I groan and grip her hips a few seconds too late. I throw my head back as my cock repeatedly pulses deep inside of her. "Keep going," I bite out and rub circles on her clit with my thumb as she bounces up and down on me. The sensation is incredible just after my orgasm, but once again she's sent me into oblivion too fast, and I owe her.

Less than a minute later she tumbles into sweet bliss as well. "Holy shit," I grumble as her hips slow, and her orgasm clutches at my still erect cock. I can't help but chuckle as she dramatically collapses on my chest, her panting breaths tickling the hair there.

The urge to admit that sex with her is the best I've had hits me hard. I don't because that seems all kinds of wrong, especially in a room decorated by my late wife. I wonder if my feelings for her would have grown as much as they have if we weren't having spectacular sex. I force the thought out almost as immediately as it creeps into my head, knowing that almost since day one she's been more to me than sex. If anything, she's my savior and she doesn't even know it.

Thinking about her in that capacity reminds me of the relationships I've only begun to try to rebuild this last week. Several I need to work on the most include my parents.

"Hey," I whisper. I feel myself slide out of her wetly as she shifts her body so she can look me in the eye. I love how wet I make her. "I have a late meeting this evening."

She looks at me without expectation, "Okay." There's no disappointment in her voice, and I suddenly feel like shit lying to her. "I can catch up on my reading."

The truth is I'm planning on finally joining my family for Sunday dinner at my parents' house, and I know taking her along would mean answering questions I'm not ready to answer. It would foster hope in my mother I'm not willing to provide just yet. Then there's always my Uncle Scott, who's inappropriate even on his best behavior. I couldn't handle having her meet my folks and deal with him at the same time. I'm certain the combination would have me snapping his neck before dinner is even served.

If I tell her my actual evening plans, I know it will hurt her feelings when I don't ask her to come along, and that's not something I want to do either. The lie only causes me distress, and that's the way I'll keep it. I can't explain to her how much I want her there with me without making certain declarations. Bringing her along would make declarations to my family as well, and I'm not ready for that either. I'm right where I always seem to find myself lately between the rock and the hard place.

"Let me make you breakfast," I say as a consolation for breaking my promise to spend the entire weekend with her.

My making breakfast consists of warming bagels in the toaster oven and offering a choice between regular or strawberry cream cheese. She eventually pushes me out of the way and makes fried eggs and sausage links. I dice some fruit while she does her magic at the stove. I love the sound of her laughter when I drag a cube of pineapple up her neck and lick the juice away. I can't keep my hands, or mouth for that matter, off of her; she seems the same way with me.

I cherish the fact that she doesn't seem to want to change me or force me to talk about what the future may hold. I know part of my falling for her is her ability to let things go and just be with me. Most days I'm okay, but then a memory hits me of Savannah, and I'm right back in the middle of the emotional hurricane I can't seem to move past.

My first appointment with the therapist is on Tuesday, and I'd be a fool not to admit that I'm looking forward to it. Well, as much as one can look forward to knowing they're walking into a situation that's going to be a catalyst for the tempest they're barely touching on their own. I do know; however, that it's the best thing I can do not only for myself but for the woman standing in my kitchen that I've grown to accept that I may need in my life. I know this with as much conviction as I know that I'll never touch another drop of alcohol. Just another thing she's managed to save me from without even knowing.

"I found a couple places I plan on taking resumes to tomorrow," she says as she sets our plates on the dining room table and turns back to grab the glasses of milk I poured on the counter.

I'm still not happy that she's decided against working for me, but I'm doing my best not to let it show. I set the bowl of fruit on the table between our plates for us to share and wait for her to sit down before I take my seat.

"Anything specific you're hoping for?" I ask before popping a grape in my mouth.

She shrugs and finishes chewing a bite of eggs before speaking. "Not really but I'll take what I can get."

"You don't have to settle, London. In fact, Cole International offers an excellent benefits package." I wink at her, and she smiles noncommittally back at me. Maybe she won't find anything she likes and will still end up at the office with me.

I have to remind myself that he's family, and I'll have to deal with him eventually when I pull up to my dad's house and my asshole Uncle Scott's car is parked out front. Hopefully, my aunt will be here and can keep him under control.

Since my warm welcome last week I don't feel like a stranger anymore, so I just walk in once I get to the front door. I head directly to the kitchen to see my mother. I say a quick prayer of thanks when I see my Aunt Diana sitting at the breakfast bar drinking a glass of wine talking to my mom.

"Ladies," I say and walk to my aunt and kiss her forehead and give her a hug.

My mom turns from the stove and closes the distance between us. I can tell she didn't know if I'd be back and she's surprised and very happy to see me again so soon. I don't dwell on it long because I know things are different now, and the distance was temporary; I have every intention of making my way back to my family completely.

"Hey, mom." I hug her back with as much enthusiasm as she's clinging to me with.

She loosens her grip on me, and I see her swipe at her eye with the back of her hand as she turns her attention back to the stove.

"Dinner's almost ready. Can you go grab the guys and have them start to make their way to the dining room?" She asks as she pulls a pot of boiling pasta off of the stove, walking it to the sink to drain it.

"Sure." I walk out of the kitchen and head to Dad's office, knowing that's where everyone will be congregated at.

I walk in on the ass-end of a filthy joke I've heard my uncle tell more than I'd like to admit. I smile at my dad when his face lights up at seeing me. I love that man and pray one day I'll have the chance to be just as awesome a father as he has been with us.

Kegan, of course, is on the other side of the room laughing hysterically egging my uncle on purposefully. He thinks it's riotous to keep him going, only because he doesn't take anything serious. I narrow my eyes at him, telling him I'm in no mood for Scott's shit tonight, and he better quit while he's ahead. He grins at me and scratches his nose with his middle finger.

I shake my head at him with a smile of my own. *Shithead.*

"Mom says dinner is almost ready and to get your old asses to the dining room." My uncle's face sours immediately. *Come on fucker say something about my mom.*

"I know better than that!" My dad says as he stands from his spot on the leather sofa. "I don't think I've heard your mom cuss since those bastards flew the planes into the World Trade Center."

He's right. My mother doesn't use that type of language, insisting anyone who does needs to increase their education level. We guys do our best to watch our mouths when we're around her. Uncle Scott is not very considerate of anyone around him. Each one of these dinners I wonder when my mom is finally going to have enough and ask him not to return, knowing it hasn't happened yet merely because my mom loves Diana so much.

Dinner was going great. We talked about future plans and vacations my parents want to take now that Dad is semi-retired. That all changed when dessert was being served, and Kegan got that look in his eye.

"So, KayKay? You told mom about the woman you have living with you yet?" Kegan says like it's just another piece of everyday news to discuss at the table.

From the corner of my eye, I see both of my parents' heads snap up and look at me. Center of attention, a position Kegan has always been better at than me. This is his payback for not spilling it about London when he asked. My mind is already thinking of things to do to get back at him; that's if I don't strangle him first.

I narrow my eyes at him before speaking. "I do have a house guest," I respond with as much nonchalance as I can muster.

"Houseguest," Kegan huffs.

"She's in the guest room," I reply and look at my mother. My explanation does nothing to keep the happiness off of her face. Seems I'm as transparent to her as I am to Kegan, and she didn't show up at the house like he did and see her braless in a tank top and yoga pants.

"And where do you sleep?" Kegan says just before popping an overly large bite of pie into his mouth.

My jaw clenches uncontrollably, and my left eye ticks periodically with my pulse. *Fucker.*

"How did you meet?" My Aunt Diana asks thinking she's saving me from Kegan's questions when she's actually only making it worse.

Kegan drops his fork on his plate loudly and sits backs far in his chair. "Oh, I love this part of the story."

Once again every head turns to me. Weeks ago I would have been drunk and thrown a fit about them being in my business and not letting me live my life how I saw fit, but I love them, Kegan I'm no longer sure about, and I need them in my life.

"London's car broke down near the cabin." I look at Kegan with pleading in my eyes hoping he takes mercy on me. He sits up straighter and nods slightly, accepting that I'd had enough.

"That's a beautiful name," my mother says with a wide smile.

"We'd love to meet her someday son," my father includes.

The conversation shifts back to safer territory, and I couldn't be happier. Not a totally terrible way to introduce the idea of London in my life. Everyone seems receptive to the idea of me seeing someone. I wondered how their reactions would be since Savannah was such a large part of all of their lives for so long as well.

Thirty

London

I did my best not to be a little sad when Kadin told me he had a meeting this evening. I have no right to dictate anything he does, but I was still disappointed to see him leave. I tried sitting on the couch and reading, but I just wasn't feeling it.

Eventually, I went to the bedroom and fired up my laptop. I hadn't been on it in forever. I was both amazed and grateful that for some reason Kadin didn't have a password for his internet. I need to talk to him about that once he gets home; it's not very safe especially for a man as wealthy as he obviously is.

I do my best to stay away from Amazon. I have hundreds of books on my eReader and have no business ordering any more, plus I have to be frugal since I'm jobless right now. I get on social media and shut down my accounts. There's no one on there I care to hear from again, and I hardly used it back in Great Falls anyway. I don't even look at the notifications and messages before deactivating.

Next on my list of things to clean is my email. I need to get a new one, but there are some things I want to transfer over. I slowly begin making my way through my emails and write down which ones I will need later. This process takes more time than I thought I'd be spending and eventually I just start clicking up the line to delete them all.

I include the emails sent from Trent. There are none from Keira which is surprising and for a split second I wonder if they are together now. I shake my head to clear the thought because honestly I wake up every morning beside an amazing man. I'd rather be here not knowing exactly where I stand than living a lie with Trent.

My blood runs cold when I get to an app reminder. One that would've been sent to my phone. The very same phone I tossed in the trash at the café we stopped at on our way back from the cabin. My heart is racing as I shift my finger and position the mouse over the 'Don't Forget to Track' subject line. I click on it and close my eyes until I have the courage to open them, even though my mind is already racing. Slowly I open my eyes, and I'm welcomed by a picture of a pretty white and pink flower. The email reminds me to track my cycle on the app, and since I didn't track two days ago, they assume I'm just forgetful. It goes further to ask if I'm having trouble using the app and gives me a reply email to contact should I need help.

Should have tracked.

Two days ago.

I'm not two days late tracking. I'm two days late. My 'here practically the exact same hour every month' period is nowhere to be seen. I go into the bathroom and tug down my yoga pants. Nothing. I sit down on the toilet and wipe, hoping for even a pink tinge or discoloration. Nothing.

I'm near tears by the time I leave the bathroom and get dressed. There's a CVS just down from the apartment, and I bundle up to face the frigid cold outside. I do it merely out of habit because I'm certain the cold wouldn't even register on my skin with the level of shock my system is in.

The wall of pregnancy tests is daunting at best. There have to be over a dozen kinds to choose from. I go with the one with two in the box that literally reads 'pregnant' or 'not pregnant' for the results. I don't remember making it back to the apartment. I don't remember opening the package and peeing on the stick. Yet I hold in my hand the white stick, PREGNANT taunting me from the tiny little window on the front.

A tear rolls down my face. Then another. And another.

Sick of looking at the evidence of my carelessness I toss the test in the trash and shove the box with the additional one in one of the drawers near the sink. I run cold water into the basin and splash it on my face. I shake my hands in front of me when I notice how much they are trembling. It doesn't help, and the tremors continue. I honestly have no idea how Kadin is going to take this news. I have to tell him. I won't keep something like this from him, even though it may destroy whatever is building between us.

For some reason the realization that I never went to the clinic after leaving Trent slams into my head. This situation lasts a lifetime, whereas most STDs can be cured with antibiotics. The disgusting thought hits my head without provocation, and then I gasp.

I go back to my laptop and run my finger over the mouse area, waking it up. I click on the link in the email that directs me to the online page and open my cycle calendar. I collapse on the floor when my suspicions are confirmed. Most fertile day of the cycle was two Saturdays ago. The same day I woke up and had sex with Trent in the shower and ended my day by having sex with Kadin.

The baby has to be Trent's, right? The thought of that turns my stomach more than the idea of having to tell Kadin I'm pregnant. I used condoms with Kadin. *Not the first couple of times*, my head reminds me. He pulled out. *Not the first night*, it tells me again. I clench my eyes shut and think about the morning after I woke up from that first night at the cabin. If I concentrate enough, I can still feel his semen snaking down the inside of my thighs.

What have I done? It's hard enough to explain an unplanned pregnancy to a guy you've got no clue where you stand with him. Nearly impossible to do that and tack on the fact that you're pretty much a whore and slept with two guys within sixteen hours of each other. I decide at some point sitting there on the floor of the bedroom that he needs to know. I can't control how he reacts, but it's not fair to him to leave him in the dark. The longer I wait, the worse it will be.

My nerves are fried by the time I hear the front door unlock and shut behind Kadin. He's returned from his meeting and for the first time since that awkward first morning after I feel mild trepidation at seeing him.

He looks for me the second he gets home, just like he does every day. I have barely enough time to stand from the floor and plaster the best smile I can find before he's in front of me.

"Hey," he says walking into the room. He holds up red and white bags. "I grabbed Chinese. I didn't know if you'd eaten yet."

He's thoughtful, always making sure my needs are met and the realization that I may lose him after I speak the words he may not want to hear almost has me collapsing on the floor again.

"Perfect," I croak. I clear my throat and hope he doesn't ask about my weirdness because even I can tell I'm failing at acting like my normal self. "Let's eat at the table," I offer with a slightly better tone.

I don't know if it is just what I was struggling with or if something else is going on, but Kadin seems skittish and pensive as well. Dinner is spent quietly at the dining room table with little to practically no conversation at all. I decide I'm going to tell him tonight as we lay in bed together, hoping he's more receptive to the news while I'm in his arms.

He tells me he's going to catch up on highlights from tonight's games and heads into the living room. I'm on edge, and he seems to be on edge as well. I don't want to be under the microscope any more than I can imagine he does so I leave it alone and head to the bedroom to change into pajamas.

I'm slipping my t-shirt over my head when I hear a knock at the door. The last time someone knocked on the door it was Savannah's twin Sierra. A chill runs up my spine as I walk to the door. It's cracked and I'm in no form with my pajamas on to see anyone who may come visit him, but I'm curious. I lean in close to the door and listen as Kadin answers.

"I told you not to come here anymore," I hear Kadin say in a hushed tone. "You need to leave."

"I need you, Kadin." That voice. That husky voice filled with seduction makes my heart stop. Sierra.

"We talked about this. You can't come here."

"Is it because of that whore you moved in?" She hisses. "I love you, Kadin. I need you with me, not her!" I can tell just by her tone she's growing agitated.

"Fuck." I hear Kadin grunt in frustration. "Wait down by the damn truck." I hear the door close.

I make it across the room and step into the walk-in closet when I hear the bedroom door open all the way. I stiffen when I feel his arms wrap around me from behind. My heart is pounding in my ears and when he says, "I hate to leave again, but I have something I've got to take care of down at the office." All I can do is nod my head slightly in understanding as he kisses the back of my head and leaves me standing there to go be with Sierra.

Thirty-One

Kadin

I knew the bullshit I pulled after Savannah died was going to come back and bite me in a big way. I also knew I had a million different things to fix and should've started exactly where I ended up tonight rather than just hoping it would go away. I spoke with Sierra on the phone after London told me she stopped by the past week, and she had me convinced that she'd agreed what we'd done in the past was detrimental to both of us and not something we should continue. I hadn't seen her in months until she showed up at the condo tonight.

I got her back to her house without incident which in and of itself is progress where Sierra is concerned.

"I don't understand," she sobs and wipes her nose with a Kleenex.

"We talked about this, Sierra. I'm trying to get my life back on track." I'm doing my best at keeping my calm but we've been at this for over an hour and a half, and all we're doing is talking in circles. I'm growing frustrated which is the last thing that helps with unstable people.

"I love you, Kadin. We can get on track together."

I close my eyes and take a calming breath. "I'm still in your life, Sierra. I'm not going anywhere, but we can't be together like that."

Eventually, she nods in fake understanding. This is how she works. She throws a fit and then when she doesn't get her way she pretends that she's going to act in the way she's expected to. She never does. I excuse myself and leave the room. Firing off a text to her parents explaining they once again needed to come and look after her. I can't keep fighting this battle. Each time she gets this way she ends up hospitalized. Her mother is her Power of Attorney so she'll be the best one to get her into a facility. She's obviously not been taking her medications as prescribed, if at all.

The text comes back immediately that they'll be there shortly. I join Sierra on the couch and play along with her as she talks about mundane stuff like shopping and a class she's thinking about taking at the local community college.

I jump up at the sound of her doorbell close to an hour later and watch her shift gears immediately. She narrows her eyes at me and almost instantly her demeanor changes. I open the front door, and not surprisingly I'm met with both of her parents and two uniformed attendants from the local mental health hospital. We've just about gotten the routine down. Her parents know that if I'm concerned enough to call that they better bring backup when they arrive. The first time we did this without help was pretty nasty.

I stand aside while they go in, and Sierra immediately goes into a rage. I wince as she struggles with the men until she's administered something from a syringe and she calms. Her parents thank me for calling as I exit the house. I sit in my truck and watch as they load Sierra in the back of a dark tinted SUV. Anyone looking at the vehicle would think nothing of it; they'd have no idea that a sedated paranoid schizophrenic is in the back.

I remain in her driveway long after the SUV and her parents' town car pull away. I would ask myself how I got in the middle of all of this mess, but I know exactly when it started. I can still see the train wreck I was the negligent conductor of.

The insistent banging on the door won't stop. I've yelled, cussed, and covered my head with my hands, but the clanging still continues. The only way to go back to the peaceful oblivion I've been pulled from is to get up and tell them to leave, drink another glass of whiskey, and get back on the couch. I pray it's not my mother again. The look of devastation on her face the last time she showed up unannounced is not something I can handle again so soon.

I roll off the couch and stumble to the door. My steps are uneven, and I've got too much booze coursing through my veins to even give a shit. The house is dark, matching my mood perfectly. I haven't left the house since the funeral three weeks ago except to restock the liquor cabinet, and that's only because my family somehow convinced the delivery service to in fact not deliver to me.

I tug open the door ready to rage on whoever dares to knock on my door. I've been more than clear about my desire to not see anyone or speak to anyone. Every thought in my head comes to a grinding halt when my tired eyes land on a sight everything in the universe told me would never happen again.

"Savannah," I gasp. My beautiful wife stands on the other side of the door glowing like a fucking angel with her back lit up from the lights in the hallway. I take an unsure step toward her, fearful if I get too close she'll disappear.

She closes the distance between us. "Kadin," she whispers, and her voice is slightly different than I remembered. The guilt of already forgetting things about her hit me in the chest, and I close my eyes. "No, baby. Stay here with me. Open your eyes."

My lips crash against hers before I can even give it a second thought. I blame the alcohol when they don't feel the same. I blame the time away from her for how different she tastes. I do my best to shove out the knowledge that there's no way my wife is here with her hands on me. She's not the one unzipping my pants and taking my cock out before I can get the door shut, locking us into the condo.

I shove all of that away and wrap my arms around her, picking her up, and walking her back into the living room. I lay her roughly on the couch while greedy hands strip her clothes off, my mouth seeking and finding the tightened bud of her exposed nipple.

Her groan is throaty and deep. "Kadin! Yes, I've wanted this for so long."

I know it's wrong. I know it's one of the things I'll regret the most when it's over, but none of that keeps me from pulling her panties to the side and slamming into my dead wife's twin sister.

I slam my hands against the steering wheel, frustrated with Sierra and the shit she pulled tonight. The anger is displaced. I put myself here and instead of explaining to London what happened I lied to her. Twice. The guilt I felt over Sierra used to be all consuming until the next bottle of whiskey showed up at my door which was consequently always followed by a visit from Sierra.

The times I tried to pull away and tell her it was wrong she'd pretend to be Savannah. Thinking back, I can see now how she's begun to transform herself over the last year and a half. Her hair and clothes have gradually become less her personality and more of Savannah's. I'd put no real effort into stopping it. In my demented mind, I needed her body against mine and the glutton for punishment in me needed the guilt afterward.

My drive back to the condo is accompanied by the revelation that London holds a place in my heart, a place in my future. I'm not in a position where I'm able to determine how much of my heart belongs to her, but she's managed to climb inside and situate herself there. I need her to know and understand that the arrangement we'd agreed to at the cabin is not where I'm at now. She needs to know that I don't see her as just someone to have sex with and if I'm completely honest with myself she never was. She began creeping inside of my soul the second she crossed the threshold of that cabin and confirmed her place when I began thinking more of her smile and less about the pills and gun I brought with me.

My hands begin to shake without warning as I pull into my parking spot in the subterranean garage. The empty spot to the right is an unwelcomed sight; the one that has been occupied by her little red car for the last week. A look at my watch makes the feeling worse. It's after midnight and much too late for her to be out for a store run.

I try to convince myself she just went out for a snack or something as the elevator crawls to my floor. The house is deathly silent, much like it was the day she didn't answer the phone, and I found her curled up on her bed. The thought calms me a bit as I make my way to her room.

The sight I was met with earlier in the week is not the one that greets me now. My first instinct is to reach for my phone and call her, but I know she doesn't have a phone. She got tired of that asshole ex of her calling all the time, so she threw it in the trash on the way back with me last week. With suddenly exhausted legs, I walk in and flip the light on in the closet. Empty. In a panic, I tug the drawers open in the dresser. Empty.

I grip my head in my hands and slowly turn in a slow circle fully taking in the room. There's nothing left of her here. The bathroom is empty as well. Her shampoo is gone. The half empty container of bubble bath we got at that hole in the wall store in Poison is the only thing left on the side of the tub. The counter no longer holds her toothbrush and lotion. Frantically I check the drawers, hoping, praying for just one thing. Something that says she's not gone. One nugget of hope.

What I find instead makes my head spin. My brain goes haywire as I look down at an open box of pregnancy tests. I slowly lift my hand and run my fingers over the top, every possible emotion flooding my body. Gingerly I pick the box up and look inside; one test is missing.

She couldn't be.

I look in the other drawers and the linen closet for the missing test and come up empty. My eyes land on the small trash can on the far side of the toilet. I approach it like the bomb squad would approach an unidentified suitcase in the airport; with uninvited anticipation and trepidation.

I don't even have to reach in to get the news that makes me collapse to my knees on the hard tiled floor. Trembling hands scoop up the positive pregnancy test of their own accord. I hold it in cupped hands and stare at it without seeing anything but the tiny oval screen; everything else fades out in a halo effect.

I stumble to my feet, clutching the test to my chest. I have no idea how I got to the bed or when I lay down, but I find myself curled on my side praying she's just a little freaked out. I close my eyes and beg the universe not to be so cruel as to pull two women from me. That's more than any man should have to suffer through in one lifetime.

Thirty-Two

London

It's been several days since I packed my things in a rush and left Kadin's condo. The first twenty-four hours were spent sobbing uncontrollably, feeling sorry for myself for once again having blind faith that I was enough for a man I care for.

Love.

I know that irrevocably. I love him. I can't even deny it. I tried; it was impossible. I may not be able to control my heart but I can control my actions, and I refuse to stay in a situation where I don't come first. Grief is one thing; competing with the ghost of his wife was hard enough. I have no desire to remain in a setting where my other competition is the exact, and all too real, replica of that ghost.

I could've stayed and let him explain. I could've listened to the excuses he would've used to explain away his blatant lie. But, I didn't.

I swore to myself when Trent carried my bloody body away from Brian's abuse that'd I'd stop making excuses for other people's issues. That's why I walked away without looking back from Trent and why I couldn't stay for Kadin either. Before crashing into Kadin's life, I knew I needed to focus on myself and find a way to be happy without the requirement of other people. Even with that knowledge, I still clung to Kadin like an emergency tether in a storm.

I plan to stay in Spokane. The city is big enough never to run into Kadin. I've poured over the classified ads and found a small two bedroom home on the opposite side of town from him so chances are slim he'll ever have to see me again. I have an appointment to meet with the owner to check it out and talk about the lease this weekend. I've also managed to snag an appointment with an OB/GYN for late Friday. I need confirmation of the pregnancy even though everything I read online says at-home tests are very accurate, and each of the six I've taken all indicate that I am.

I'm coming to grips with the idea even though I'm terrified beyond belief about not only being on my own but doing it as a single mother. I remember Kadin telling me that Savannah didn't want kids. He responded that he wanted Savannah when I'd asked him what he thought about kids. I have to keep reminding myself that Trent is just as possibly the father as Kadin is, but it's obvious what my preference is right now. The last thing I want is to see Trent much less spend the next two decades in each other's lives because of a child.

The week has been incredibly successful. My doctor appointment yesterday confirmed the pregnancy, and I found myself hoping for it to be true as I waited for the lab work to be completed. I also got an email and an interview request for today.

I tap my foot on the floor as I sit in the waiting room of Bland & Pratt, an attorney's office. I'm interviewing for a personal assistant position and can't help but think about the job that Kadin offered me. This will be different on so many levels.

"London Sykes?" a middle-aged woman in a dark blue, sharp looking business suit asks from a doorway at the far end of the reception area.

I look up and plaster the biggest smile I can muster. "That's me," I answer and stand to greet her open hand with my own.

"I'm Theresa Gilson with human resources. I'll be conducting your interview this morning."

"Nice to meet you, Ms. Gilson," I answer.

"Just Theresa," she says with a smile and my nerves are instantly calmed. "Follow me, please." She walks with purpose down a long hallway and turns left down another hall when it ends at a huge office.

Just as I reach the turn to follow her, the dark, solid wood door pulls open, and a hulk of a man stands inside the frame. I nod my head slightly, whisper good morning, and continue to follow Theresa to her office.

She waits for me to enter before closing us into her comfortable office. Sitting down at her desk, she restacks an already perfect stack of papers as I take a seat in the chair directly in front of her desk.

"I want to say right off the bat I was very impressed with your resume." I smile at her. "The fact that you've been a PA before is a huge plus. You're interviewing for Mr. Bland today. Do you know anything about Bland & Platt?"

"I'm sorry; I don't. I've only just moved to Spokane." I shift slightly in my seat, suddenly nervous about why it seems I'd need to know about the organization prior to getting the job. I immediately wonder if he's horrible to work for. "Is that a problem?" I ask trying to judge her reaction.

"Not at all. He's just really known here in the city." She shifts her eyes down to the papers on her desk, and I can tell she didn't mean anything by her question. Now it seems more like small talk than the ominous warning from before.

We go through the basic interview questions. I answer appropriately telling from the smile on her face. Next we shift gears to the benefits package and schedules.

"Mr. Bland keeps a pretty basic schedule. Most, if not all, of his appointments, are kept here at the office. There may be an occasional lunch you'd need to attend, but that is, of course, an exception to the everyday routine."

I nod my head as she continues to speak about holidays, vacation pay, and insurance.

I paid out of pocket for the doctor's office visit yesterday, grateful he had an in-house lab rather than having to go to the hospital to have the bloodwork done. The latter would have cost an arm and a leg.

Deciding I need to be one hundred percent honest with anyone I interview with I asked a question that may have me shot straight out the door. "Do you know what kind of coverage there is for preexisting conditions?"

She tilts her head slightly to the side. "Like diabetes?"

"Pregnancy," I answer quietly.

"When are you due?" Her demeanor has changed slightly as she cuts her eyes to my stomach.

"In the fall," I reply.

I see her look at my left hand before asking her next question. "You're not covered on your husband's insurance?"

I hold my head as high as I can. "I'm not married."

She restacks the papers again, tapping the small pile repeatedly. "We have supplemental insurance, but I'm almost certain that your condition won't be covered under that either."

Somehow my perfect resume means absolutely nothing because I'm having a baby. I knew I'd get some looks and possibly snide remarks when I started showing, but I never thought it would start so close to me finding out.

"That's okay. I can manage without it." *Like I have a choice.*

Her face twists in mild disgust. "Well, Ms. Sykes I'll review your application." She emphasizes Ms. as if it's now a filthy word.

Her phone rings before I can stand from my seat. I know I need to go, but I don't want to be rude even though it's obvious I'll still be looking for a job after I leave here. I can only hear her side of the conversation.

"Hello."

"Yes, sir."

"Very well, until," she cuts her eyes at me and I know instinctually that the conversation is somehow about me.

"No, sir."

"Of course, sir."

She hangs up the phone, and she's practically dripping with disdain. "Are you able to start Monday?"

I nearly fall out of my seat at her words. It leaves me speechless, and I stare at her and back to the phone she just cradled the handpiece on.

"Well?" She says, even more, annoyed. I want to ask her who was on the phone, but I'm not going to push my luck.

"Sure. Yes. Of course." I'm grinning from ear to ear at the fact that something is finally going right in my life.

"See you then," she huffs and turns her attention to her computer screen effectively dismissing me.

I get up and see myself out. She's got a major attitude and some serious issues with me being pregnant, but I'll be Mr. Bland's PA not hers. Hopefully, that means my interactions with her will be very limited.

The next day the luck continued when I signed a six-month lease on a cute little two bedroom cottage. I may not still be living here when the baby is born, but the second room is perfect for a nursery if I am. It comes furnished, so that was a huge selling point for me.

The woman renting the home, unlike Ms. Gilson, had no concern for me being pregnant without being married. I think she likes the idea actually, presumably because pregnant women aren't going to throw parties and damage property. She did ask if I anticipated problems with the baby's father and seemed satisfied when I told her there was no chance of that.

The house was move-in ready, so I got keys the second I signed the lease agreement. In a matter of hours, I was comfortably situated in my very own rented home, on my own for the very first time in my life. I have all day tomorrow to stock the kitchen and buy the odds and ends that accompany moving into a new place for the first time.

I spend that night the same way I'd spent every night this week, crying myself to sleep and wishing Kadin had never lied to me, wishing I were enough. As much as things are looking up with the house and job my heart is still shattered. It feels like this time it's much worse than any time before. I reason with myself that it's because this last heartbreak happened before my heart was healed from Trent's betrayal. The truth is my feelings for Kadin are solely what makes it almost unbearable.

No amount of praying has brought her back. The hours spent driving all over town have remained fruitless. I am; however, fully stocked on anger, sadness, and guilt. I've spent the last week recollecting as much detail from each one of our conversations as possible, picking them apart. I tried to determine what I may have said or how I may have reacted that would cause her to think leaving after finding out that she's pregnant is the best thing.

It's taken days and more patience than I thought it would to track down the bar that her ex-Trent works at. As I sit in the parking lot of the bar, I close my eyes for a brief second. I'm exhausted, having spent most nights wrapped in the covers on her bed, tossing and turning with sleep remaining elusive.

I've done my best to keep up my end of the agreement with the board, running on steam most days at the office; which is still a vast improvement over my days there before my trip to the cabin. Before London.

My boots crunch over the gravel of a nearly empty parking lot. As much as I need to see her again I'm glad her car isn't one of the five parked out front. She was adamant about this chapter of her life being closed, but this asshole is the only other connection I have to her.

I pull the heavy door open and walk across the sticky floor to the bar. A man, who looks questionably old enough to drink himself, is behind the bar loading beer into the in-counter ice chest, obviously gearing up for Saturday night patrons.

He sees me approach and wipes his hands on a bar towel before speaking. "We don't open for another half hour, man." *Not the most aware businessman is he?*

"I need to see Trent." He doesn't say a word just walks away from the bar and through a door to the left.

I turn my back to the bar and look around. It's nothing special, just a slightly rundown, not quite clean hole in the wall.

"Can I help you?" I turn towards the voice and want to laugh, and then cuss London and her choice of men.

A tall, skinny man with almost white hair and freakishly, clear blue eyes approaches me with his hand out. *Not today fucker.* I cross my arms over my chest, a clear indication I'm not here as his friend.

"When was the last time you heard from, London?" I all but growl. I hope he's just as aware of the hate in my voice as I am.

He switches gears from shitty business man to apparent enemy instantly. My lip twitches at the corner satisfied that I can get him riled with just one simple question.

He looks me up and down, clearly evaluating the situation before he responds. I'm waiting to see if he's as dumb as he fucking looks.

"Who are you?" He finally asks. The fact that he answers my question with a question of his own rubs me the wrong way. I take a step closer to him, and his eyes widen slightly and he takes a small step backward. Not a complete idiot it seems. "You're the guy who answered her phone aren't you?"

I see a girl walk through the same door that Trent just came from. I'd put money on her as being Keira, the friend London said she caught fucking Trent. The flush in her cheeks and the dishevelment of her hair scream post-sex.

"That's not important. When was the last time you saw London?" I've lowered my voice and can hardly manage to keep the growl out of it, this time, growing more agitated as each second passes.

"Weeks ago. What's it to you?" I sneer at him, and he takes another step back, colliding with the slut who's slinked up beside him, placing a possessive hand on his back.

He looks at her with disdain, but she's too busy raking her eyes down my body. *Not interested skank. Move on.*

"That didn't take long," I say nodding at the contact between them.

Trent takes a quick step away from Keira, and her face falls.

Satisfied that he hasn't seen or heard from her since she left three weeks ago, I begin to turn to the door.

Finally growing a pair of balls at the sight of my back, he crosses a line I don't tolerate. "What did she do? Fuck you and run?"

I don't even think before I close the distance between us, swing my arm back, and pop him in the fucking nose. He splays back half lying on the table behind him. Keira is trying to help him up, but he continues to shove her away.

I strode to the door, incredibly satisfied with the slight throb I feel across my knuckles. Just before stepping outside I turn back to them. "You know," I say. "I should thank both of you. You sent her right into my arms." I point at Trent. "You are a fucking idiot for downgrading from London to that." I shift the direction of my finger to the woman who's wide-eyed and unsure of her station.

He keeps his mouth shut but I watch him cut his eyes from me to Keira, and I can see the awareness in his eyes. He's very cognizant of what he lost and clearly regretting his choices.

On my long drive back to Spokane, I'm antsy. There was no reason to get a hotel room in Great Falls even though driving straight through will put me back home early in the morning. I wouldn't have slept even if I wanted to.

I drive by the entrance to the cabin's property near midnight and have no desire to stop. I'm not a fan of the pain in my chest and walking into that cabin, where every night I spent there was with London, would kill me. I hate feeling helpless. I hate not being able to find her.

I'm not even sure what I'd tell her if I saw her again. What kind of promises can I make to her? I regret canceling the appointment with the therapist. I could use the fact that London left as the reason, but I'm not certain I was going to keep it to begin with, so it's not fair to place any of the blame on her.

I have nothing to offer her if she would've stayed. Financial support is about all I can manage right now. I'm disgusted with myself when I realize that her leaving may be the best thing to happen. I'm in no position to be a father. I can hardly deal with my own life much less the responsibility of raising a baby.

She's better off alone than even further wrapped up in my shit. I lose the battle I've been fighting furiously since she left as the thought that she may choose not to have the baby creeps into my mind. She never put off vibes that she was purposely trying to get pregnant, so it had to of been a big surprise to her as well. Raising a child on her own could be daunting enough that she'd choose not to. I slam my hands on the steering wheel.

It's at that exact moment that I realize I want the baby. As unexpected and horribly timed as it is I can't even stomach the idea of her aborting our child. I drive through the city as the first sign of the dawn is peeking in my rearview mirror with renewed determination to be a better man on the off chance that she comes back and gives me the opportunity to be a father.

Thirty-Four

London

I've been at Bland & Platt for a couple of weeks now, and I can say that I actually love this job. I found out on the first day of work that the bulky man I'd seen standing in the doorway on my way to Ms. Gilson's office was my new boss Justin Bland. He and his best friend Hawthorne Platt, Hawke as he preferred to be called, started this firm right out of law school and have turned it into one of the most lucrative corporate law firms in the city.

My last personal assistant job required me to fetch coffee and dry cleaning and such, which is what I thought I'd be doing here as well. I think I'd only used the skills I'd learned in college a handful of times at that job. Gladly I was wrong. I'm not running errands and being bossed around the office like a slave; rather I'm managing Justin's day, planning his trips, and serving a purpose as more than just a glorified hood ornament. I record minutes in important meetings and make sure accommodations for clients are up to the standard the firm has set.

I've somehow managed to find a job I can take pride in; one I actually enjoy and can look forward to each day rather than being bitter and angry. That doesn't mean that my hormones aren't all over the place because they are.

Along with the emotional roller coaster I ride every day without choice is the sheer exhaustion. I've spoken with Justin about the baby, and he's given me no indication that he has an issue with it. If anything he's supportive and attentive to my needs, that and he's an awful flirt.

I can admit that Justin Bland is an incredibly handsome man and whatever woman finally lands him will be incredibly lucky. He's caring, intelligent, and sex appeal drips off of him by the gallons. Unfortunately, he's not Kadin. It's almost like my heart has instructed my brain and body not to respond to anyone but him.

"You look lovely today, London," Justin says I set his weekly schedule on his desk.

I smile at him. Most people would be offended or find his compliments offensive, but I don't; I look forward to them honestly. He's always respectful in what he says and never crosses the line into creeper territory.

"I don't feel like I look lovely, but thank you, Justin."

"Sick again?" he asks as he scrunches up his nose.

"Every day this week," I admit sitting in the chair across from his desk so we can go over his schedule and make the appropriate changes if need be.

He opens the desk drawer to his right and pulls out a large bag of cookies, setting them on the desk in front of me. "I grabbed these for you this weekend. My sister swore by ginger snap cookies when she was pregnant with my nephew. I figured they might work for you as well."

"That's incredibly sweet." I say and reach for the bag. "Why is it a woman hasn't been able to snag you up yet?" I say it as a joke, but I can tell by the look on his face that he's taken me seriously.

"I have incredibly high standards, London. Not many women can meet them." He smiles brightly at me as if he's just realized something and can't wait to share it. "Go to dinner with me."

I open my planner to the week's schedule. "Which client will we be meeting? Would you know of cuisine preferences?"

When he doesn't answer I look back up at him, his penetrating eyes are holding mine hostage.

"Not to woo a client, London. Dinner. Just you and me." He looks uncharacteristically nervous.

"We can't do that, Justin," I answer.

"You're seeing someone." It's a statement, not a question.

I smile weakly without a clue how to even avoid the topic of not dating and why. "I'm not available." Sadness clutches me, and I furrow my brows at the knowledge that I'm pining over a guy who isn't even in the equation anymore. Furthermore, I question his sanity for wanting to get involved with a pregnant woman when he's just expressed how high his standards are. No man in this day and age should want a ready-made family.

"Is he in prison?" Justin offers like it's the only other possibly explanation for my dinner refusal.

I laugh uncontrollably for several long moments before I can respond to him. Finally managing to look up at him I see the confusion he had on his face when he asked the ridiculous question has transformed into amusement at my response, indicative by the smirk he's giving me.

"*He* is *not* in prison, and we're not together either. I just have too much emotional stuff going on to get involved with anyone right now." Admitting that out loud is sobering to my previously cheerful mood.

"It's just dinner, London," he says quietly without losing the smile from his face.

I study him and after a while I decide just to lay everything on the table. "Just dinner?" I emphasize. "So you're saying you have no other interests in me than feeding me a meal?"

His face falls. "I'm not saying that at all." That's what I thought.

"I'm not dating right now," I say as I stand and scoop the bag of cookies off of the desk.

"But when you start?" He prods.

"You'll be the first to know." I wink at him and leave his office.

"I won't stop asking," he says to my retreating back.

"What do you mean you turned him down," Jillian scoffs even though she has a mouth full of food.

Jillian is Hawthorne Pratt's personal assistant and we made fast friends the first time we met after I started working at the firm. She's bubbly and always in a good mood and exactly what I need most days to pull me out of the self-pity that always seems to want to consume me.

I take a sip of water to help wash my last bite down before responding. "He asked me to dinner, and I told him I couldn't."

"Yes, London. I heard that part. What confuses me is why in the hell did you do it?" I shrug my shoulders in response, unwilling to go too far in-depth about my past.

Suffice it to say I have major trust issues. I had them long before the whole Trent and Keira situation, and now they've grown exponentially after Kadin. I see keeping at a distance emotionally from people as a means of mandatory self-preservation, knowing my heart couldn't take any more disappointment.

"You realize he's perfect boyfriend material right?" She's put her fork down, and I have her now undivided attention.

"I guess. I don't know him that well." I continue to eat even though my stomach is in knots. I don't know if it's the direction the conversation is heading or if my morning sickness is going to ruin another meal.

"Well, I've been working here for past six years, and I've only seen him with one girlfriend and that woman did something that pretty much ruined his view on all other women."

I lean forward in my chair. "What did she do?" I hate knowing someone hurt him but haven't we all been hurt? I see this as the perfect opportunity to turn the spotlight off of myself and put it on someone else even though I hate gossip. Unfortunately, Jillian is not easily distracted.

"That's not the point I'm trying to make. Besides, no one really knows what happened. All I know is it didn't end well, and he hasn't really dated since. That was five years ago, London."

I keep my eyes focused on her but don't say anything to encourage the conversation. "Ugh," she huffs in frustration. "My point is, for the first time that I know of in forever he's interested in someone. He's interested in *you*."

She picks her fork up and begins to eat again like she just solved the hardest problem in physics and should be rewarded for her observations.

"Okay? He's interested in me, but I'm not dating. It's not just him. I have no desire to get involved with anyone. Sadly, that includes Justin," I answer and continue to eat as well.

"I wish I had your willpower," she mutters before taking another bite of her salad.

I'd ask her what she meant by that, but I know digging into her past opens the door for her to attempt to do the same with mine. Not that it's stopped her in the past, but it's a can of worms I'd rather not open right now.

"What are your plans this weekend?" She asks thankfully switching gears into safer territory.

Certain 'crying myself to sleep and feeling sorry for myself while missing a man I love but can't have' wouldn't be the best thing to say, I shrug my shoulders. "Probably going to hit a few estate sales if I can find them. I'm looking for a few more things for the cottage."

"How old are you, London? Sixty?" She laughs. "You should go to the club with us this weekend."

I don't even want to know who *us* is. "I'm twenty-six, but I'm also pregnant. So going to the club isn't the best idea."

She gives me a strange look. "You can go to the club while you're pregnant. You're not even showing, and I'm not saying go on a bender. Drink water and have a good time dancing. You need to get out of that tiny house you live in and have some fun."

The idea still isn't appealing to me even though I know now she won't judge me for still having some sort of life even though in eight months I'll be responsible for two instead of one.

"I'll think about it," I placate her and finish eating my lunch.

I can't decide if I want to get my mind on something else by going out and forgetting about my troubles if even for a short time; or if I want to continue to bathe in the heartache that engulfs me every time I don't have something else to distract me.

Thirty-Five

Kadin

Weeks. London has been gone for weeks, and I wish I could say that I'm in a better place. I wish I could, but I can't. The only thing I have done besides wallow in grief over my deceased wife and the girl that got away is start therapy.

I thought going back to the same therapist I saw shortly after the accident would keep me from having to talk about, in detail, the events leading up to my desperate need for professional help. I was wrong. I was seeing Dr. Long twice a week in the beginning but the emotional turmoil I was in after each visit wasn't something I could continue to do to myself, so we dropped it down to one agonizing day per week. When I say agonizing I mean I pay her double to see me on Saturdays, so I have Sunday to try to get back to some semblance of normal before work on Monday.

I could barely function the first week I saw her, which left me wondering if I was going to shift back to prior coping mechanisms. Needless to say, the very next visit was spent more on how to deal with the bombardment of emotions and less with the subject matter causing the distress. So now I work-out until muscle fatigue every night, hoping for a few hours of sleep as a result.

"Are you ready to talk about Sierra?" Dr. Long asks.

I shift my weight in my chair, uncomfortable with anything pertaining to Sierra but knowing I have to deal with it at some point. With everything that's happened most of my shame revolves around what Sierra and I've done.

"Now's as good a time as any I guess." I crack my neck preparing for her battery of questions, reminding myself to answer openly and honestly because that's the only way this works.

"Have you heard from her?" She asks keeping in safe territory to begin with, easing me into the topic I despise the most.

"No. She's still hospitalized. I spoke with her mother last week. They can't find the right mix of medicine to keep her leveled out."

"But when she gets out?" She prods gently.

"When she gets out, she'll be right back at my door. Expecting…" I trail off even though I know she won't allow it. She remains silent, so eventually I continue, "She'll expect to pick up right where things were left off before I went to the cabin. If I know her, she'll pretend like her last breakdown didn't happen. She'll act like I didn't tell her we couldn't continue."

She waits silently again and stubbornly I remain quiet.

"Couldn't continue what, Kadin?" This is how she works and although it's been extremely helpful in the past it's a rough time getting to the end.

"Pretending," I tell her.

I wake up on the floor of my condo, my head throbbing from the obscene amount of whiskey I drank last night. I groan and curse my existence as I roll over on the carpet that only feels soft under your feet but grows unbearably inflexible when you lay on it if for several hours.

I don't want to open my eyes. I don't want to accept what I did last night. I know it happened even though the details are blurry and almost ungraspable, skating on the very edge of lucid thought. I pray she's gone, but I know she's not. I can hear her breathing deeply beside me. I can feel the slender arm she has thrown over my waist.

I try to slip out from underneath our connection but stiffen when she mumbles something in her sleep. If this seemed like a bad idea last night, I can't even begin to explain how atrocious of a choice it is in the full light of day.

While contemplating how to handle the situation and coming up empty, my hand is forced into action. "Good morning." Her voice is soft and hopeful.

This is the last woman I'd ever want to hurt. Savannah adored her sister, and no doubt would be very disappointed with what I've done. Not only did I sleep with her sister but my actions may compromise her delicate mental health.

"Hey," I respond and climb to my feet.

I wrap a throw blanket around my waist and hand one to her, hoping she'll follow my lead and cover up. She doesn't, and I can tell by the glimmer in her eye she's trying to entice me, but all I feel when I look at her is regret and shame. Even though she and Savannah were identical twins, to me, they are worlds apart. A man knows his wife like the back of his hand and this woman is most definitely not my wife.

I knew that last night. I knew it when my hands touched her when my mouth tasted her, but I still followed through and used Sierra. If I wasn't going to hell before, I sure as shit am now.

"Listen, Sierra," I begin.

"Don't," she pleads and climbs onto the couch to sit beside me.

I do my best not to wince when she runs her fingers through my unruly hair and kiss my shoulder.

"We can't do this again, Sierra. I'm sorry I let it get so far last night." I tell her even though what I want to say is: "Please don't have a breakdown in my living room. I can hardly deal with my own shit, let alone someone else's even though I created this situation."

She sits quietly for a minute, her hand continuing its stroking along my back.

"You called me Savannah," she whispers. I squeeze my eyes tight wishing I had a bottle of Jack Daniels in front of me. "I can pretend to be her. If that's what you need."

My eyes go wide, and I scoot away from her, breaking our connection. She grins at me. I discovered a long time ago that Sierra finds amusement in the most uncomfortable things. "I was drunk," I explain, even though we both know that's no excuse.

She stands from the couch and begins to get dressed, and I'm grateful for her intentions to leave. Once fully dressed she stands in front of me until I lift my eyes to hers. "So then drink, Kadin." She bends down and kisses my head like a mother would a child and leaves my condo. The click of the door closing behind her rattles around in my head for hours, until the bottle of whiskey I put in my system, silences it.

"How long has this continued?" Dr. Long asks as I finish explaining just how the chaos got started between Sierra and me.

"It wasn't an ongoing thing. It happened five, maybe six, times. Sierra spends most of her time in and out of psych wards so there were long periods where it wasn't even possible." I explain.

"Did you ever seek her out?" I shake my head no. "How did it happen then?"

I scrub my hands over the top of my head before openly admitting my weaknesses. "A bottle of whiskey would be delivered to my door. Later that night it would be followed by a visit from her."

"And each time she pretended to be Savannah?" I nod. "And each time you let her?" I nod again and hang my head in shame.

The rest of that session was spent on ways to finally let go of the grief I felt over Savannah's death and giving a voice to the shame and coming to terms with it. Dr. Long emphasized that I'd not be able to move on until those two things were accomplished. She reminded me that I'd always love Savannah and moving on from the idea of a future that is no longer an option doesn't mean I forget her.

"You think it's time for me to let her go?" I'm trying my best not to let my anger bubble over. The doctor means well, but frankly she's not the one dealing with the loss of a spouse.

"I'm not saying 'let her go' Kadin. I'm telling you it's time to start moving on. You won't heal until you do." Her voice is firm and shows no sign of pity, of which I'm grateful. I've had my fair share of pity for both myself and my family. I can't stomach another ounce of it.

That particular conversation is on a constant loop inside my head. It sounds simple enough, but every time I make a plan to follow through with goals we set while in session, I always find a reason not to. Then the next week's session begins reviewing what we discussed the week prior. I've reached an expert level on reasons and excuses for why I haven't done the things I agreed to try the week before. Work is too hectic; I've been spending more time with my family, etc.

I've got reasons for days when the truth is the idea of packing Savannah's things from the home we share physically makes me sick. Dr. Long says keeping her side of the closet like it was when she left it, along with her things in the bathroom and shower, is detrimental to my recovery. Recovery. That's what she calls this since my sudden turn into alcoholism after the accident is always a consideration of hers.

She reminds me weekly that getting rid of all but a few mementos will help the healing process along much quicker. I know she's fully aware of what her request means. She said she'd offer to come over and help me, but she knows it's something I have to do on my own. It's exactly what I repeated to Kegan when I mentioned what she wanted me to do, and he offered to help.

There's no reasoning I can find in keeping her clothes in the closet or the blazer on the chair she carelessly tossed aside the morning of her death because she found a snag on the sleeve. I can't voice one sane reason why her toothbrush is beside mine or why her face cream, even though it is now dried out because she left the lid off, is still on the bathroom counter. What I can admit to is not being ready to see it all gone; not having the strength to let her go.

I've spent eighteen months rolling around in my grief, torturing myself with it every chance I got. Feeling remorse and derision if I caught myself smiling or showed the slightest hint of moving on became a pastime I frequently sought.

I haven't breathed a word about London to Dr. Long. I didn't mention that I have felt happiness; no matter how short-lived it was, since Savannah passed away. I've not mentioned how I'm not grieving the loss of just one woman but struggling at the deprivation of two. There is no reasoning behind leaving that little nugget of information out other than feeling the need to deal with one thing at a time.

Thirty-Six

London

"What excuse are you going to come up with this weekend?" I gasp at the sudden intrusion into my work.

I turn to look at Jillian and find her standing in the doorway of my office. I complete the email I was working on as she settles in the chair across from me, making herself at home like she always does.

I know exactly what she's asking because it's been the same thing week after week, but I play coy just because it riles her up. "I don't know what you're talking about, Jillian. Please elaborate." I smile at her innocently and playfully bat my eyes at her.

"Cut the shit, London. I won't let you turn me down this weekend. You're going out with us."

She crosses her arms over her chest like a petulant child, and it makes me laugh. Even though she's only a few months younger than I am our maturity levels are years apart, and she proves it every chance she gets. I envy her carefreeness, knowing it means she's not been tainted by the cruel world. I hope she never is.

I've run out of excuses, so I go with as much shock value as I can. I know she's already gearing up to give me the riot act about being so young and sitting at home just like she does every week when she's trying to guilt me into going out. "Sounds like fun. Can't wait."

"You say that every damn...wait. What?" She looks confused, and I smile.

"I said," I speak slowly pretending she's hard of hearing just to annoy her. "Sounds like fun. I can't wait."

She narrows her eyes at me. "Are you fucking with me?"

I chuckle. "No. I'll go out. But no seedy ass bars with cigarette smoke. That I can't handle."

"Only the best for you, London." She claps her hands together like a preteen and stands from her seat. "I'll be at your house at six on Saturday so we can get ready together."

I groan but nod my head in agreement. "I can hardly wait," I say flatly as she leaves my office.

The second she's out of earshot I laugh quietly again. I'm actually looking forward to getting out for a change. My morning sickness seems to be subsiding, so I'm not as fearful of getting sick as I have been the last couple of weeks.

"Who exactly are we meeting?" I ask as we valet her car at *Prime*, a club she's assured me is the best of the best.

"You know," she shrugs her shoulders in a very unlike Jillian manor. "Just a few people from work."

I glare at her as we make our way into the club, waiting to interrogate her until after we clear security and find a table.

Walking side by side deeper into the club I finally reach out and grab her arm. "Jillian there is only a handful of people who work at that office. Please don't tell me you invited…"

"London," I hear a familiar voice say before I can finish my plea with Jillian.

"Justin," I say in greeting as well as completing my sentence directed at my soon to be ex-friend. "So nice to see you outside of work."

I reach out to shake his hand, suddenly awkward in the situation and not knowing what to do. He takes my hand rather than shaking it; he brushes a soft kiss on the top.

He's remained mostly professional at work; except for the occasional requests for dinner since our conversation about being emotionally unavailable. Things weren't weird between us until the last sixty seconds.

"I ordered you water with lime," he offers, remembering my drink order the handful of times we've been out with clients.

I thank him and take a seat on the high stool he's pulled out in offering. Jillian talks to Hawke and ignores me even though I'm shooting her daggers in my mind. This is the kind of thing she does. She always feels like her interventions will help people along, and they end up backfiring.

I don't even want to talk about what happened last week at lunch when she tried to set the guy in line ahead of us at the coffee shop up with the barista. Things were going great between them until his wife came out of the restroom and caught him flirting with another woman. Needless to say, she's got no clue what other people need romantically even though she continues to interject herself in other people's love lives like some deranged cupid with a broken bow n arrow.

"Are you here under duress as well?" I ask Justin as I sip my water and watch as Jillian strangely flirts with her boss.

"No," he says with a playful smile. "I'm here because Jillian said you guys were going out and thought Hawke and I should join you."

"Did she?" I say and cut my eyes to her. "Would you be surprised if I told you that I had no idea you'd be here, and she's set me up?"

His smile gets bigger before he answers. He looks over at Jillian and then back to me. "Not surprised one bit. I've known Jillian for a while, and this seems like something right up her alley."

"Yep," I answer.

"It's not the first time she's pulled this with me so if we're doing the full disclosure thing I have to admit that I had an idea it's what she was doing again tonight."

"Yet you came anyway? Why is that?"

"I knew it was you she was trying to set me up with." He holds a hand up effectively stopping my response. "I know where you stand, London and I'm not trying to infiltrate myself further into your life, but heaven help me, I couldn't turn down a chance to see you outside of the office."

I just glare at him, even though I'm not really that upset.

He raises an eyebrow at me. "I won't apologize for it," he says and winks at me. "Want to dance?" He asks holding his hand out as the DJ begins to play a popular, fast-paced song.

I should say no, just because I don't want him to get the wrong idea or read too much into it, but instead I jump off the stool and place my hand on his. I love to dance, and I haven't done it in months. I vow right then to start doing more things that make me happy.

We dance for what seems like hours. By the time I make it off the dance floor, I'm so sweaty it's embarrassing.

"That was great," I say patting the sweat off of my face and arms with a cocktail napkin.

"I agree!" Justin says while flagging down a waitress. "Water?"

"Yes, please."

"Are you glad you came tonight?" He asks as the waitress leaves to retrieve our drinks. I notice he's drinking water also.

I grin from ear to ear. "I really am!" I sway in my seat to another favorite song of mine as it rumbles through the packed club.

The waitress gets our drinks lightning fast, and I gulp almost all of mine down before she even walks away.

I grin at Justin and in a very unladylike manner wipe my mouth with the back of my hand. I freeze instantly when I realize that I've grown so used to being around him over the last few weeks I don't even pay attention to appropriate mannerisms anymore. The thought sends a chill up my spine because I was the same way with Kadin. I quickly push the thought out of my head.

"Want to go somewhere we can chat?" He points to one of the loud speakers nearby. "Can't really hear anything right here."

I raise an eyebrow at him. "Let me guess? Your place?"

His eyes widen, and he holds his hands up in mock surrender. "London, I'm not the type of guy to do that sort of thing." He points to a staircase that leads to a balcony on the back wall. "I was thinking more along the lines of VIP."

I automatically feel like shit for assuming that all of a sudden he would turn into a douche that thought a few dances meant I suddenly had a change of heart. I know him better than that, but I still jumped to the wrong conclusion first. When did I become the person who stopped trusting everyone? *About the same time everyone you trusted betrayed you,* my brain reminds me.

I give him a look of apology and place my hand in his, allowing him to guide me through the crowded room to the staircase. A quick nod to the security guard is all it takes for them to unclip the velvet cord and allow us to past. It seems Justin is well known here, which I find surprising since Jillian says he doesn't date.

Just because he doesn't date doesn't mean he doesn't fuck. This is the twenty-first century, I remind myself.

The chaos from down below doesn't quite reach the half-moon shaped lounging area Justin chooses for us to sit in. A waitress provides drink services almost before we have time to sit down.

"You must come here a lot," I say nodding toward the guy at the rope as he turns a couple of inebriated guys away.

"Not really," He answers and thanks the waitress as she hands him two more iced glasses of water, one with lime.

I take mine from him. "Must come around enough that you don't have to bribe anyone to get into the VIP section."

He laughs loudly, throwing his head back. I smirk because I just can't help it and he's quite enduring when he's this animated. "The guy at the rope," he says pointing at the security guard who let us up here. "That's my cousin Anthony. I called him earlier and begged him not to give me shit if I came up here with a pretty girl."

"Seriously?" I shake my head slightly. "Why wouldn't you just let me believe you were popular enough just to breeze past him? Why tell me your trade secrets?"

I watch his eyes with amusement and look down when I feel him take my hand, resting the combination on my knee.

"Two reasons, London. First, I don't want you to get the idea that I run around and go trolling for women so often that the bouncer at a club knows me." He pauses, and I blink up at him, amazed at his sincerity. "Secondly, I'll never lie to you. Ask me a question and I'll always tell you the truth, even if it's something you don't want to hear or may cause you pain."

I look down as his thumb casually rubs circles on the back of my hands. "Not a very good trait for a lawyer is it?" I chide.

"What's that?" He asked distractedly.

"Not being willing to lie." I raise my eyes back to him and notice the change in his. They're softer, more inviting if that's even possible considering how kind and thoughtful he's been since day one.

"Can I kiss you, London?" He asks softly already moving on from the previous conversation.

I gasp. "I can't, Justin. I'm just not…" I trail off because I feel like shit.

"Available. I know. Can't blame a guy for trying." He releases my hand and grabs for his water, moving slightly to give me some much-needed space. I wait for him to turn into an asshole. I wait for him to accuse me of being a cock-tease, all of the things Brian did leading up to the first time he raped me. I know when I get home I'll analyze every word we've spoken tonight, every action of mine to determine at what point the gears shifted leading us into the direction.

He never becomes that person. Not once does he even hint or insinuate I'm a horrible person for dancing with him, spending time with him, and yet still refuse to move past the friendship that we have. It makes me curse the past men in my life even more, knowing if it wasn't for the heartbreak and pain they've caused I wouldn't be one hundred percent on board the Justin Train.

"So I can ask you anything?" I ask playfully and smile when he turns his head from watching the writhing crowd down below back to me.

"I'm an open book." I'd ask him about the woman Jillian mentioned weeks ago but once again I don't want to open a door he'll expect me also to walk through after he's shared his sob story.

Instead, I keep it safe and ask something that's niggled in my head since I first walked into Brand & Platt. "When I came in for my interview with Ms. Gilson, did you call her while I was still in the office?"

His smile answers my question, but he verbalizes it anyway. "Yes."

"You know she was about to kick me out of her office don't you? She had no intentions of hiring me once she found out I was pregnant." I can't even hide the disdain in my voice if I wanted to.

He grins sadly. "That's Ms. Gilson," he sighs. "She can't have children and pretty much hates any woman who can. She's bitter to say the least."

"She's rude," I add.

"Well, it's a good thing I called then, huh?" He winks at me, and I smile at his continued flirting.

Apparently Jillian had no intentions of hanging out with us tonight. She and Hawke disappeared sometime after Justin and I hit the dance floor because I didn't' see her again after that. I make a mental note to bitch her out first thing Monday morning and refuse to ever go out with her again.

I can't deny I had a great time tonight. But I don't know how awkward things are going to be Monday morning.

Justin insisted on driving me home and walking to my door even though technically the evening wasn't a date. He assures me my car will be waiting for me in the morning, and he'll drop my keys in the mail slot. I know he doesn't read it that way either, and he's a gentleman all of the time, not just tonight.

"Thanks for coming out tonight," he says as we reach my front door. "I had a great time." He holds open the screen door as I find the right key and unlock it.

"I did too," I reply honestly.

I turn to tell him goodbye and close my eyes briefly when I find him only inches from my face. I feel his finger trace my jawline from my ear to my chin.

"I can't," I whisper.

"I know," he says, and I look up into his eyes. "I'll wait until you're ready."

"I'm not asking you to do that."

"I know," he says kissing my forehead and walking back to his car. He remains parked out front until I get inside, lock the door behind me, and wave goodbye to him from the window.

Thirty-Seven

Kadin

I haven't felt London's touch or kissed her lips in six fucking weeks. Since the doctor's offices around town refuse to tell me if she's a patient I'm still nowhere as far as finding her. I've even called several places pretending to be a forgetful dad to get appointment times, but they didn't fall for that either. I've been relegated to spending hours in the evenings and most of Sunday at stores that sell baby shit in an attempt to run into her. Needless to say, I haven't yet.

"What are you planning on torturing me with today doc?" I ask with only half playfulness as I situate myself on the padded chair across from her.

She gives me a stern look; one I know for a fact she doesn't mean. I've been more open and honest with her in our sessions even though I've struggled with the follow through on my own. We've built a trusting relationship, and I even make my appointments with more willingness and less detriment these days.

"I want to hit on the motivator for you deciding on trying counseling again after well over a year since the one and only appointment you made after Savannah passed."

I wince and realize her mentioning my late wife is not the reason. We've talked about it so much that I can now speak freely about it without getting angry or worse yet, breaking down. That is what happened those first couple of weeks I began seeing her.

I rub my beard with my hand. "You don't pull any punches do you doc?"

"You pay me to be completely real, Kadin. Is it something you'd like to discuss today?" She asks setting her iPad on the table beside her. She must have a great memory to take notes later, or she records our conversations on her tablet. I'm too distracted by what I'm going to disclose today to focus even too long on that, though.

"I told you about my trip to the cabin," I began knowing the majority of the session will be me spilling my guts and her asking poignant, yet sporadic, questions peppered throughout. "What I left out is I spent the nine days I was there with a woman whose car got stuck right off of the property."

I proceed to tell her every detail. My suicidal intentions, the sex, bringing London back with me, and her staying at the condo with me. She remained mostly silent but was completely shocked when I got to the part about coming home from dealing with Sierra, finding London gone, and discovering the positive pregnancy test in the trash can in her bathroom.

"You haven't heard from her since?"

"Not for a lack of trying on my part," I huff thinking about the two hours I trolled around a high-end baby boutique before coming to my appointment today.

"How do you feel about a baby?"

"Always with the feelings, huh?" She raises her eyebrows at me in mild annoyance at my attempt to avoid talking about this particular subject.

Begrudgingly I continue. "At first I was pissed that she left. Pissed that she took off and didn't tell me. Then I realized that she deserves better than what I have to offer her and a baby."

"Deserves better or deserved better?" She says simply.

"Excuse me?" I can't distinguish the difference in the two.

"You've been working through a lot in therapy. Do you feel like you're better prepared to be a father now than you were six weeks ago?"

"No," I answer honestly.

"Have you packed away Savannah's things?" She gives me the 'put two and two together, Kadin' look she's grown famous for.

"You think it would help?" I ask solemnly.

"I think it's a step in the right direction," she says without inflection. "Why didn't you and Savannah have children? Did one of you suffer from fertility issues?"

We're just going to cover the entire gamut of shit today it seems.

"Not that we were aware of. We never tried to get pregnant." True to form she remains silent forcing me to continue. "Sav worked with child victims all day long and said she didn't want to bring an innocent person into the world only to run the risk of them being destroyed by the evil in it."

"What did you want?"

I stop myself before I give her the 'I wanted Savannah' retort I'd been giving my mother for years when she asked about grandbabies.

"I think we would've made great parents."

"Be more specific, Kadin," she presses delicately.

"I wanted to coach t-ball and go on family vacations. We talked about it often. Well, *I* talked about it often. I begged for children. I knew we could protect our children. We were diligent people. I know *I* could've protected my children." I scrub at my face with rough hands. "She never relented; instead she worked longer hours at the office. She gave all of her time to other people's children. She'd shut me down every time I brought it up. Eventually, I stopped thinking about it all together."

My voice has grown angrier with each word until I'm nearly breathless.

"You're still pissed about it," she says stating the obvious. "Tell me why."

Unable to stay still I bolt up from my seat and pace in front of the faux mantle on the far side of her office. I clench my hands open and closed, trying to calm my now thundering heart.

"She refused me. She denied me the right to fatherhood."

"It's deeper than that, Kadin. Reach for it."

I bellow at the top of my lungs. She doesn't react, prepared for my outburst. "If we had kids she would've been home with us that night. If we had kids, she *never* would've died!" I all but crumple to the floor as waves of sobs wrack my body.

Dr. Long stuffs a Kleenex in my hands but other than that she remains silent and lets me work through my pain alone. "I'm angry at her." I finally manage to mutter.

"It's okay to be angry, Kadin. It's natural." Her voice is calming, and my breaths become more fluid, the jags of desperation growing fewer.

"I can't get mad at my deceased wife. It's horrendous." I explain with my head down, still unable to face her.

"Of course you can," she reassures me. "Your emotions are just as legitimate as the next person. Whether you want to waste time denying them instead of working through them, moving past them, is also completely up to you."

I huff loudly. "Give it to me straight, doc." I look up at her.

Her eyes squint in mild amusement. "Always."

Sunday I wake up with as much renewed determination as I came home from Great Falls with all those weeks ago, only this time my focus is on beginning the process of moving on. Dr. Long had been 'giving' me permission since my first appointment with her when I went ballistic after laughing at some stupid ass sitcom. It wasn't until my revelation about my anger with Savannah yesterday that I truly gave myself the same consideration.

Her instructions were to keep a box of the most prized sentimental things, disburse family heirlooms back to her parents, and donate the rest to a women's shelter, citing they would get more use out of her clothes than the closet they currently inhabit.

Seemed easy enough. I called down to the concierge and had them bring a stack of boxes up. My mind was focused as I worked them from flat to actual box form and taped the bottoms. When it came time to leave the living room and actually go to the bedroom to begin the process is where things grew difficult.

That's why I find myself sitting on the closed lid of the toilet in the bathroom with an empty trash can repeatedly tossing a container of Clorox wipes from hand to hand. This should be the simplest part. Other people can't have previously used cosmetics; it's unsanitary I reason with myself.

All I want to do is sweep all of it in the trash and wipe the counter clean, not even thinking about, but Dr. Long was very specific. I needed to work on letting it go rather than just completing the actions without thinking about it. She promised I'd regret it if I didn't. I'm already growing angrier and angrier, blaming everyone on the face of the Earth for trying to force me to give up my wife. Realistically I know these are my issues and not anyone else's but blaming has always been a part of my coping. Yet, another thing I needed to work on.

An hour later the counter is clean, and her drawers have been emptied. I'm also in need of a new shower curtain. It lost the battle of my rage when I grew angry once again at the tasks set before me today. I don't exactly feel sorry for it; I'd always hated that flowery, lacy thing anyways.

Wasting time slowly tying up the trash bag from the bathroom, I keep my focus straight ahead as I carry the bag of trash to the front door and set it down. I drink an entire bottle of water at the dining room table before I finally tell myself to man-up and get it done.

I start with what I'd thought would be the least emotional, her clothes. Things were going fine at first I was taking clothes from the far end of the closet and working my way forward, but the closer I got to the most recent stuff, the heavier her scent became. It was clinging hardest to things like her winter coat and an evening gown she'd worn two years ago to an advocacy fundraiser, items that weren't laundered after being worn for only a few hours. Those items I clung to like the devil himself was trying to snatch them from my grasp and sobbed.

The process took hours. Pack some clothes, cry; pack more clothes, cry some more. It was utterly exhausting. After the clothes, I moved to the belts, shoes, and other miscellaneous fashion accessories. From there I dragged out the boxes from the top of the closet, knowing I could only handle this once and knew I had to be completely thorough.

The easiest ended up being the things she had from her childhood, items she kept for sentimental reasons that were important to her before our life together. I put those boxes together with the things I plan to give to her parents.

I only thought I was having a bad time dealing with all of this until I found the photo albums ranging from high school through college until they began to taper off after our wedding. I do my best to ignore the unopened bottle Lagavulin we'd received for our ten year wedding anniversary as a gift from her parents that has somehow been forgotten in the box containing her preserved wedding bouquet and my boutonniere.

It taunts me from the top of the dresser as I turn page after page in the final photo album that recorded our happy lives, the years before she became obsessed with work and I became complacent in my marriage. It's hard to admit the problems after wearing the rose colored glasses I put on after she died for so long. Removing them was a bitch and at times today made me feel even more guilt than I ever had before as if I'm cleaning out her things in retribution for having the audacity to die and leave me alone to deal with all of this shit.

I gingerly slide the last photo album into the box with the others even though at this point I want to toss everything in a pit and set it on fire. It's not rational, but in my head it would temporarily take away the pain at least until the guilt hit full force moments later. Dr. Long told me to keep only one box, but I'm certain she underestimated the number of photo albums we would have, so I don't feel shame in the three that I've ended up with.

Exhausted from the emotional day, I make trip after trip through the condo carrying the boxes for donation along with the things I'm sending to the Price's. On the last trip out of the foyer, I notice at some point in my dozen or so trips I brought the bottle of whiskey from the bedroom and placed on the entryway table. Without a second thought, I scoop it off of the table and crack it open as I walk into the living room.

I press the top of the bottle to my lip and tilt it up. The second the expensive liquor hits my lips I snap out of it, flying into a rage instead. The bottle crashes against the brick of the fireplace, and the damage doesn't stop there. I topple furniture and rip pictures off the walls. Nothing in the room is left sacred. It isn't until I'm surrounded by utter chaos and destruction that I take a calming breath. Leaving the living room in complete disarray, I enter London's room and fall onto the bed. Crying myself to sleep has never been so cathartic.

Thirty-Eight

London

My tiny baby bump isn't even noticeable with most of the clothes I wear, but I'm totally in love with it, as if it's the proof I needed that there really is a life growing inside of me. I know each appointment to the doctor is verification as well, but now I have the ability to reach down and run my hands over the proof anytime I need to.

I'm talking to the baby I'm not even certain has ears yet about what to have for lunch when Jillian wanders into my office. The first time she caught me doing it I felt like a complete idiot, but her 'tell him auntie Jillian says hi' reaction set me at ease.

"Has he decided what we're having today?" She asks and sits down in her usual spot.

"He *or she* thinks Chinese food will be best," I answer with a smirk. "But I don't think I can handle all the sodium. We're compromising with that buffet place down on Chamberlain."

"A little bit of everything. Good choice." I make sure I have everything I'll need and stuff it all in my purse before she begins speaking again. "What are you doing this weekend?"

I glare at her. "No."

"What?" She smirks at me.

"Don't even ask. I learned my lesson the last time. You know Justin asked me if he could kiss me."

"Did you?" She leans in closer like we're sharing gossip no one else should hear.

"Of course not," I huff.

She arches a brow at me. "Why not?"

I shake my head in response.

"You can talk to me you know." She's sincere. I've learned that Jillian is always sincere, even when it's something you don't want to hear, she's brutally honest.

"Okay," I agree needing to talk to someone; the emotional roller coaster I ride every day is becoming exhausting. "This weekend?"

"Of course. I'll come to your place and bring chocolate and a chick flick." She grins from ear to ear. "Let's go feed that baby," she says nodding to my invisible bump.

Saturday has arrived quicker than I'd anticipated. I don't know why but I'm nervous about spilling my guts to Jillian. I know she won't judge me, but that doesn't stop me from judging myself. Hindsight is always twenty/twenty and looking back I can see all of my mistakes like they should have been blatantly obvious while they were occurring even though I know when you're in the situation perception is always different.

I inwardly wince at the look of pure shock on Jillian's face after completing my history about Brian. I clear my throat to keep from crying as she clutches my hands and a tear rolls down her cheek. She tries to speak, but it seems her throat is just as blocked as mine. She slowly just shakes her head back and forth in disbelief.

I move onto Trent and Keira next, and like any good friend she gets madder than a wet hen. I honestly think if I wanted to go seek vengeance on either one or both of them right now, she'd offer to drive and pay for the gas. As a woman, she knows the detriment we all have when a friend betrays us. Most aren't double-crossed as thoroughly as I was, but we all know the pain when someone we trusted stabs us in the back.

"Are you fucking kidding me?" She finally asks.

"Nope. They were going at it in the office at the bar. He used the same pet name on her that he'd used with me for years." I explain.

"What was the pet name?"

"Kitten," I respond.

"Ick. Really, London? You let that man call you kitten?" She crinkles her nose, and it makes me laugh.

"It was enduring when I thought it meant something to him," I admit with mild disgust. "Now that I heard him use it with her I hate cats all together!" We both laugh and it lifts my spirits slightly, but I know the rest of the story is coming and even though I suffered the abuse for years and Trent ripped my heart out, it's the last part of the story that hurts the most.

"So the baby is Trent's?" Here we go.

I sit back further on the couch and curl my legs under me, getting comfortable for the emotional devastation I'm sure is going to hit.

"That's the thing," I admit softly. "I haven't told you about Kadin yet."

I continue my story up until the day I left Kadin's condo, and she's sitting beside me with her mouth gaping open.

"You've dealt with more shit in the last ten years than most people go through in several lifetimes!" She finally says.

"Don't I know it," I mumble.

"He just lied to you and left with that woman?"

I nod because words are too difficult at the moment.

"What are you going to do?" Her voice is soft, and I appreciate her ability to read my mood and respond in kind.

I shrug and wipe a stray tear from my eye. "I'm doing it. I'm taking care of myself. Saving money for when the baby gets here. Living my life. I'm okay with where I am. It's not the situation I ever dreamed I'd be in, pregnant and single, but I'm making the most of it."

"What about Kadin?" she asks gently.

"What about him?" I look up at her.

"You love him."

"And he loves her," I say referring to Savannah. "I can't compete with a ghost, Jillian. He spent seventeen years with her; the couple of weeks I was in his life don't even compare."

We sit in silence for several long minutes. "Plus, let's not forget about the twin. I don't even know what's going on with her, but there's enough there that he lied to me to go be with her. I refuse to play second fiddle to anyone else. Ever."

"Believe me I get that." She agrees, but then looks away.

"What? Just say it, Jillian." I may be asking for trouble, but I want everything out in the open.

"You've had no closure," she finally says. "I think if you had some-good, bad, or indifferent-it would help you move on. I know you put on a brave face, but I notice the times at work when you grow distant. I've seen your eyes begin to water and how hard you fight to keep the tears at bay some days. If you spoke to him and laid it all out, I think you could *actually* move on, rather than pretending like you have."

"Tell me what you really think," I mutter with a small laugh.

She's right even if I don't want to admit it. Most days at the office are hit or miss when it comes to my emotional stability. I usually blame it on the crazy hormones, but I know it has more to do with my unhealed shattered heart.

"I don't know if I can face him," I admit somberly.

"You need closure. That's if it's what you actually want." She shrugs her shoulders. "I'm all for kicking an asshole to the curb, but you should confront him about it. The situation with Trent and Keira was different than what happened with Kadin. There was no room for misconstruing what they were doing, but the thing with Kadin could possibly be different."

I sit quietly for a while and mull over what she just said. This whole time I've pushed reasoning with what he did to the back of my head, telling myself I'm tired of making excuses for people who hurt me. I turned Kadin's lie into an all-or-nothing; myself, of course, ending up with nothing.

"You think I made the situation with Sierra into more than it actually is?"

She shakes her head vehemently. "I'm not saying that at all. There's something there, but without him explaining it you'll never know just how deep it goes with her. Did you get a vibe he was sneaking around the week you were at the condo with him?"

"No," I answer truthfully. "I mean he retreated into himself a couple of times and I'm certain that had more to do with Savannah than anything, but it wasn't until that Sunday that things got weird."

"You need to let him explain," she says resolutely.

"And if he feeds me a line of shit?"

"You walk away because you've done everything you can. But you know as much as I do that he deserves to know about that baby." I hate when she's right.

We left the subject alone after that and tortured ourselves with *The Notebook*... twice. When she left, I went to the park nearby and sat watching the moms and dads play with and chase after their children. The smiles on their face brought one to my own.

I know I have to tell him even if there's a chance this baby is not his, but that's not the reason I'm sitting in the parking lot of his building gripping the steering wheel with sweaty hands. I'm here because I miss him more than I could ever explain. I left months ago, but I can still close my eyes and see his handsome face; I can still hear his voice as if he's standing behind me whispering in my ear.

I'm terrified that he'll lie to me or worst yet tell me he has no room in his life for me. I'm scared to death that he won't be happy to see me. Certain I'll walk away from here today rejected by him has my stomach in knots. I haven't been on this side of town since the day I left; I've avoided it like sure death would come if I crossed over into his territory.

Stepping out of my car, I can't stop the tremble of my hands and the thunderous pounding of my heart. I'm full blown trembling by the time I get off the elevator and stand in front of his door. I've raised my hand to knock more than a half dozen times and each time I've lowered it and paced up and down the hall.

Taking a final deep breath, I lift my hand one last time and tap gently on the door. I wait a few seconds and turn to get back on the elevator, suddenly relieved and heartbroken at the same time that he hasn't answered. Before I can take a solid step, I hear the door tug open. I freeze momentarily but eventually turn around to look into the eyes of the man I dream about on a nightly basis.

I gasp when my green eyes meet blue ones instead of the chocolate brown I'd grown to love.

"Can I help you?" The elderly man asks from the doorway.

I try to look over his shoulder, but he steps to the side, further blocking my view. "I'm." I clear my throat because that just came out in a squeak rather than English. "I'm looking for Kadin Cole."

He blinks at me a few times but doesn't respond, and I have to wonder if he's senile. "He used to live here."

He tilts his head up as if he's checking his memory for the name; he comes up empty. "Names not familiar, but I've lived here the last forty years." Clearly he's senile.

"Okay, thank you." I tell him respectfully and get back on the elevator.

He's moved, and now I have no way to reach him. I've waited too long, and I'll never see him again. This hurts almost as much as the day I walked away. In the back of my mind I'd always assumed I'd have the chance to speak to him, tell him about the baby; apparently I was wrong.

Thirty-Nine
Kadin

I didn't have even the slightest clue what therapy would bring to a head. It's been a very eye-opening experience to say the least. After my tantrum in the condo the night I packed away Savannah's things I realized I'd never wanted to live in that damn condo in the first place; being in the middle of town was what Savannah had wanted. Once again I bent and compromised because I wanted her happy more than anything in the world.

Dr. Long also helped me realize that staying there not only forced me to hold onto the past but also the hope that London would return. Not one word from her in three months made me face the realization she wasn't coming back. The two weeks we spent together obviously didn't impact her life as much as it did mine.

I know I'll probably never find her, but that hasn't kept me from calling around to doctor's offices and hanging around baby stores. It's become second nature that I stop in and roam around every time I see a sign that even hints at having baby items. I know I'm wasting my time, but I have nothing else to do.

I moved out of the condo a month and a half ago. I figured three months of her not showing up proved she never would. If it weren't for the fact that she was possibly pregnant, I might have given up looking for her altogether. I may stop looking for her eventually, but I can't imagine I'll ever stop caring for her. She somehow has become part of my soul, and that never goes away.

I bought a home that's rural to Spokane on a large part of land. As a distraction, I've actually spent the time to furnish it just how I want it. I left every piece of furniture I owned in the condo, except for the queen sized bed London and I slept in when she was there. Creepy I know, but it's the only thing I have from that time that she'd touched.

I also got a dog. Dr. Long felt like some form of companionship was a necessity, and since I don't see myself jumping into the dating pool anytime soon, seemed like the best alternative. Pudge, the mixed breed mutt I rescued from the local shelter, and I roam the property around the house most evenings, and he has free range of the land when I'm gone.

I've gotten things under control at work, and I've been going to the Sunday dinners with my family. After a long heart to heart with my dad, I've cut my hours back at the office and only work a regular workweek rather than the sixty to seventy hours I'd been putting in before Savannah passed. I explained to him that I didn't want to work that much in the first place, but did since she was at work herself. My saving grace was Lisa reconsidering and coming back to work after she had her baby. I'm certain the full-time day nanny and nursery I set up onsite convinced her.

I don't work at all on the weekends anymore which is why I'm sitting on the front porch watching Pudge chase after a half deflated basketball. The thing is in tatters and reeks to high heaven but it came with him from the shelter, and he loves it. Who am I to deny the guy of something he loves?

I'm mid-laugh when I see Kegan's truck making its way up the driveway. I no longer feel dread when I see a family member drive up, and the sight of my baby brother climbing out of his truck makes me happy. We've spent quite a bit of time together since I moved here. He constantly bitches about having to drive so far out, but I refuse to go to his nasty apartment. I told him I could meet him there if he ever got out of his bachelor phase and cleaned shit up. He hasn't complained about coming out here since; clearly he's not ready for that big of a step in his life.

He reaches down and scratches Pudge's head and has to hold the pizza he's carrying higher so the dog can't jump up and get it.

"He seems much healthier," he says as he walks up the porch steps.

"He eats like he's starved every day. He's filled out quite a bit since I got him home." I reach down and pat Pudge's head as he wiggles excitedly never taking his eyes off of the pizza box Kegan sat on the patio table.

"I think I should get a dog," he says absently.

I laugh. "You can hardly take care of yourself. Why would you want to torture an innocent animal like that?"

He smirks back at me. "Maybe you're right." He flips the lid to the box and takes a slice out then slides it closer to me.

"Let me guess?" I say looking at my watch. "You're here to watch the game?"

He nods and continues chewing. He doesn't wait until he swallows before saying, "Your TV is bigger than mine."

I grimace as food falls out of his mouth. Pudge is on it in seconds. I shake my head knowing my brother may remain single for the rest of his life.

We sit in silence for a few minutes, enjoying the impromptu meal. I toss the crust of my last piece to Pudge and stand. "Pregame is about to start." I head into the house; Kegan and Pudge follow.

Kegan left shortly after the game, and I spent the next fifteen minutes cleaning up after him. He's like a tornado that manages to leave destruction in his wake. I hear the doorbell chime as I wad up the Clorox wipe I used to get his finger prints off my coffee table.

He must have left something; I think as I pull open the door. "What did you…?" I stop mid sentence and cringe when I see not Kegan, but Sierra standing on my front porch.

I haven't seen her since she was carted off by the employees from the mental health institution. Her parents let me know last week that she was out and seemed to be doing better. I figured it would take her longer to find me.

"Hey, Sierra," I say as platonically as I can but remain in the doorway, apprehensive to let her in the house.

"Hey, baby." I wince at her use of the nickname. "Can I come in? I brought a gift." She holds up exactly what I would expect from her, but the bottle of whiskey doesn't hold the same power over me that it did five months ago.

"I don't think that's such a good idea, Sierra." I try to keep the tone of my voice neutral.

"You didn't tell me you moved. It's almost insulting that you'd leave and not tell me where you went." She bites her lip, and I know it's a failed attempt at seduction. "Imagine my surprise to see an old man answer your door at the condo."

"How did you find me?" I know she has unlimited resources considering her net worth, but I'd like to know what she did exactly so I can let her parents know. She seems to grow more unstable as the years go by. She was what I'd call quirky when Savannah and I started dating, but this is borderline stalking.

She ignores my question which is typical of her. "I was hoping we could have a drink and make love. I've missed you. It's been months since I've felt you inside of me."

I close my eyes and squeeze them tight hoping she'd just disappear but knowing it's never that simple.

"Sierra." The word sound like a plea, which in a way it is. "We've been over this." I keep the chastisement out of my voice as much as I can knowing she doesn't do well with feeling like she's being talked down to. "I don't drink anymore and what we… did. Can't happen again." I can't even put it into words.

"Made love, Kadin. We made love." She says her voice growing louder, the agitation becoming apparent in her demeanor as she begins to pace the front porch.

"We didn't," I say softly. "We had drunken sex."

"You love me!" She rants.

"Not in the way you want me to," I admit not for the first time.

She stops pacing and glares at me. "You used me."

I hang my head. "And I'm sorry." There's no sense in pointing out that she arranged each and every one of our encounters. I'm man enough to admit my wrongdoing; pointing hers out will serve no purpose, especially considering her level of agitation.

"You need to let her go," she spits. "She doesn't love you. She never did."

"Savannah's been gone for almost two years Sierra." I can finally say it without it bringing me to my knees.

"I'm not talking about her. That bitch that was at your condo. She doesn't want you!" She screams the last sentence, and I immediately wonder why she's even bringing London up.

I stand quietly hoping my semi-calm demeanor rubs off on her; it doesn't.

"She's working across town and doesn't give a shit about you!" My eyes widen.

"You know where London is?" I hate the maniacal look in her eyes, but I ignore it at the mention of London.

I grab her arms roughly. "Tell me where she is!" I demand.

She smiles in my face like the psychotic person I know she's become. "She's working as a secretary or some shit for Justin Bland. She's moved on Kadin." His voice grows calmer like I'll accept her news and move on with her instead.

I release her arms and take a step back sure she's just fucking with me like she's become an expert doing the last two years. "How do you know that?"

"I saw her at a grocery store the other day, and I followed her home." She shrugs like stalking and following people is completely normal.

I narrow my eyes and try to determine if she's telling the truth. She's so hard to read these days, but I won't take a chance. I know exactly where Justin Bland's office is. He's worked a couple of contracts for mutual clients of ours.

"I've given you enough time to get over Savannah," she says angrily. "I won't allow another woman to come between us. I've waited almost twenty years for you already."

Ignoring the craziness of her last words, I turn my back on her to enter the house to get my truck keys. It's late, but I'll wait outside in the parking lot until the sun comes up if I have to.

"If you go after her, Kadin," Sierra vows. "I swear to Christ I'll kill her too."

Forty

London

I was so upset when I left Kadin's condo that I didn't even realize that I could track him down through his work, but by the time I realized that, the truth that he'd moved on, literally as well as figuratively, had already settled in my gut. I've been on my own five months now, and I've grown somewhat used to the situation. My heart still hurts, but the pain is not as acute as it was. I'll wait until after the baby is born and then revisit telling him about it. For now I'm trying to focus only on myself and the life I'll be responsible for soon.

Jillian and I have grown closer, and we spend almost all of our time off either shopping or just hanging out at each other's houses. I get the feeling that something happened between her and Hawke, but she refuses to talk about it even though I spilled my guts to her a couple months ago. The vibe around the office has been off ever since we all met up at the club yet no one seems to be willing to talk about it.

"I don't think being supportive of a friend is an indication that you want to have a baby, Jillian." She's once again barged into my office so I put her on the spot, asking her if she'd go to my next appointment with me. I'd love to have someone to talk to since the wait seems to take forever.

"People will think we're lovers," she says comically waggling her eyebrows. I sigh in frustration. "Fine, I'll go and be the supportive best friend slash gay lover."

I smile big at her dramatics. "Thank you for the sacrifice."

"I won't stay in the room while he checks your vagina." She crosses her arms over her chest in resistance.

"It's not that kind of appointment, Jillian." I glance back at my computer. "Don't you have work to do?"

She sighs suddenly, and I can tell she looks dejected. "Hawke has a visitor, so I decided to come visit you." She looks at her nails.

It doesn't go unnoticed that she said visitor and not client which hints at the person in his office is there for personal reasons and not work. "Want to talk about it?" *Maybe this is the time she actually opens up about it.*

"Nope," she says standing up and walking out. *Maybe not.*

The ringing of my phone doesn't let me dwell on it any longer.

"London Sykes," I say into the handset.

"Can you come in for a minute?" Justin.

"Sure," I respond but find it weird he called rather than messaged me on the office's instant messenger.

I enter his office without knocking. I used to knock, but he told me to stop, said it made him feel like I thought he was doing something creepy in there if I felt the need to ask permission to enter.

"What's up?" I sit in the chair across from him.

"Why do I have travel plans on the calendar for the end of the week?" I shake my head in mild amusement.

"I swear you never listen to a word I say," I tease him.

His face grows serious. "London I've heard everything you've ever said to me."

He's incredibly sweet, and I've really come to value his friendship these last few months. Jillian continues to push me in his direction, even more so since I discovered the old man living in Kadin's condo.

"If that's the case then you'd remember me telling you that you'd have to travel out of town to meet Mr. and Mrs. Hofstetter. They're loaded and will be excellent clients, but they're a little reclusive and refuse to travel. If you want them, you have to go to them." He looks at me as confused as ever. "Ringing any bells?"

"Nope," he answers with a smile. "What would I do without you?"

"Besides not show up for half of your appointments?" I laugh. I thought it was weird for the two men in this office to need personal assistants, but it was apparent very close to the beginning of my employment that we were needed desperately. Hawke isn't quite as bad but some days I wonder how Justin's ever shown up on time for anything on his own. He constantly loses track of time.

"Have dinner with me?" His words are soft and random in respect to our current conversation.

"Justin, I can't." I hate the way his face falls for the split second before he corrects it. He's always taken my rejections in stride, and they've even practically stopped, but every once in a while he'll ask. He told me from the beginning he'd continue to ask until I told him to stop. "I'm huge," I say in jest and pat my growing stomach. I'm almost to the halfway point in my pregnancy. "You don't want to be seen with me."

"You were beautiful when you first started working, but you're even more gorgeous now." He leans in slightly before continuing. "You're smiling more these days."

I blush. He's completely sincere, and the attention is a huge boost to my ego. I think his complimentary nature is the main reason I've yet to put an end to the mild flirting and requests for dates. It's almost as if I need the attention to feel validated. Feeling wanted works wonders for my self-esteem.

"You were broken when you first got here." I wince because I'd thought I hid it very well.

"I'm still broken," I say softly looking at my hands.

"You can't tell from here," he assures me. His comment validates that either I've gotten very good at hiding my true emotions or I'm beginning to move on. Most days I don't know the difference myself.

"I feel incomplete," I admit raising my head and looking into his eyes.

"You still love him," he states, referring to a man he's never met but still feels in competition with.

I can't answer him. I can't give a voice to that fact right now. I know I need to move on but I'm not ready, and I don't know that I'll ever be. Knowing that, I feel like I just need to jump off of the cliff into the unknown.

"Ask me again," I whisper.

"Will you have dinner with me?" His eyes are on fire, and I can hear his foot tapping under his desk betraying his excitement.

"Yes," I answer with a small smile. "I don't want you to have high expectations, Justin. I know I'm not ready for anything serious."

He leans back in his chair and attempts to act nonchalant. "Casual dating?"

"Let's start with just friends who have dinner together," I say in rebuttal.

"Sounds like a perfect start. When?" He asks with a smile, knowing I'm more aware of what's on his calendar than he is.

"Next Thursday," I answer. We both have work the next day, so it seems safer and less date like.

"I'll pick you up at seven?" His grin ear-to-ear grin is contagious.

"Seven sounds perfect." I stand from my seat. "Don't miss your flight to Utah," I tell him pointing to the itinerary on his desk.

Forty-One

Kadin

Did she just say? The room tilts and my head begins to swim. I turn my body around to face Sierra, but it takes a minute for my eyes to focus on her.

"The fuck you just say?" I had to have heard her wrong. There's no way that she would go so far as to kill her own sister just to get a shot at being with me.

Her eyes go wide as if she can't believe she just said what she did and in that second I realize she'd been telling the truth. My hands begin to tremble and in my rage a tear rolls down my cheek. "You crazy fucking bitch!"

She hates the word; I know she hates the word. Everyone had been very careful never to use the term around her. Hell, I was just as guilty as the rest of her family for skating around her mental health issues and making excuses for random crazy shit she did.

I watch as utter rage takes over her face, but I'm beyond caring at this point. "You killed my wife? Your sister?"

She sneers at me. "And I'd do it again in a heartbeat."

"Even knowing I'd never be with you? Knowing that because of what you did I'll hate you forever?" I grip my head with both hands because it feels like I'm in the twilight zone. "She was in a car accident, Sierra."

I remember the accidents report. They presumed that she fell asleep behind the wheel because there were no signs of her trying to avoid driving off the ravine they found her car in.

"You can find anything on the internet, Kadin. Even how to cut brake lines." She says it so matter of fact that it sends chills up my spine.

I take a moment to finally take a long look at her. At first all I see is pure evil, but the more I take in, the more I notice just how much she's transformed herself into Savannah. I notice her haircut is similar to the way Savannah wore hers. Sierra's clothes, which were usually a little edgy and hip have now been replaced with slacks and a sweater set, identical to what my late wife would've worn to the office.

"I didn't take out my twin to have some two-bit whore come in and take what's mine." Her second reference to harming London makes me see red.

I whip around and run back into the house frantically looking for the phone. The woman outside just admitting to killing my wife and is now openly threatening the woman I love.

The woman I love.

The thought slams into me, but I don't have time to consider it now. I need to call the police and have her put away for good this time. I fly up the stairs, grab my phone, and I'm dialing 911 before I make it back to the porch.

The bottle of Jack Daniels is shattered in the spot she previously occupied, and her car is already gone out of the driveway. The call connects and I relay to the operator everything she just admitted me.

I'm told that a detective will make contact with me, and I'd need to come to the station to give a proper statement tomorrow, but there is nothing that they can do about it tonight. The case would be transferred to the Criminal Investigation Division; they would take it from there.

They didn't care that she has a history of mental illness. The operator sounded bored as if she took calls from people admitting to murder numerous times a day and she was reading from a cue card.

Remembering a detective I know I search my phone, hoping I still have his number. I'd worked with Henry Bates on more than one occasion when properties we were under contract to build were vandalized.

I eventually find his name under Spokane Police and press send. It rings three times before he picks up.

"Henry?"

"Hey, Kadin. What's up?" I can hear the background noise fade out as he walks away from whatever he was doing.

"I have a situation. My sister-in-law just came to the house and admitted that she cut the brake lines on my wife's car and caused her accident."

"Fuck, Kadin. Didn't your wife…" he trails off.

"Die? Yes. She killed my fucking wife and I called to report it to the police, and they said…"

"You'd have to wait for CID," he says cutting me off.

"Yes! Is there anything that can be done?"

"I wish there was, man. They may be able to pick the case up first thing in the morning," he says, and I can tell he's not happy about the way the law is set up either.

"She'll fucking kill herself before that happens and then she'll never pay for what she's done." I sit on the couch and hang my head in defeat.

"Does she have a history of mental health problems?" He asks with renewed expression in his voice.

"She's been hospitalized more than half her life for suicidal ideations and manic-depressive mood swings. She's a paranoid schizophrenic." I confess to him her secrets; the one her family always insisted we keep because of her dad's public persona are no longer ones I'm willing to keep.

"I can call and have dispatch do a well-check on her. If she seems unstable, they can commit her for a few days for evaluation." He offers.

"Seriously? That'd be awesome, Henry. Keep me informed?"

"Of course, Kadin," he says before hanging up.

I grab my keys and wallet and head for my truck. It's after ten at night, but I can't sit still. I have every intention of driving to the attorney's office even though I know no one will be there. I have to keep myself busy because if I think about the revelations that were made tonight I'll drive myself insane.

As I head down the driveway and again as I near the empty office space where London has been working for God knows how long, I try to convince myself not to take up sentry in the parking lot tonight and wait for her to come to work in the morning.

Rather than park and wait I just drive around in concentric circles, knowing that most people live within a few miles of their job. I let my mind wander as each road starts to look the same and her car is not parked on any of them.

"You know she walked in on me in the bathroom again," I tell Savannah as we pack to get ready to leave.

It's our junior year at college, and we spent Thanksgiving with her family this year and plan to spend Christmas with mine.

"You left the door open again?" She's hardly paying attention to me.

"Seriously?" I say growing annoyed. "She's busted in on me three times this week alone. I think she waits until I head in there and plans her attacks."

"Attacks? You're so dramatic, Kadin," she says with a laugh. She finally zips her suitcase closed and wraps her arms around my waist.

"You need to say something to your parents. Her behavior is getting worse." I kiss her head, but she pulls away from me.

"She's eccentric, Kadin. She's harmless." She turns her back to me, and I know the conversation is closed for discussion.

Her behaviors only got worse as time went on. Everyone felt sorry her because she wasn't able to go to college or have what most people would consider a normal life because of her issues. Her father, being a local politician, did everything he could to avoid any type of awareness or stigma as far as Sierra was concerned.

I knew from day one that had more to do with his reputation and less to do with her well-being, and she's suffered because of it. She's been shuffled around to different mental health institutions around the states for the last twenty plus years, most times only receiving minimal help.

My ringing cell phone startles me. I pull to the side of the road knowing I'd never be able to drive and concentrate on a call. I look at the screen. Henry.

"Hey, man," I answer.

"Kadin," he says softly. My blood runs thin. "You made the right call on the well-check. Patrol found her with two slit wrists."

I remain silent because I don't have it in me to give a shit if she's dead.

"They were able to stop the bleeding and got her in an ambulance, but it doesn't look good. One of the officers on patrol said she was white as a ghost. You still there?" He asks when I don't respond to a word he's said.

"I'm here. Have her parents been called?" I pinch the bridge of my nose at the first sign of a major headache that is about to hit me.

"Yes. Kadin, you need to make sure you go to the police department tomorrow no matter what happens with the sister tonight." He says.

"I'll be there first thing in the morning," I promise before ending the call.

I'm numb and decide on the way back to the lawyer's office that I'm in no position to seek London out. As hard as it is I know I have to get all of this mess cleaned up once and for all before I see her again. I bypass the turn for Bland & Platt and head back to my house. The next few days may possibly be some of the worse I'll ever have to face.

Forty-Two

London

"So. Today's the big day."

I narrow my eyes at Jillian across the table of the café. "Today is not a big day."

"You're going on a date with Justin right?" She says.

"We are having dinner. As friends. That doesn't make today a big day." I correct her.

She's been hounding me all week about agreeing to go out with my boss. I think she's more excited about it than I am.

"When is it?" She asks then stuffs a bite of chicken salad in her mouth.

"He was going to pick me up at the house later this evening, but we decided to go ahead and leave from work." I sip my water and watch her stuff her face.

Taking a break from her food binge she says, "Is that why you're dressed extra nice today?" She angles her fork at my new dress.

"I'm not extra nice today. My stomach has gotten too big for my old clothes, so I'm wearing my new maternity clothes." I explain. "Wait. Do you think he'll think I'm more dressed up than usual just for him?"

She grins at me in response.

"Shit," I mumble.

I don't want him to think that; I don't want him to read too much into the evening. Honestly, I was feeling incredibly fat when my clothes seemed to be shrinking at an alarming rate, so I bought extra dressy clothes at the maternity shop to help me feel better about myself. I still feel like a plumped up cow, but at least now I look like a nicely dressed cow.

"It's no big deal. It's like you guys think alike. Did you notice the new suit he's decked out in today?" I had noticed the new suit, and I have to admit he looks incredibly handsome in it.

I kick myself once again for holding onto a past that isn't a possibility. Justin Bland, I've come to realize, is an insanely great catch. His personality now, including all of the kindness and nurturing behaviors, is exactly how it was when I first started. I'd thought there was no way a man was that sweet and knew he'd change over time, but he hasn't. He's one of the most genuine men I've ever met and I kick myself every time he smiles at me that all I feel for him is friendship.

"He's dressed very nice today," I agree with her.

"Nice? Are you blind or do you just like to be obstinate? That man is hot as fuck, and you're crazy for not jumping on that," she tells me with mild annoyance in her voice.

I look away from her and don't respond. I know she's right, but I'm not going to act like I have feelings for him other than the platonic acceptance of his good looks. I refuse to pretend to care when I don't. I've been on the receiving end of that fake affection, and it's not something I'll ever do purposely to another person.

"I should just cancel," I say distractedly.

"You do that, and I'll shoot you." She holds her fingers up in the shape of a gun and flexes her thumb in mock firing.

"You look beautiful today," Justin whispers in my ear as he guides me to his car. The hand he has on the small of my back is comforting and feels protective all at the same time.

"Thank you. You're exceptionally handsome today as well." I wonder if I should've said that, and I want to groan, knowing I'll second guess everything I say tonight in fear that he'll take it to mean more than it actually does. He winks at me and closes my door once I've settled into the passenger seat.

I take a few calming breaths as he makes his way to the front of the car and smile softly as he gets in behind the wheel. I ignore the soft music playing through the sound system as we drive to whatever restaurant he's chosen for this evening.

In true 'only the best for Justin Bland' fashion he's pulled up outside of one of Spokane's swankiest restaurants, something I'd expected, hence the super nice dress. He gets out, handing his keys to the valet and walks around and opens my door for me, offering me assistance with an outstretched hand.

Within moments of walking through the double glass doors, we're seated in a quiet corner near the back. I know we said this dinner was just friends, but it's obvious Justin's hoping I change my mind. I once again curse Kadin for stealing my heart; then I curse myself for leaving it behind with him months ago.

We sit perpendicular to one another rather than directly across from the other. If I'd even questioned the romantic feel of the restaurant, the candles on the table leave no room for doubt. I'm not uncomfortable about the situation yet, but I can feel the discomfort hovering right on the edge.

The waitress comes by and takes our drink and appetizer order. It isn't until she leaves and I know I'll have a few uninterrupted minutes to speak with him and try to manage his expectations.

"Justin," I say and look at the candles with an arched eyebrow.

He holds his hands up like he had nothing to do with the romantic gesture. "London. I swear; the candles were not my doing."

I look at him in disbelief. "Look around." I sweep my head to the other tables, noticing not one of them has flowers and candles in the center. "This is the only table lit up like a runway."

He laughs softly. "I promise. I had Jillian make the reservations. You know I'm not good at that stuff."

I roll my lips inward between my teeth before I start a tirade on the woman who I was beginning to refer to as my best friend. Of course, she had a hand in this mess. I can tell he's truthful, and this is exactly something Jillian would do.

He bends his head forward and blows out the candles. I watch as the black smoke twirls to the ceiling. "Better?" His eyes are lit up with amusement.

"What?" I finally ask him when his face doesn't change.

"I was wondering how long it would take before you said something about them," I smirk at him.

He honestly knows me pretty well. I haven't left much unsaid these last few months, taking a page out of Jillian's book and deciding just to lay everything out there. If the thought came to my head and I had even the slightest urge to share it, it usually came out of my mouth. I was tired of keeping things bottled up inside.

"I just don't want you to read too much into this dinner," I repeat the words I said when we scheduled tonight after the waitress drops off our drinks and fried calamari.

"Believe me, London. I know exactly where I stand." I'm saddened by the slight disappointment I see in his face.

A huge grin spreads across my face when I feel the sudden jolt in my stomach.

"You don't have to look so happy about it," he mutters.

I laugh gently. "I'm not smiling because of what you said. The baby just moved. I never get used to feeling it." I place both of my hands on my stomach and wait for the next round of movement.

Justin holds out a tentative hand. "May I?"

I reach for his hand and place it on the spot I felt the last movement. His eyes go wide when the fluttering begins again. "That's amazing," he whispers as if he has to stay quiet or it will stop. "When do you find out what you're having?" he asks without moving his hand.

"Week after next." I honestly can't wait. I haven't bought one single thing for the nursery, and I'm anxious to get started.

"Do you have a preference?"

I shake my head no. "I just want to know so I can have everything ready when I bring him or her home." It's a lie of course. I want a daughter that looks exactly like Kadin. A son with his features would just be too hard, and I'd never be able to get over him, even though that prospect isn't looking possible right now anyway.

He clears his throat and pulls his hand from my stomach. With complete sincerity in his eyes, he looks at me. "You don't have to do this alone."

I'm not surprised by his offering. He's never given me one indication that his desire to date me excluded the child I'm carrying and what an amazing man for being willing to step up and take the place of an absent father.

"My life is too messed up, Justin. You deserve better." I blink my eyes rapidly to keep the tears at bay. I'm well aware of what I'm turning down.

"What do you want, London?" I don't know if he's asking in general or in relation him and me.

"I wish things were different." It's a simple response to a loaded question.

"But they're not." His voice is soft and almost pleading, but it doesn't carry an ounce of derision.

"I love him," I respond.

"And if you can't have him?"

"I'd rather do without." I look up and watch him wince at my brutally honest answer.

"Forever?" He asks with a broken voice.

"For now," I respond even though forever would've probably been more accurate.

Forty-Three

Kadin

Paramedics got Sierra to the hospital just in time. Her parents were upset when they found out she'd hurt herself again. They were devastated when she admitted to hospital staff that she'd set into motion the events that led to Savannah's death. There's a very slim chance that she will go to trial, but police assure me she'll never see the outside of a mental hospital again.

I spent days dealing with the police, giving reports, and trying to come to terms myself with my anger at Sierra. For almost two years, I grieved over the loss of a woman to what we'd all thought was an accident. To find out her own sister murdered her? That brought on another wave guilt and shame. If everyone, including myself, didn't dance around the fact that she was insane, Savannah would still be here.

My therapy session with Dr. Long yesterday focused on forgiveness. When I grew angered at her suggestion, she reminded me that forgiving myself for the things I couldn't change were the first steps, and she understands that I'll never be able to forgive others before I can do that first. She also reminded me that Savannah was just as guilty as anyone else for tip-toeing around her sister's illness. Needless to say, it's been an emotional week.

It's Thursday, and I couldn't wait another minute for London. I have no idea what she'll say when she sees me, but I can't live the rest of my life with the unknown.

I'm parked at a neighboring business, watching the front doors of Bland & Platt. Her little red car is in the parking lot indicating that for once in her life Sierra told the truth. I've been parked here for hours, not sure when she'd get off work but afraid to miss her if I showed up too late.

I don't realize just how much I missed her until I watch her walk out of the front of the office. I move to open my truck door but stop when I see no other than Justin Bland himself walks out beside her with his hand on her back. I can see the happiness on her face from here, and it makes my blood run cold.

Has she truly moved on? Has she moved on with him?

The last thing I want to do is cause her more pain or ruin any happiness she may have built since we were together. I'd almost convinced myself to walk away but then she turned to her side. I gasp at the sight of her rounded stomach. A tear rolls down my cheek unbidden as I take in the most beautiful sight I've ever seen. She didn't have an abortion, and that realization means there may be hope. Hope that we can be together or at a minimum I can be a father.

Just before she lowers into the car, I see a small hint of pain on her face and that's all I need to seal my plans. There's no way I can walk away from her. My heart won't allow it. She may not want me when it's all said and done, but I won't walk away from a child.

I watch them drive away, and it's the hardest thing not to follow them and confront her wherever they stop. I call Kegan instead and invite him over to hang out this evening before I can decide to sit in this parking lot and wait for her to return to her car. Seeing me beat the shit out of Justin won't win me any points in her favor.

For the first time in as long as I can remember I want a drink. Not because I feel like I need one but I know passing out drunk will keep me from going back into town and searching for her. I'm glad I called Kegan over, and I've decided to talk to him about London. Other than Dr. Long her name hasn't crossed my lips but I feel the need to work out a plan with someone and Kegan, although he's my brother, is also the only friend that I have. Making friends was another thing on Dr. Long's long list of things to do that I never got around to.

"There isn't shit on TV," Kegan says leaving the station on ESPN and setting the remote back down on the coffee table.

"It's Thursday. What do you expect?" I tell him. "I wanted to talk to you anyways."

He turns his body, so he's facing my more and bats his eyelashes. "Are we going to gossip?" He asks in a girly voice.

"Sure and then you can braid my beard," I respond flatly with the same thing London said months ago at the cabin. "I'm serious. I have some shit to say."

"Is it about Sierra? Mom told me about what she did. I'm so fucking sorry, man."

"Thanks. I don't want to go into detail too much; I'll save that shit for therapy but Sierra and I messed around a couple of times, and she went crazy and told me about what she did to Savannah's car."

"I guess it's a good thing. I don't know if the truth makes it better or hurts even more than the lie everyone believed," he says.

"It's honestly hard to tell right now," I admit to him. "That's not the only thing she disclosed." I pause.

For a long minute, Kegan just waits patiently, but patience has never been his strong suit. "Am I going to have to drag it out of you or are you just going to torture me with hints until I guess?"

"She saw London at a grocery store and started following her."

"Fuck. Did she tell you where she lives?" He shifts his weight on the couch sinking in deeper into the leather.

"No. But she did tell me where she works." I explain.

"Are you going to go see her? Beg her to come back?"

"It's more complicated than that, Kegan."

"How is it any more complicated than going up to her, telling her how you feel, and begging her to take you back? Seems pretty simple to me." He crosses his arms over his chest and nods his head, ecstatic he just solved my problem.

"She's pregnant, man." He gasps and if the conversation wasn't so serious I'd laugh at the look of complete shock on his face. He looks terrified like I just mentioned his worst nightmare.

"Holy shit," he mutters.

"Yeah," I agree with him.

"And you don't want the baby?"

"What kind of man do you take me for? Of course I want the baby." I glare at him for even opening his mouth and let that bullshit fly out of it.

"What's stopping you from going and getting your girl then?"

"I went to her work yesterday, and she was getting in the car with Justin Bland."

"The contract lawyer?" I nod. "Stiff competition, Kadin. He's a pretty decent man."

"I fucking know that. You should've seen her, Kegan. She's even more beautiful than I remember. Her stomach is out about this far," I say indicating with my hand about six inches from my own stomach. "Most incredible thing I've ever seen."

"You have to try," he says.

"I know but what if she doesn't want me?" I sound like a whining child, but the idea of her rejecting me makes me want to break down and cry. Some man I am.

"Well, then at least you'll know, which is much better than sitting here each day wondering about what might have been." He is one hundred percent accurate. It's exactly what I'd do. I know it's exactly what I'll do tonight once he's gone and all day tomorrow as I sit in the parking lot and watch her leave work again.

"You don't seem like you want her to say no, but are you ready for her to say yes?" Leave it to my wild-ass, take nothing serious, brother to come up with some poignant shit like that.

"I've been in therapy since she left. I've known she was pregnant since then. I found the positive pregnancy test in the trash," I admit.

"And you're just telling me this shit now? What kind of brother are you?" He playfully shoves my shoulder.

"I've had a ton of shit to work through. I knew if I wanted even a chance of being worthy enough to be a father then I had to get things straight in my own life. I had to compartmentalize my issues and work on them individually. I would've gone insane had I not." I swallow roughly. "Besides she left and never came back. Until Sierra told me what she did, I was working on accepting that I'd never see her again."

"Did you look for her?"

I huff a light laugh. "I went to her old hometown and punched out the boyfriend that cheated on her. The one that sent her running in the first place, but he hadn't seen her. I had a private investigator looking for her but since she hadn't filed income tax for the year and all of her stuff was showing up as her old address in Great Falls. Everything was a dead end."

"You were just going to give up?" Here's the asshole brother I know.

"I had to accept eventually that she knew where I worked and never came to me. She could have come to the condo." I sigh. "I've spent hundreds of hours over the last five months hanging out in baby stores hoping I'd run into her."

He chuckles and the ridiculousness of what I just admitted to. I can't help but laugh with him.

"It scares me how much I want her; how much I need her. It took all the strength I had not to chase them down today and demand she come back to me." I scrub my hands over my face.

"When do you plan to go up to her?" He leans in closer, anxiously waiting for the answer.

"Tomorrow evening when she gets off of work," I respond. "I can't wait a day longer. That's if I don't go sit in the parking lot at her work and surprise her when she gets to work first thing."

He smirks at me and shakes his head. "I don't think first thing in the morning is going to work. I'll stay here tonight and hang out with you tomorrow to keep you from doing anything stupid," he offers.

"Don't you have work tomorrow?"

He winks at me. "I'm sure my boss won't mind."

Forty-Four

London

"Quit huffing," I tell Jillian as we walk down the hallway to the doctor's office. "Find a seat when we get in there and I'll find you after I pee in the little cup."

"Ugh, London. Keep the fucking details to yourself." She sticks a finger playfully in her mouth and pretends to gag. "Why the hell do they need you to pee in a cup or anyways?"

"I'm not exactly certain, but they run tests on it or something." I shrug. "I have to do it every time I come in."

"It's moments like this I realize two very important things. One, I love my job, and I'm glad I decided NOT to go into the medical field. Two, I never want kids. Just getting to the birth is absolutely disgusting." I think she's joking but when I cut my eyes to her she's shaking her head slightly and is completely serious.

As usual I'm put into a room very quickly but this is where the long wait happens. I don't know why they don't leave us in the waiting room where I can at least people watch. Plus, the sign on the wall instructs me to turn off my cell phone. The last time I came I was brave and read a book on the kindle app on my phone but got a tacky look from the nurse when I couldn't put it away fast enough. I think a half a second after knocking is not a long enough time before barging in on someone. "What are you doing?" I ask Jillian with a light laugh as she stares at the 3D replica of a uterus and ovaries. "Haven't you been in OB/GYN's office before?"

"Yes," she says scrunching up her nose and leaning in even closer. "But the handful of times I've been I've been in a paper gown on the table. I didn't have the ability to look at things up close." She points to the uterus. "Do you think that is a healthy one or a diseased one? I honestly can't tell."

"I think that's a healthy one. Will you sit down," I beg, pointing to a chair beside the table I'm perched on. "You're making me nervous."

Giving it one last scrutinizing glance, she appeases me and takes a seat. "Tell me about your date last night."

I narrow my eyes at her. "About that," I say sharply. "You've got to stop pushing Justin on me. It's not fair to him. He gets his hopes up. I try to keep things platonic, and you do things like make sure we have the most romantic table in the restaurant with fucking candles on the table."

"I was just trying to help," she replies with an uncharacteristically gentle voice.

I soften my own voice because I know she means well. "I've been telling you for months there is too much other stuff I'm dealing with right now. I can't get into anything with Justin."

"Okay," she finally agrees. "I won't do any more sneaky matchmaking. Seriously, though, how was last night?"

The quick knock on the door prevents me from relaying last night events and the doctor walks in.

We go through the basics, and he asks some questions about some elective tests I'm due to have if I feel like it, mostly genetic type stuff. I realize that I know nothing about Kadin's family history and what I'm aware of from Trent's family is just what he'd relayed to me in passing. I have no way of knowing the things that could affect my baby without knowing who the father is and getting that information from them.

Just as he's finishing up and turns to wash his hands before exiting the room, I finally speak up. "Dr. I want to know about," I clear my throat. "I'm curious about how a paternity test would work."

Ever the professional, he takes the question in stride. "You could have an amnio now to determine paternity, but it carries some risks. The safest thing to do would be to wait until the baby is born and do it then."

"What all does that entail?" I question.

"Buccal swabs. The testing center will swipe the inside mouth of the baby as well as the suspected fathers and the tests would be run from that." He uses a couple paper towels to dry his hands and takes a step near the door. "Do we have your anatomy sonogram scheduled?"

"Yes, sir. Next week." I answer.

"Very good," he says with a gentle smile. "See you next month Ms. Sykes." He nods his head at Jillian and exits the room.

"That was a tough conversation to have," Jillian says as we get in my car outside the doctor's office. "What are you going to do?"

I don't hesitate. "I'm going to wait until the baby is born. Poor thing is already going to have enough of a hard life with only one parent. I don't want to take the chance of complications just because Mom is a slut who doesn't know who its father is." I'm near tears. I'd thought I'd accepted the fact that the baby could be either Trent's or Kadin's but apparently I'm not even close to being over the shame from it.

"Stop that shit right now," Jillian says harshly.

I sniffle and use a tissue from the console to dab at my eyes. "Sorry. I cry all the time."

"Cry all you want. That's not what I'm talking about." She turns her body toward mine in the passenger seat. "There is no shame in the situation that you're in. It's not the most ideal, but it is far from unmanageable. Now dry your pretty face. We still have a half day of work at the office before the weekend starts."

"You're right." I steel my spine and will my eyes to be clear and dry by the time we make it back to the office.

"Besides," she says speaking for the first time since we pulled out of the parking lot at the doctor's office. "Either one of those assholes should be honored to have knocked you up."

I glare at her then nearly fold over in laughter. She knows just what to say and exactly when to say it.

I smile as I open the door to my office and see an outlandish vase of flowers on the corner of my desk. My assumptions are correct when I pluck the card that's nestled in them and read the little note that Justin wrote on it.

Had a great time last night, hope to do it again soon. It's signed *Your Friend*, J.

I lean in close with a smile on my face and breathe the bouquet in. I'm not a flower person, and Trent only sent some on my birthday a few times, so I have no clue what half of them are but the reds, pinks, whites, and greens make for one stunning display.

"Wow," I hear Jillian say from my door.

Suddenly a wave of uneasiness comes over me. "Jillian," I sigh. "Did you send me flowers from him?"

She shakes her head no and walks up to smell them just like I did a moment ago. "I had nothing to do with this," she says with astonishment. "But he did a damn fine job."

She walks and leaves with that little tidbit.

I don't know how Justin has been both patient and persistent at the same time, but he's seemed to have perfected the combination. I can't deny that I slept better after our date last night. I was happy that someone was willing to show me interest even though I now come with baggage. Both physically with the baby and emotionally with my past.

As wonderful as he is, he's not Kadin. As much as I know he would work every day to make me happy, I don't think I can be completely happy ever again. He needs to find someone who still has a heart to give away.

I sigh again and turn on my computer, hoping some work will push all thoughts of both Justin and Kadin out of my mind.

I've been here before. A feeling of unease sweeps through me as the fog glides around my ankles. I can almost remember what happens next, but the events seem blurry. Familiar yet oddly different at the same time. The trail I'm following in the woods opens up into a clearing filled with a slow moving fog. It clears just briefly enough to expose London's beautiful face. She looks at me tenderly, and I follow her gaze down to her arms but can't tell what she's holding. When she looks up, I see a tear roll down her cheek, and she turns and disappears into the mist. The sound of a baby crying makes my heart stop and propels me into action at the same time. I search for her, but the fog is too thick, and my hands come back empty each and every time I reach out for her.

"London!" I sit upright in bed covered in sweat and barely able to catch my breath. I scrub at my face with my hands and try to wipe away the dread I feel in my stomach.

I'm no stranger to nightmares; I have them all the time. The one that has haunted me for months was with Savannah. This one with London and the sound of the baby crying is brand new and puts me on edge. I grab my cell phone from the table by the bed. Four in the morning; more than twelve hours before I'll be able to see her. Twelve hours of nothing to do but drive me crazy.

A couple of hours later Kegan finds me on hands and knees scrubbing the kitchen floor. I'm determined to clean the house from top to bottom on the off chance she may want to come back here with me. The house was pretty damn clean to begin with, which Kegan pointed out, but at least it gave me something to do to pass the time.

The last hour before I left the house, I spent making room for her. The house is huge, so that's not even an issue, but I made room for her in my space. I moved my clothes to one area of the closet; I cleared off one of the bedside tables, and I arranged things on the bathroom sink for the things I remember seeing on the sink at the condo. I can tell her all day long that I need her, but I want her to see truly that I have room in my life, in my heart, for her. I want her to know that I want her to fill all of the voids in my life; that I'm incomplete without her.

Kegan and I part ways on the front porch, ending with a back slap man hug and wishes for the best outcome. He assures me since I'm a Cole, I've got it in the bag. I hope with every atom of my being that he's right.

Waiting in the parking lot is miserable. Knowing she's less than a hundred yards away kills me as each second ticks by agonizingly slow. I hope she comes out alone because I won't be able to refrain from approaching her if she tries to leave again with Justin Bland. I'm pleased to see her car parked in a different spot than it was yesterday; it leads me to believe that she actually went home last night rather than stayed with him. I had to realize and accept last night that I may not be fighting only against our pasts, along with my mistakes, but I may also be up against another man. The thought sits heavy in my already turning stomach.

Five o'clock rolls around and no one exits the building. I'm growing impatient by the second. What kind of man keeps his staff after five on a Friday? At five-fifteen the front door opens and a small group of people walks out, heading to the small parking area.

My heart stops just like it did yesterday at the sight of London. Watching Justin Bland walk her to her car with a hand at the small of her back enrages me. They get in separate cars but not before Justin leans in and places a kiss at her temple. I may be charged with murder if they end up at the same place. I watch as he leaves the parking lot, turning right. I breathe a sigh of relief when she turns left.

I'm in a company truck with no real identifiable features. It's purposeful because I didn't want her to recognize me and put herself in danger by trying to get away. I don't think she'd do something like that, but she did leave with no warning and not so much as a note, so I didn't want to take my chances.

I wait at a distance in the parking lot of a small grocery store for twenty minutes while she shops, resisting the urge to get out and help her load up her groceries when she's done. The more I sit and watch her, the creepier I feel. I'm not trying to learn her routine; I just need to know where she lives. I can't lose her again, and I'm afraid if I reach out to her at any place other than her home I may never see her again.

The grocery store appears to be her last stop, and I park on the street when she pulls into the driveway of an adorable cottage style house. The driveway is empty which leads me to believe that she either lives alone or is currently the only one here. My hope, of course, is for the former.

She doesn't notice me as I make my way up the driveway. She's huddled near the trunk of her little red car, grabbing groceries out of the trunk.

"London," I say startling her so bad she swings around, and apples go rolling down the driveway.

"Kadin!" She gasps and brings her now empty hands protectively to her stomach.

I tried working out what I was going to say to her at this moment. I pondered over it for hours last night and again today while I did my best to keep busy. Standing before her right now, my mind is a complete blank other than the urge to sweep her in my arms and run my nose down the side of her neck.

We stand, just looking at each other. The first tendrils of anger at her leaving begin to creep in.

"You just left," I say harshly.

I watch as her face changes from shock at my presence to anger.

"You went to go fuck your dead wife's twin. Excuse me for not staying around to put up with that shit!" Leaving the hatch open on her car and the groceries inside, she turns and begins to storm away to the front of the house.

"London! Don't walk away from me again." She ignores me and continues walking into the house. This is not how I saw this going at all. "How can you walk away from me when you're carrying my baby?" It's an honest question. The last amount of venom in her words tell me why she left, something I'd been wondering about since the day it happened.

"I don't know that!" She seethes as she turns around to face me.

What the fuck did she just say?

Forty-Six

London

I watch as confusion and some other unnamed emotion, sadness maybe, sweeps over his face. I'm shocked that he's here and more than a little excited, but I don't know how to handle the barrage of feelings as they all collide with me all at once. I regretted the words the second they came out of my mouth and I'm terrified he will run, but it's not relief washing over his face. From the fall of his mouth, he seems distraught at the possibility of the baby not being his.

"What are you saying?" he finally whispers.

"You want me to spell it out?" I ask with a tremble in my voice. I take his silence as a yes. "I conceived the weekend we met."

"So it has to be mine," he says. "We were drunk but I… we didn't use… you fell asleep in my arms that night."

A tear rolls down my cheek. "I woke up in Trent's arms that morning."

Understanding marks his already crestfallen face, and I want to sob when I see the slight tremor in his chin. He reaches out for the banister of the porch to steady himself, his eyes closing briefly.

"So that means…" His voice trails off as if he can't fathom the possibility that I may be carrying another man's baby.

"That I'm a whore, and I have no clue who the father of this baby is?" I press my trembling hands to my stomach. Saying it out loud to him makes me sick to my stomach.

"London," he whispers reaching for me. I take a step back. "I'd never say that about you. I'd never *think* that about you."

I close my eyes and let his words wash over me allowing myself to believe him if only for a minute. He takes a step closer but doesn't reach for me again.

"When you woke up that morning, you had no clue how your night was going to end. I got you drunk. I took advantage."

"You didn't," I argue. "I kissed you first, remember?"

His face softens, and his eyes flutter closed as if he recalls the memory this exact second. "I could never forget." His eyes pop open. "But, I knew you were vulnerable, and I let it happen. You're not a whore, London. You're a beautiful, amazing woman, who is carrying my child," he says stubbornly as if he believes it enough it will be true.

We watch each other for long moments, and his twitching fingers do not go unnoticed. I wonder absently if he has the urge to reach out and touch me as I do him.

"Can we go inside and talk?" He finally asks in a hopeful voice.

Without a word, I turn from him and finish unlocking the door. "It's not much," I explain as he follows me inside.

He closes the door behind him but keeps a small distance between us. I turn the lights on in the living room and hold an arm out, directing him to sit on the sofa.

"It's exactly how I would have imagined your place," he says and sits down in the middle of the sofa forcing me to either stand or sit beside him, knowing if I sit our legs would be touching.

The cottage is very small, and the sofa is the only place in the living room to sit. He pretends it wasn't intentional as I take a seat beside him, keeping a protective arm over my stomach.

"Were you ever going to tell me?" He asks nodding at the ever-growing bump I can no longer hide even if I wanted to.

"The answer to that question has changed quite a few times over the last couple of months, Kadin." He looks at me patiently, waiting for me to explain. "I was going to find a way to conduct a paternity test after the baby was born." I stupidly remember Trent's hairbrush I somehow ended up packing when I left Great Falls, but with what the doctor told me this morning that's not how the tests are conducted.

"Why would you get a paternity test? Do you plan to go back to him if the baby is his?"

"No." I shake my head back and forth.

"Then it doesn't matter, London."

I stare at him. His mood has completely changed from the anger he had when he first arrived to now.

"I went to your condo," I admit softly. I watch his head snap up. "It was weeks ago, but some old man was there, and he said he'd lived there for years, and I knew he was confused so I didn't question him any further."

"You came back to me?" He reaches out and grasps my hand bringing it to his chest.

I almost moan at the heat coming off of his body. I've missed his touch so much.

"I came to tell you about the baby," I clarify.

"I've missed you," he says softly and touches my cheek with his free hand.

It takes every ounce of power and control I have not to lean into his touch. "You don't seem surprised that I'm pregnant. How did you know?"

"I found the test in the trash."

I nod. I remembered the test after I left the condo but had no way to go back and get it. I have to admit selfishly that in my anger I'd hoped that he would find it.

"I was going to tell you that night." I swallow roughly trying to fight back the pain I still feel from his lies. "I heard you talking to Sierra."

He winces.

"I could tell something was going on between you two. It wasn't my place to get in the middle of whatever it was, but then you came and lied to me about needing to take care of something at the office." I pause, doing my best to choke back the sob that's trying to climb up my throat. "You lied to me. I told myself when I left Trent that I'd never let another man treat me like that."

"So you left," he sighs.

"I left." I reach a hand up and wipe the tears I couldn't stop if I tried.

"Sierra and I," he huffs quietly. "We were never together, but that situation was a train wreck at best. I put an end to our... fuck I don't even know what you would call it. That was over long before I met you. Months before we met."

"You had sex with her to try to feel like you still had Savannah." He doesn't even have to explain it to me. I came to the conclusion long ago. There were two possibilities, either he was having an affair with Sierra or in his grief he gravitated to the closest thing to her he could find. Even in the short time I was around him, I could easily tell that he loved and was completely dedicated to Savannah, so the first part of my reasoning wasn't even a possibility.

"Pretty fucked up, huh?" He admits.

"Grieving is messy," I tell him.

"I want you back, London." His voice is almost pleading and I look up and into his beautiful eyes.

"We were never together, Kadin." I clarify.

"Tell that to my heart."

My pulse doubles at his words. *His heart?*

"You're still grieving, Kadin. I can't compete with her memories." I look down at our clasped hands which now rest on his lap.

"London." I refuse to look up at him.

"I need to be first in your life." Another tear rolls down my face, and he reaches up and catches it on the end of his finger. "Can you love me like that? Can you love me like you loved her?"

"No," he whispers softly, destroying what little repairs my heart had made over the last five months.

Forty-Seven
Kadin

"No," I answer honestly. The pain that immediately crosses her face guts me and makes me happy all at the same time. Obviously not the answer she was wanting and her reactions prove she cares for me; it proves I have a chance.

I reach up, clamp my finger and thumb on her chin, and pull her face up, forcing her to look into my eyes. "London, I already love you more."

She gasps and her eyes go wide at my admission. "I've spent the last couple of months working through a lot of my problems," I tell her not wanting to lose steam. "I felt incomplete when Savannah died. Her death destroyed me. She took a huge part of who I was with her." I take a deep breath because I've thought all of these things but never said them out loud, not even with Dr. Long.

"That's how I felt without you," she admits.

"Even in your absence, you've already replaced that missing piece, London." She watches my hand as I reach out and place it on her stomach. "I love you, London." I flex my fingers. "I love this baby. Look at me," I plead as her eyes drift down to where I'm touching our unborn child. "Biologically or not, this baby is mine. I need you, London, and I need this baby, too."

She smiles softly and places one of her hands on top of mine. "Love?" she whispers so low I can hardly hear her.

"With every atom of my being," I proclaim gently.

"I can't take the lies," she says. "Even if you're trying to protect me."

"Never again," I vow.

"I'm not going to compete with Sierra for you." She turns her face to look in my eyes.

I can't control the mild tick I get above my right eye when I think of that murderous bitch. "Sierra is even more of a non-issue than she was months ago. I'm not going to go into all of it right now, but we'll never have to deal with her again. I promise you, London. You're it for me."

She shifts her gaze back and forth between my eyes, more than likely trying to determine if I'm telling the truth.

"Do I have anyone to worry about?" I don't think right now is the right time to bring up the fact that I've practically stalked her outside of her building.

Without hesitation she replies, "My heart is possessed by yours. I couldn't love someone else if I tried."

The smile in my heart matches the one creeping over my face. "You love me?"

"I think I had loved you before we left the cabin, Kadin."

Her words bring pain and understanding with them. I know without a doubt had she had said those words before she left, I would've more than likely rejected her. I can admit that I've needed every second of the time we've been apart to heal and move past my own demons. I only hope that I can repair what I broke because of the lies I told her.

I lean in closer to her, hoping to kiss her softly when she stands abruptly. "I forgot the groceries!" She exclaims. "My frozen yogurt is going to be ruined."

I stand with her. "Let me help you," I offer.

I convinced London to let me order pizza for us when her stomach started to growl after we got the groceries into the house. She offered to cook and as much as I'd love to spend the evening in the kitchen preparing a meal together I can tell how tired she was after a long work week.

"Thank you," she says pushing her plate away.

"For what?" I ask gently. We've been in the same room for hours, and my fingers itch to touch her, my mouth waters to taste her. I know we have to go slow, and we can't just go back to the way things were the weekend before she left.

"The pizza," she says pointing at her plate.

"I plan to give you the world, London." I wink at her. "Pizza is only the beginning."

She smiles timidly in response. "Want to watch some TV?"

Watching TV is not exactly my first pick but being in the same room with London is more than I thought I'd ever have again. "I'd love to," I tell her.

We end up with some ridiculous Lifetime movie on with the volume turned almost all the way down. Her eyes seem to glaze over almost immediately, and I know she's exhausted.

"Come here," I tell her and pat my lap. "Lay down." I shift my body to the very far end of the sofa and watch with relief as she lies on her left side and places her head on my lap.

I pull the few clips she has in her hair out and toss them on the coffee table in front of us. I stroke her hair gently and resist the urge to bring it to my nose to smell. We didn't discuss where we plan to go from here, but we know we both love each other, so I'm hopeful of our future together.

Before long she's gone completely still, and her breathing has evened out. I continue to stroke her hair absently and lean my head back, closing my eyes. A sense of calm I've never felt before in my life settles over me and know I've found my place in the world; I know that place is wherever she is.

Not wanting both of my legs to fall completely asleep, I lift London in my arms and cradle her to my chest as I make my way down the narrow hall. There are only three doors to choose from. One is the bathroom and the one at the very end of the short hall is open, and I can see a queen sized bed taking up almost all of the space in the room.

I walk inside and gently put her down on the unmade bed, thankful the covers were already out of the way, clearly left from when she threw them off of her this morning. I settle her in, pulling the covers over her shoulder and turn to walk away. I have no plans to leave fully but decide it may be best to sleep on the couch.

"Please stay," she whispers as I make my way to the door.

I turn back to her and see her peering at me with tired eyes. "London, if I get in that bed with you…" I let my words trail off because I don't even want to give my hunger a voice yet.

"Hold me, please?" I kick off my shoes, unable to resist her plea and climb in behind her.

I wedge one arm under her head and wrap the other one around her waist, settled firm against her amazing bump.

"I love you so much," she whispers into the dark.

"I'll love you for the rest of my life, London." I squeeze her a little tighter as I feel her body match up to mine like the very last piece of a puzzle I've been waiting my whole life to find.

I wake up holding onto the most beautiful woman in the world. It's not a fairy tale, open your eyes and smile at each other kind of moment, because the second she opens her eyes, she jumps up on the bed and scrambles out of the room. I laugh when I hear her mutter something about the baby jumping on her bladder.

A few minutes later she's crawling back in bed with me, lying across my chest. I stroke her back gently and kiss the top of her messy head. We're both still in our clothes from yesterday and looking pretty ragged.

"I missed you so much," she says hoarsely, and I can hear the pain in her words.

As much as I want to point out the obvious I keep my mouth shut. She knew where I worked; she knew how to find me. I know my anger over it is something I'll have to work through in therapy, but I refuse to let it cloud the moment we're having right now.

"I looked for you almost every single day," I admit to the top of her head.

She shifts her weight and turns her head so she can look at me. "You did?" She asks as if she doesn't believe me.

I nod. "I drove around for hours trying to find your car. I called almost every doctor's office hoping they'd give me your information." She frowns. "They wouldn't. I didn't know if you left Spokane. I didn't know if you," I have to clear my throat at the next thought. "If you had an abortion." I reach down and place my large hand on the swell of her belly.

"I'd never…" I hush her by placing my fingers to her lips.

"When all the driving around didn't produce you I starting being the creepy guy that hangs out at baby stores." I laugh. "I'm certain I've been in every store in this town, at least, a dozen times each."

"I haven't even started shopping for the baby yet." She runs a finger down my cheek. "I didn't want to go until I knew if it was a boy or a girl."

My heart rate increases and my hand begins to tremble slightly, excitement coursing through my veins. "Have you found out?" I hate that I've missed everything with her pregnancy up to this point.

She grins at me. "Not until next week." My face hurts because of how big my smile is. "Something you'd be interested in?"

"It would mean the world to me, London." I'm ecstatic knowing that I haven't missed every single thing.

"Do you love me, Kadin?" She asks hesitantly.

"More than anyone in this world," I answer her.

"You haven't kissed me; you've been hesitant to touch me." She lowers her eyes, but I hook my finger under her chin, gently forcing her to look at me.

"I don't want to push you. The last thing I want is for you to feel overwhelmed or like I forced my way back into your life. I want nothing more than to make love to you for the rest of my life, London, but I need to know that's what you want too." I let my finger roam down her neck and feel a sense of pride when she quivers from my touch.

"We have a lot to talk about," she says finally.

"Yes, we do. Do you want to do that now? Some things are difficult for me to discuss, but I won't shy away from your questions." I need to be an open book for her. I need her to be the same for me. I need to know that she feels comfortable talking to me, able to ask me anything because I can't lose her again.

"Right now?" She asks and scrunches up her nose like it's the worst thing in the world. "Right now I want you to shower with me."

"London," I groan and scrub my hand over my face. "That's not such a good idea. I won't be able to keep my hands off of you."

She winks at me and climbs off the bed. "I don't expect you to. Besides, the shower is super tiny so we'll be practically on top of one another."

I don't think I've ever moved so fast in my life.

Forty-Eight

London

The libido that vanished the second I walked away from Kadin months ago showed up yesterday almost the same second he arrived in my driveway. I stepped away from him on my front porch because I didn't think I could keep my hands off of him once he touched me.

The wanton woman who just invited him to the shower with her? I have no idea who that woman is, but I have a feeling she's not going anywhere anytime soon. The cottage is nothing like his condo or the cabin was as far as luxury. I reach in and turn on the hot water, knowing it takes several long minutes for it to warm.

Kadin stands at the sink rinsing his mouth with mouthwash. I brushed my teeth when I used the restroom earlier hoping that he would pounce on me the second I climbed back into bed with him. I don't know this cautious and tentative Kadin. It's sweet and endearing, but right now I just want to attack him, and my restraint is faltering as the seconds tick by.

He turns from the sink and takes a step toward me. The bathroom is beyond tiny, so there's not much room at all to maneuver. I reach my hands up to the top button of his shirt, flicking the first one open.

His chest rumbles in approval when my fingers touch his hot chest as I slowly unbutton his shirt. I stand on the tips of my toes to gain the height I need to push it over his shoulder, making sure my hands stay on his golden skin the entire time. He closes his eyes and takes in every sensation as it flutters to the floor.

I rake my nails down his chest and abdomen on their way to the button and zipper of his jeans. He hisses as they slightly score his skin. The tension builds in the front of his pants at an amazingly swift rate. My mouth waters and the apex of my thighs grow slick as my ears register the rasping sound of his zipper being lowered; Pavlov's dog at its finest.

I see his hands open the fist as he attempts to maintain his control. I know he wants to touch me, but it's almost as if he's enjoying the agony of making himself wait. I watch his face as I rub my hand over his length still covered by his now tight boxer briefs. His groan is rewarding and echoes my own need.

Unable to wait a second longer I push his jeans and boxers down his thighs, causing his cock to spring from its confines. I missed the glorious sight of him. I take a step back and let him finish tugging the pants free from his feet, watching as he carelessly tosses them aside on the floor.

I stand there innocently as if unaware I just provoked a bear in a very tiny room. I want him wild and lustful; I need him to want me as much as I want him. From the look of his narrowed eyes and the way he's staring at me as if I'm prey, I don't think that's going to be a problem.

"Your turn," he growls. His demeanor is aggressive, but his hands are calm and reverent. He bends forward as he pulls my tank top up, placing the sweetest of kisses on the very top of my bump.

He tugs the tank top over my head efficiently and tosses it toward his own pile of discarded clothing. He hesitates and looks in my eyes as his hands glide up my ribs and his thumbs caress the underside of my breasts, still covered in the lace of my bra. It's almost as if he's asking for permission to go forward. I want to slap him for being so apprehensive but at the same time I want to kiss him for being so considerate. I nod my head, giving him permission to continue.

Not wasting another second, he flips open the snap of my bra and my heavy breasts spring free.

"Fuck," he whispers reverently. I let the lace fall off of my shoulders as he raises his hands and delicately cups each of them in his hands. "They're bigger than I remember." He places a kiss on the top of each globe and looks in my eyes.

"I've gone up a cup size since getting pregnant, and all of the books say they'll get even bigger than that after the birth," I explain.

He keeps his eyes locked on mine watching my reaction as he sweeps his thumbs over the tender, hardened tips. I moan and close my eyes momentarily.

"Still sensitive I see."

"Ah!" I gasp when he lowers his mouth and gives one a hard lick. "They're more sensitive."

He releases me and slides his strong hands down my back, taking my wrinkled slacks down with them. The best thing about maternity clothes is the easy on/easy off. We're both standing stark naked in my tiny bathroom that long ago filled with the steam from the shower.

Somehow maintaining his control when I want nothing more than for him to bend me over at the sink and fuck me stupid, he pulls the shower curtain aside and holds my hand, helping me step over the lip of the tub and into the spray. My lips remain kiss free as he quickly washes his body and then turns his attention to me.

I'm almost okay that he only cleaned my most delicate spots just as quick and efficient as he did his own as he massages soap and then conditioner into my long hair. I close my eyes as his long fingers work my scalp with a magical touch. Once he deems us both clean he reaches past me and turns off the water.

I give him a sexy pout when he dries me with just as much economic grace as he did when he washed me. I'd almost believe he wasn't affected, but the thickness of his fully erect shaft betrays his false calmness. He wraps the towel around my body, hiding it from his eyes and sits me on the edge of the tub.

He may be doing his best to ignore the big horny elephant in the room but when he starts to comb out my long hair, there's no way I can ignore the straining erection bouncing in my face. I place my hands gently on his thighs, lean my head in, and without warning suck the mushroom head of his cock into my mouth.

He pulls back suddenly, wrenching himself from my mouth. "London," he gasps. "What are you doing?"

I give him a mischievous smirk and shrug my shoulders. "You put it in my face. I was just getting reacquainted."

He narrows his eyes and drops the comb to the floor. "Reacquainted, huh? How about we both get reacquainted in the bedroom?" *Finally.*

He stands me up and tugs the towel free of my body and uses it to quickly run over his own skin before discarding it on the floor.

"I think that's a great plan." I say and squeal when he sweeps me up in his arms and carries me down the short hallway to the room.

He places me gently on the bed and covers my body with his own, taking care not to put pressure on my stomach. Our faces are mere inches apart; I can feel his hot puffs of air as he sweeps damp strands of hair off of my face.

"I can wait, London. We don't have to jump right into this. Sex is not the reason I'm here with you." His words falter at the end when I rotate my hips and grind my heat against him.

"I swear, Kadin. If you don't make me come I'll..." He cuts my words off when his mouth covers mine.

I wrap my arms around him and hold onto him with everything I have as his tongue strokes along mine, reorienting their selves. My body is pure liquid under his touch, better now than I remembered because I know how he feels about me. Having passionate sex is nothing compared to making love to a man you want to spend the rest of your life with.

I open my eyes and crane my mouth searching for his when he pulls away, aching at the loss. Slowly he makes his way down my body kissing, caressing, and nibbling.

"What are you doing?" I mutter as he places his forehead on my stomach.

He doesn't respond until he's had his minute then begins to move his mouth lower, over my hip, along my thigh.

"Please, Kadin. I don't need that right now. I want you inside of me." I moan loudly when I feel his hot breath tickle my delicate flesh.

I look down, and he raises his eyes to mine. "I'd last about three seconds inside of you, London. I'm good, but I'm not 'give you an orgasm in less than three seconds good.' I don't know exactly what you plan to do to me if I don't make you come, so I'm rectifying that first."

All I can see is the very top of his eyes over my stomach when he swipes his tongue through my neglected folds. My body arches of its own volition and I press myself hard against his working mouth. He presses his big hands against my thighs holding me open as my body tries to clamp them together at his intrusion.

His talented tongue skates and flutters over my core with wicked skill and my body grows warm as the tingles I haven't felt in months begin in my lower belly. "So good," I hear him whisper against me reverently.

"Kadin, please. Oh God." He's placed his hands under my body and back over my hips to hold me in place as I squirm and wiggle under his attention. "Kadin!" I screech when the orgasm hits me full force, and I begin to convulse and my core clenches at the emptiness I so desperately need to be filled.

Kadin moves quickly, lining himself against my center and slowly pushing into my still quivering body. My eyes go wide as he pushes further inside. I don't remember him being so big. I press a hand to his chest and clamp my eyes together. His hips still immediately.

"Am I hurting you? Fuck you're so tight, London."

I can feel his body trembling, urging him to move. "Just go slow," I whisper to him.

I whimper when his thumb rolls over my clit, the attention to the bundle of nerves eases some of the discomforts of his invasion. My legs tremble when I bring them up and lock the around his thighs.

His thumb presses harder, and my body clenches him tighter. He pushes forward slowly as his talented hand manipulates my swollen clit. I hum appreciatively when he finds the end of me and the tell-tale signs of another orgasm begins to creep over my body. My already flushed skin grows even warmer as a light mist of sweat covers my forehead.

"I'm going to come just like this, London. Buried deep inside of you." He closes his eyes briefly. "I can feel you quivering. When it hits you, you're going to take me with you." His thumb strokes faster, the circles becoming concentrated exactly where I need them.

"Kadin," I gasp breathlessly.

"Take me with you, beautiful." The second my orgasm forces the first ripple of pressure against him I feel the pulsing beat of his own orgasm inside me.

He prolongs mine, at the same time completing his when he flexes his hips back a few inches and thrusts gently inside of me. His thumb continues to absently stroke against my oversensitive nub until I have to pull my hips away and swat at his hand to make him stop.

Still inside of me, he rests back on his heels between my spread thighs. "You're absolutely amazing."

I smile up at him. "Kiss me, Kadin. I've missed your lips."

He obliges willingly until we decide it's best to get cleaned up and we reluctantly force each other out of the bed. After quick showers, we eat breakfast but end up right back in my bed holding each other.

"Want to have that talk now?" I prod as I lay my head on his chest.

Forty-Nine

Kadin

"I'm an open book," I tell her holding her close to my chest. "You may not be completely happy with my answers or my explanation on some things, London. But I won't ever lie to you again."

She runs her fingers up and down my chest, and it's one of the most relaxing things I've felt in a very long time.

"Now that I have you back in my arms," I begin my confession, "I can honestly say that I'm also glad you left."

She swings her head up and looks painfully into my eyes.

"Let me finish," I admonish and tap her nose with my finger. "I don't know that I would've worked through everything I have if you would've stayed. In the end, my grief and bitterness would've destroyed us. I realized on the way back from Great Falls that I needed to be a better man if I ever expected you to allow me to be a father."

"You went to Great Falls?"

I nod. "I did everything I could to try to find you."

"You went to the bar didn't you?" She asks softly.

"I did. I could tell he hadn't seen you. So I punched him in the face and left."

She stares at me with a shocked expression on her face. "You punched him?"

"Yes. He popped off at the mouth, and it pissed me off."

"What did he say?" She asks.

"It's not important, London. It was on the drive home that I understood what I had to do to be a man worthy of you; worthy of this baby." I caress our unborn child with my hand. "I didn't know if I'd ever see you again. I wasn't particularly hopeful since I hadn't been able to track you down, but I knew I had to be ready if I was ever given the chance again.

"I'd canceled my therapy appointment after you left, but realized very quickly that I'd get nowhere without it, so I've seen Dr. Long weekly since shortly after you left," I explain.

She remains silent, allowing me to get everything off my chest without the expectation of answering questions, just as I had done for her in the cabin when she told me about her abusive history.

"It took forever, but I was eventually able to accept that Savannah was gone. I was able to work through my anger at her and choices we made. Choices I let her make for me that weren't exactly what I'd wanted."

"Like what?" She questions gently.

"The condo for one. I never wanted to live there. I hate being inside the city not able to see the stars at night." I lovingly touch her belly again. "I wanted children. I knew even then that parenthood was something a couple had to enter into together, so I eventually let it go."

She places a hand over mine on her stomach. "This wasn't exactly something we planned, Kadin."

"You have no idea how much I want this with you, London. I can't picture my life without you, without this baby, in it. We may not have planned it, but I feel like things, even with the winding path we took to get here, is exactly where we're supposed to be." I kiss the top of her head and continue my admissions.

"I tried everything I could think of to find you, and when I couldn't, I went looking for Brian." She goes rigid under me. "Don't worry, beautiful. He'll never hurt anyone again."

"Oh God, Kadin. Did you?" She raises her head and waits for my answer.

I chuckle at her response. "I didn't touch him. I had a private investigator track him down, and he found a tombstone rather than an abusive asshole. Brian Webster was murdered by an angry father shortly after you left college. The relationship he got into after you left turned abusive very quickly. The father of the girl he was abusing sought retribution and beat him to death with a baseball bat. Brian must have hurt her pretty bad because the jury convicted the dad of manslaughter rather than outright murder."

I see a tear roll down her face and wipe it way, almost angry at the idea that she feels sorry that he's dead. "I should've done something before I left. It's my fault someone else was hurt by him because I just took off and didn't file charges on him."

I squeeze her to my chest. "You did what you needed to do to be safe, London. His choice to hurt other people is not on you. Don't let him take up any more space in your head. It's over. You never have to worry about him hurting another person. He's been dead for years."

She settles on my chest again, and I continue to rub her back and belly simultaneously. "What else do you want to know?"

She remains silent for a long moment before she whispers, "Sierra."

"Sierra came to the condo that night, and I knew things were going to be bad. I'm not making excuses for my lie, London, but she's not stable. She has a history of mental health issues, and I wanted to get her away from you. With everything I know now, that lie was the best thing I could've ever done."

She lifts her head off of my chest once again and looks like she's going to argue with me. "Let me finish," I say hoarsely.

"I let things between Sierra and I get very muddled since Savannah passed. We slept together a handful of times. I can tell you that I was drunk every single time, and that's the truth, but I knew each and every time she showed up and let me pretend she was Savannah that it was wrong." I shake my head slightly, not wanting to vocalize my sins to her but knowing full well we can't go forward until she knows all my secrets.

"I knew Sierra was obsessed with me since we were teenagers. Everyone did. We ignored all of the behaviors. She was so out of it the night I took her home from the condo that she had to be hospitalized. I'm pretty certain she's spent more of her life institutionalized than in the free world."

"So sad," she whispers against my chest.

I huff. "She was released a week or so ago. She tracked me down at my new house." My chest constricts painfully. "She was angry. She saw you at a store and followed you home and to work. She's how I found you."

"She's stalking me?" His face is full of alarm.

"Was." I kiss her forehead. "She was angry with my response to the news of where you were. Those words out of her mouth were the most beautiful thing I'd ever heard. She," I have to pause and clear my throat. This is the most recent revelation in my life and still one that is the most painful. "In a rage she admitted that she cut the brake lines on Savannah's car." She gasps and grips me tighter. "She admitted to killing my wife, her sister."

"Oh, Kadin. No!" Nodding my head is all I can do. If I try to speak, I'll lose it, much like I did in Dr. Long's office the first time I talked about it there.

At least, ten minutes pass before I continue; even then my voice is still gravelly and full of painful emotion. "She left my house that night in a rage before I could get the cops there. They did a well-check on her later that night. She'd slit her wrists down to the bone."

"She's dead?"

"No. They got to her in time. She admitted later at the hospital what she'd done. She'll never walk free again." I explain.

"Kadin, that's a horrible thing to deal with," she says softly.

"But I am. Dealing with it, I mean." I shift her weight, so she's on top of me, her legs straddling my hips.

I cup her face in both my hands hating that her panties and my boxers separate our bodies but instinctively knowing using sex at this moment is not fair to either one of us. I'm still learning to feel and work through painful emotions rather than using a coping mechanism to dull them.

I watch a tear roll down her cheek, saddened by my own pain. This woman is amazingly perfect. I bring my mouth to hers. "I love you," I whisper against her lips and kiss her thoroughly hoping she can feel my words rather than just hear them. "I want to spend the rest of my life making you happy. Will you let me?"

She smiles against my lips but doesn't answer.

"I'm serious, London. I can't leave here without you and this little house is way too small for the four of us."

She pulls her head back slightly. "Four?"

"The three of us." I place my hand on her stomach indicating our child. "And Pudge."

She laughs gently. "What is a Pudge?"

I smile big at the idea of her meeting my dog. "Pudge is the dog I adopted."

"You have a dog?" Her grin widens at the knowledge.

I nod. "*We* have a dog, London. Come home with me. I have an amazing house in the country."

She places both her hands on my chest, leans in, and places a delicate kiss on my lips. "I have a lease here, Kadin." The look on her face tells me that she's considering it, but she's not one hundred percent sure if she should say yes.

"Do you remember the days at the cabin?" I kiss her cheek. "The way we woke up every morning at the condo and made love?" I kiss the tip of her nose and run my hands down her back. "How perfect we were just sitting on the couch in the evenings?" I let my fingers trail up her inner thigh. "It's either me here with you or you there with me." I sweep my fingers through the slickness already forming at her center. She moans slightly and closes her eyes.

"Do it for Pudge, London. He loves the country. He'd be very sad cooped up in the tiny back yard you have."

She opens her eyes when I pull my hands away and whimpers when I move them to her knees, my touch losing its sensual intention. "How do you know I have a tiny backyard? Pudge may love it here."

I tilt my head at her. "London, I can stick my hand out of the window and touch your neighbor's house. I don't have to see the backyard to know that it is smaller than the dozen or so acres I have to offer him at our house in the country."

"Our house?" she says softly.

"Ours." I run my hands back up her thighs, taunting and teasing her.

"I wouldn't want Pudge to feel deprived. That would be a very selfish thing for me to do." She taps her finger on her chin playfully.

"Don't be selfish, London." My cock throbs at her moan when I slip my thumb past her panties and into her tight heat.

"As long as Pudge is happy," she gasps as my fingers continue to work her.

I pull my hand out of her panties. "Is that a yes?"

She nods her head, grasping my hand, and placing it back inside her panties. Who am I to deny her?

Fifty

London

Losing his wife was horrendous. Finding out her twin sister murdered her? That is unfathomable. Even with his news and the pain, I know he still feels about the entire situation, he seems happier than he ever did in the cabin or the condo.

The second he asked me to move in with him, I already knew my answer I just didn't want to seem overeager and needy. I wouldn't mind staying here with him, but it is pretty small especially with a dog and a baby on the way. I only have a month left on my lease so breaking that contract won't be too bad. Kadin assures me that he'll pay whatever he needs to get me in his arms and keep me there for the rest of his life.

He seems much more eager to get me out of here than I could ever have been. I went to the kitchen to cook lunch, and he left in his truck for twenty minutes and came back with a pile of industrial strength cardboard boxes. It seems he wants me out immediately. After lunch, we spend a few hours packing my meager belongings.

Much of the furniture in the house will stay, but I insist that the eclectic pieces that I bought over the last few months go with me. I almost thought he'd put up an argument, considering the very modern, sleek look I remember of the things in his condo, but he just smiles and agrees. He tells me that we can go ahead and bring what will fit in the bed of the truck today, and he will send a moving company by on Monday to get the rest.

We touch, kiss, and caress each other if we get within arm's length of one another. We both know we have a lot of time to make up for. He carries another box to the truck after insisting that I don't lift a thing. I sit on the sofa and look around the quickly emptying room. He must notice my sudden melancholy when he comes back in because he sits beside me and clasps my hand in his.

He tilts my chin up with a gentle finger and looks into my eyes. "What if you only think you want me? What if parenthood is more than you bargained for? What if the baby isn't…?" His fingers on my lips halt my words.

"I told you yesterday, and I meant every word I spoke. This baby," he says as he places a gentle hand on my stomach. "This baby is mine regardless of what a test would say. I'm not changing my mind, London. I've never been more certain of anything in my life. I don't want to spend another day away from you, but if you need time to decide I'll give you all the time you need."

I look into his eyes, and my heart grows at his words, doubles in size at the sincerity not only in his voice but in the depths of his gaze. The longing he feels for me is almost palpable, and it makes my heart rate calm and grow stronger if that's even possible.

"Promise me," I whisper. "Promise me I'm enough for you."

"You're more than I could've ever dreamed of, London. Am I enough for you?" There is not a hint of cocky Kadin to be found; the slight flash of fear in his eyes proves he's concerned I find him lacking.

"Yes, Kadin. Forever." He gently places his lips on mine sealing our impromptu vows with the most tender of kisses.

"That is not a puppy, Kadin!" I exclaim as we pull up outside of the most beautiful country home I've ever seen. "He's as big as a pony."

He laughs. "The people at the shelter said he was only about a year old. It's clear he's going to be a huge animal."

"Well, I'm glad I didn't decide to move him into the cottage." I wink at him, but my face falls. "He's going to knock me down when I get out." I cross my arms over my stomach protectively.

His eyes follow my actions. "Stay in the truck and I'll get him inside. He's much calmer in there than out here. He's a maniac outside."

I watch as he gets out. Pudge senses I'm in the truck and is not happy when Kadin begins to practically drag him toward the house. I can hear him telling the dog about me and his expectations of his behavior when I get inside. I grin wide when I hear him mention the baby and how he's going to be a big brother, and the last thing he should do is hurt his sibling before his momma even gives birth.

When he shuts the dog inside, I open the door to the truck. Kadin runs to my side to help me jump out of the big monstrosity. I'm grateful for his help because it is a pretty big leap.

"I'm going to have to start using the car when we go places," he says absently.

"I don't think you'd fit in my car, Kadin."

He laughs and points to a five car garage. "No offense, beautiful, but I wouldn't be caught dead in your car."

The happy gleam in his eye prevents me from feeling offended that he's unimpressed with my Mini Cooper.

"You ready to see the house?" I nod and let him take my hand, leading me into the home we'll raise our child in.

Kadin is able to calm Pudge with the snap of his fingers and a quick scratch on his head. I crouch down in front of him and let him sniff my hands. I pet his head gently and coo to him watching his tail thump against the wall at the attention.

He follows us around the house as Kadin gives me the grand tour. "This is nothing like the condo," I eventually say as we make our way upstairs.

"Savannah decorated the condo," he informs me. "This is more my style."

We walk toward the end of the hall, and I can't help but notice how open and inviting it is. All of the doors are open and welcoming, even the master suite at the very end of the hall. He lets me walk in first and wraps his arms around my waist, resting his head on my shoulder as I look around the room.

Noticing the bed, I smile. "Is that the…"

"The bed from your room in the condo? Yes." He turns me in his arms. "It's all I had of you. I know this may seem sudden to you, but I've felt you with me every single day that we've been apart. I've built this life for us, hoping I'd find you again. This isn't something I impulsively decided the last couple of days."

"I want to show you something." He grasps my hand and tugs me to a door on the far side of the room.

I'm a assuming it's a bathroom and immediately hope it has all of the shower heads that the shower in the cabin had. He swings the door open wide, and I gasp, clamping a hand over my mouth. My eyes rake over everything in the small adjoining room.

"Is this okay?" He asks suddenly unsure about the entire situation.

Tears are running down my face as I look at the dark cherry crib and matching rocker with ottoman. The beautiful changing table in one corner looks like an antique and fits perfectly in the room.

"You need to say something, London. I don't know how to interpret the tears." He sounds nervous.

"It's beautiful, Kadin." I wrap my arms around his neck and bury my sobs into his hard chest. "You really want us here."

He pulls away slightly so he can look in my eyes. "You're home, London." He kisses my lips delicately. "Welcome home."

We stand in the small nursery holding each other for a long time until I eventually pull away to have a better look. I run my hand over the changing table. "I love this," I tell him.

"That was mine and Kegan's when we were babies," he informs me. "My mom can't wait to meet you."

I turn back to him with wide eyes. "You told your mom about me?" He nods. "When? Does she know about the baby?"

He chuckles. "I told her about you earlier this week; that's how I got the changing table. I didn't know if I'd get you back, but I knew," he pauses like he doesn't want to finish his thought. "I knew even if you didn't want me I still wanted to be a father."

I turn my attention back to the small dresser and the closed, dated book on top. I flip the cover open and see the sweetest little red headed child smiling back at me.

"Is this you?" I whisper.

"I told you I was a ginger." I watch as he runs his hand over his mahogany colored hair. "The red disappeared completely by the time I was in Jr. High, but I was born a ginger. My mother's side of the family apparently."

I trace my finger down his jaw. "I'd wondered. When the sun hits your beard a certain way I can see hints of red in it." I kiss his lips and whisper in his ear. "I've always had a thing for gingers."

"Is that so?" He asks gripping my ass cheeks in his hands and pulling me as close to his body as my stomach will allow.

"I love this home, Kadin. I can't wait to build a life with you here, raise this baby here." I smile down at the bump that keeps me from being able to rest flush against his hard body.

"Babies," he counters. "I want lots of babies."

Fifty-One

Kadin

We had a long conversation last Sunday after making love in our bed for hours. I was concerned about her going back to work. She finally admitted to me that Justin, although a very sweet guy couldn't seem to let go of the crush he had on her. I get it; she's an amazing woman.

I told her I'd love nothing more than to go to her job and inform him of just how unavailable she actually is, but she wouldn't let me. She promised she'd discuss it with him, and if she felt like he couldn't let it go completely, she'd quit.

She came home on Monday and informed me that she wasn't quitting altogether, but she'd be working from home most days. I shifted some things at work so I could spend a day or two working from home as well. We've spent the past week incorporating her things amongst the things I already had in the house and spending as much time in each other's arms as we could stand.

Just like at the condo we've quickly managed a routine that we both seem happy about. We spend quite a bit of time wandering around the property and walking with Pudge, but today is an exciting day. Today we find out what we're having, and I think I'm just as excited as she is to start buying things for our child.

"London," I whisper to her back. She's been sleeping on her left side which means I've had to get used to sleeping on the opposite side of the bed I've been used to sleeping on my whole life, but change is a good thing, right? "You have to get up. I'm serious this time. We have to get going."

She grumbles incoherently until I pull her shoulder back, forcing her buried face upward. "You shouldn't have fucked me stupid."

I slip my hand between her thighs and laugh heartily when she parts he legs for me, her body ready for more already.

"If you don't get up now," I chastise in her ear as I slip two fingers inside of her. "You won't have time to shower and the doctor will know exactly what you've been doing all morning."

She moans and opens up even wider, unconcerned about my warning. "I'm going to make you come one more time, dirty girl then you have to get up. I want to know if I'm having a son or a daughter."

I pull her back to my chest and pin her leg down with my own, biting her shoulder I set my fingers into motion until she's a quivering mess and I have to carry her to the bathroom to get cleaned up.

"I called this place a half dozen times," I tell her as we pull up to the small family practice. "They wouldn't tell me shit."

She's still laughing when I make my way to her side of the truck and help her out. I told her we needed to start taking one of my cars so she's not so high off the ground, but she insists on the truck. I think she likes when I lift her out and let her drag herself down my body. If I'm completely honest, I'd rather do this every time also.

Half an hour later we're in a small dark room as a middle-aged woman in scrubs squirts a blue looking jelly on London's stomach. We spent the next twenty minutes in anticipation as she points out all the body parts that the baby has except what I need to know most. I can't be mad, though. Tears are running down my face as I look at the most beautiful black and white baby I've ever seen.

Perfect little legs and arms.

Beautiful little arms and fingers.

Amazing head and pouting mouth.

"This here," the technician says moving the mouse around on the screen "is the labia majora of your little girl."

"A girl?" London says quietly looking up at me.

She reaches up and wipes tears from my face. "A daughter," I whisper to her. "I've always wanted a little girl."

She smiles as I lean down and kiss her with the salt of my tears still on my lips. Unable to resist I deepen the kiss, my hand instinctively reaching for our sweet princess and then lower on her body. I pull back when the other woman in the room clears her throat, realizing my hand is now covered in the jelly from London's stomach. I shrug my shoulders, unashamed of loving this woman.

She hands me a Kleenex but not before giving me a disapproving look at my inappropriate celebration. She hands another tissue to London, but I take it from her and clean her stomach myself, planting a soft kiss to her stomach when I'm done.

The technician then hands London a long strip of tiny pictures of our little girl. I want to ask her for more, but I won't press my luck with the look she has on her face. I'll take her for a dozen more sonograms later if she wants.

"Let's go shopping for our little girl," I tell her as I unroll her yoga pants back up onto her lower belly.

She tilts her head to the side. "You actually want to go shopping for baby stuff?"

I laugh. "Are you kidding me? Do you know how hard it was all those months to walk around those stores for hours and not buy anything?" I place my hand over our growing bundle. "She will have two of everything." I kiss her forehead and help her off of the table.

"She doesn't need two of everything, Kadin," she admonishes me half-heartedly.

"I never said anything about need, beautiful." I clasp her hand in mine and tug her out of the office and back to the truck.

I hoist her inside of the truck and make my way around to my side. I barely have enough time to shut my door before she's climbing on my lap.

"Where were we," she pants against my lips "before she interrupted us."

I moan loudly as she reaches between us and grips my already thick cock in her small hand. "Don't, London. I'll fuck you right here in broad daylight if you don't stop."

She pulls away from me when I start to tug her yoga pants over the globe of her ass. "That's what I thought," I say in short huffs. I groan uncomfortably and adjust my hard-to-ignore erection in my jeans.

She settles back in her seat, and I tilt my head back and to the side so I can look at her. A mischievous look crosses her face. "I still have the keys to the cottage."

I can't get my seatbelt on fast enough considering I was wondering how upset she'd be if I suggested getting a hotel room for a few hours, five stars of course.

We ended up staying the night at the cottage and didn't get any shopping done until the next day. We're home now, and I've unloaded the truck, filling the nursery and a guest bedroom with more things than one little girl could ever use in a lifetime.

London hums softly to herself as she removes tags from clothing ranging from newborn to some she assures me she'll be able to wear once she starts kindergarten. She seems happy and content, and that knowledge makes my heart smile. Pudge has just about given up on me and has become her dog. He ignores my existence if she's near. I don't mind, though; if anything I completely understand. I'm drawn to her much the same way.

I've helped her move things around and been her insistent pack mule for almost everything. I don't want her hurting herself, but I also don't want her to overtire either. I have plans for her this evening that will require her full attention.

"What about this one?" I hold up a medium sized box.

She angles her head, slightly confused. "What's in it?"

I shrug my shoulders and hand it to her. "No clue."

She pulls back the tabs, opening the box. "Looks like a box inside of another box. I don't remember getting this…" Her voice trails off when she pulls a pale blue box with a tiny white ribbon on top from the large nondescript box.

The larger one falls to the floor when she raises her eyes, finding me on one knee. Her hands tremble as she holds onto the blue box with one hand and lifts her other one to cover her mouth, preventing a sob from escaping.

I gently wrap my hand around hers and pull the box from her unsure fingers.

I clear my throat and pray for strength and courage to get through this without becoming a blubbering fool myself.

"London, I, of all the people in the world, know how precious life is. I know just how fast life can change. I know that one tragedy has led me to a destiny I'm certain I was always meant to find." I clear my throat again as I begin to be overcome with emotion and use the back of my hand to swipe away a tear from my cheek. "You are my future, London. You saved me that day you ended up at the cabin with me, and you've saved me each and every day since. I swear I'll be everything that you need for the rest of your life. I'll provide for you and our children. I'll be the man of your dreams. Marry me, and be the woman of mine?"

Her answer is a guttural sob as she launches herself into my arms, nodding her head frantically. "Yes," she finally whispers in my ear. "You're already the man of my dreams, Kadin."

Epilogue

London

I smile from the kitchen window as I watch my amazing husband chase my redheaded daughters around the back yard. Daughters. Plural.

I went for my checkup eight weeks after having our first angel only to find out that Kadin apparently has super sperm. I practically forced him to make love to me four weeks after she was born; consent was dubious on his part at best. So my girls are just under ten months apart.

Anastyn was born in late September and came out looking exactly like her ginger daddy. There was no denying her paternity, so we never bothered with a test; the results wouldn't have mattered anyway. She just turned five last month. Her late birthday means she missed the cutoff for school by just a few weeks, which I don't mind. I never went back to work at the office and eventually helped Justin find someone else to fill my spot. I don't know how I'm going to handle three, I think, as I gently stroke over the little boy growing inside of me; but Kadin is beyond ecstatic about having a son.

His relationship with his family has grown by leaps and bounds over the last few years, and he strives every day to be the man his father was for him and Kegan. His mother treats me like the daughter she's never had and spoils the girls beyond anything I could've ever imagined. For the first time in more than half my life, I have a family, and I'm surrounded every day by people I love and who love me back.

I still can't believe how close both Kadin and I came to not ever having this. I was devastated and relieved at the same time when he disclosed to me shortly after we got back together that he was in that cabin in Poison to take his own life. Just the idea of living a life without ever meeting him is unfathomable to me and still brings tears to my eyes. I'm beyond happy with the life I have now, and I would suffer through every ounce of heartache and pain all over again if it meant this is where I'd end up.

The girls are running around kicking through piles of leaves Kadin has been trying to rake up all morning. He chases them away, playfully turning his back so they can do it again. He notices me watching and makes his way across the yard to the sliding glass door off of the dining room.

I open the door just as he clears the patio, and he first kisses my stomach and then wraps his arms around my waist.

"I love you," I whisper in his ear.

"You make me happier than I'll ever be able to show you," he returns.

"You can at least try," I tease seductively letting my breath warm his neck. "As soon as the girls go to bed I want you to put on those suspenders so we can play lumberjack."

His laugh registers secondary to the heat in his eyes that say he's more than ready to chop some wood.

More by Marie James

Marie James Facebook: Marie James

Author Group: Author Marie James All Hale Fans

Twitter: @AuthrMarieJame

Hale Series

Coming to Hale

Begging for Hale

Hot as Hale

To Hale and Back

Hale Series Box Set

Psychosis

Matthew Hosea FanFiction Novella

Co-write with Gina Sevani

Acknowledgements

This is the 6th time I've been blessed enough to write this part. Each and every time, I'm humbled by the people who are right beside me through this journey. As the support grows so does the number of people I have in my corner. Had I known years ago the support I'd have in the Indie Author World, I would've had the courage to begin this journey long before this year.

My husband remains my number one fan. Without his support and dedication to my brand, I'd be lost. He helps me plot, he works on some of the research, and then he suffers through the editing. On top of all of that, he spends extra time with the boys when I just can't manage to pull myself away from a story.

My betas have been imperative every step of the way. So more thanks than I'd ever honestly be able to give go out to Brittney, Tammy, Brenda, Jessica, and Diane. These ladies have been my sounding board and read and reread this book more times I think than I have personally!

Brittney C....lady you're amazing! If it weren't for your help plotting and the back and forth for weeks this book would've never seen the light of day! You're an amazing woman and an even better friend!! Can't wait to talk to you about the next one!!

Huge thanks to Shauna Kruse for her awesome photography for the cover. As always I'm impressed with each and every picture Mr. Justin James Cadwell takes. Thanks for agreeing to be my lumberjack!! Kari Ayasha did the incredible cover and I couldn't ask for a better person to work with! Kari Nappi helped out with teasers for the book and they're amazing!!

Give Me Books did an amazing job with the cover reveal and release day blitz. Kylie is incredible to work with! I look forward to the process each and every time because she makes it so stream line and easy!!

Last and certainly not least my fans have been incredible. I thank each and every one of you! Each purchase, each and every teaser share, every single mention of my books to others looking has been amazing!! I'm grateful to you for helping me in this journey. Couldn't do it without you!!

One Destiny

~Marie James

About the Author

Marie James: I'm a full-time, working mother of two boys and wife of 11 years. I've spent almost my entire lifetime living in central Texas, with only short stays in South Carolina, Alabama, and Florida. I've always wanted to write novels and just recently had the gumption to sit down and start one. My passions include reading everything under the sun and plotting out new books to write in the future.

Love Me Like That is my 6th book. I've also written the Hale Series and a FanFiction named Psychosis, featuring up and coming cover model, Matthew Hosea, as the main character. This book was done for fun, and all of the proceeds are going to charity.

My current work-in-progress is titled Kincaid and is a spin-off motorcycle club novel from the Hale Series. Fans begged for Diego "Kincaid" Anderson to have his own novel since he was first introduced in Hot as Hale, book 3 of the Hale Series.

Made in the USA
San Bernardino, CA
10 November 2017